PR 6069 .U4 G47

Summerton, Margaret

The ghost flowers.

DEC 1991

MAY '86

APR 1977

FEB '82

KVCC KALAMAZOO VALLEY COMMUNITY COLLEGE LIBRARY

25860

THE GHOST
Flowers

BY *Margaret Summerton*

THE GHOST FLOWERS
SWEETCRAB
THE SAND ROSE
THE SUNSET HORN
THE RED PAVILION
A SMALL WILDERNESS
THE SEA HOUSE
THEFT IN KIND
NIGHTINGALE AT NOON
QUIN'S HIDE
RING OF MISCHIEF
A MEMORY OF DARKNESS

Margaret Summerton

THE GHOST
Flowers

PUBLISHED FOR THE CRIME CLUB BY
Doubleday & Company, Inc.
Garden City, New York 1973

All of the characters in this book
are fictitious, and any resemblance
to actual persons, living or dead,
is purely coincidental.

ISBN: 0-385-07736-x
Library of Congress Catalog Card Number 72–89348
Copyright © 1972, 1973 by Margaret Summerton
All Rights Reserved
Printed in the United States of America
First Edition

The village of Kessima in Cyprus, in which the action of this book takes place, is a purely imaginary one. If by chance one of the many hundreds of villages—some of them remote—in Cyprus has this name, it is not my Kessima.

THE GHOST
Flowers

ONE

The curtain raiser to those September days in Kessima was a cone of white paper afloat in a down-current of draught blowing through the sitting-room window I'd flung open when I'd arrived back at the flat at midnight. A sheet of typing paper that danced a skittish pirouette before subsiding half underneath the sofa. It landed face-side up, flaunting its message written with a scarlet felt pen by Mrs. Pratt, who cleaned the flat on Wednesday and Friday mornings.

With a jolt I set the tray of coffee and toast I'd been carrying back to bed on the hall table, made instantly aware of a leaping excitement. With telephone messages Mrs. Pratt operated a grading system. When she needed soap powder or polish she pencilled the items on the shopping list hanging in the kitchen. What she categorised as non-urgent ones from friends or my mother she scribbled on the telephone pad. But when the message was from Matthew she helped herself to a sheet of my typing paper and purloined by fieriest pen.

Once or twice I'd speculated uneasily whether my life's secret was in fact a secret from Mrs. Pratt, then dismissed the notion. In two years I'd become so highly skilled in the art of keeping it, I was confident that no one guessed its existence. The sheet of typing paper, the red pen were no more than a signal from Mrs. Pratt that the message was from my boss and therefore merited top priority.

Crossing the room, my excitement was diminished by a hand-sized cloud of guilt. When, arriving home at midnight, I'd riffled through the pile of mail, I'd missed the most important item because Mrs. Pratt, normally super-conscientious, had failed to weight down the flimsy sheet. More than likely the draught as I'd opened the front door had sent it careening across the room. Even so, if I'd not been so bleary-eyed from driving, so eager for bed, I'd have spotted it, not slept away seven hours in ignorance of its message.

Lurking behind the small guilt was a larger one. On the first page of the loose-leaf notebook Matthew carried in his breast pocket were my sister's address in Launceston and her telephone number, plus the date I was due to arrive and the date, a fortnight later, when I would be returning to the flat—Thursday night. But I hadn't made it until midnight on Saturday.

With her husband attending a conference in Edinburgh, I'd stayed on to comfort and support Diana, whose two-year-old daughter, an hour before I was due to leave, had fallen down a flight of stone steps, concussed herself, and fractured her femur. During the weary hours of waiting in Casualty, back at the house, easing the two of them out of shock, there'd been an odd ten minutes during which I could have telephoned Matthew at his Beirut hotel, explained why I'd be two days late in returning to London. Instead, on Friday, I'd sent duplicate telegrams to Beirut and his flat in Curzon Street. The excuse: my distraught sister's chalk-white face, and Arabella's non-stop piteous wailing. But as an excuse it failed to stand up, and I knew it. Consequently my professional pride that was overweening—after all, it was all I had—took a knock.

At first the clammy apprehension that by not being where I'd said I would be I'd failed him sent all the lines that might have been written in blood running together. Then reason preached that there was a chance the message meant no more than, whereas I had been late, Matthew had returned from the Lebanon earlier than planned. Instantly the secret half of me was cradled in joy: I'd see him today, maybe within the hour. While the cool, practical half on public view reminded me that, if that were so, I'd have to telephone my mother and explain why I wouldn't be coming to eat her traditional Sunday lunch. She'd be upset; worse, mortally offended at being robbed of first-hand reports on her younger daughter and injured grandchild. My mother, being a woman who spoke her mind loud and clear, wouldn't spare me. But love, especially a love that is unwanted and unrewarded, has the effect of neutralising any emotion that isn't committed to that love.

In underlined block caps Mrs. Pratt had written my name. MISS MARIA CARON, added Friday 1 P.M.

> Mr. Grant telephoned from Cyprus at 11.15. He was very put out that you weren't home as you'd told him you would be. I gave him your sister's telephone number but he said he hadn't time to get through again, and I was to take down a message and make sure I wrote exactly what he said. You are to catch the plane to Nicosia on Sunday morning that arrives at 4.50 in the afternoon and he'll be at the airport to meet you. That's about all I can be sure of. After that the line went bad, and I couldn't make out half he was saying. Maybe he had a bad cold. I think he said something about you bringing his nephew straight back to England but I couldn't swear to it. And there was some message about his stepsister, Mrs. Mitchell, but exactly what, I don't know. Then right at the end, he said he wanted you to bring a file from his safe. Just as he was going to tell me which file, we got cut off. As he'd made the call, I took it for granted he would ring back, and I've hung on until 1 o'clock, but the phone hasn't rung once, and I have to go now as I'm due at Mrs. Spencer's at two.
>
> Hope you had a good holiday with your sister and her little girl. We've had lovely weather while you've been gone. Thanks for the p.c. Leave me a note if you'd like me to rinse through the net curtains on Wednesday.
>
> Yours truly,
Janet Pratt.

I read it through three times, the third with such slow deliberation that every blood-red word imprinted itself inside my head. Coming from Matthew, a summons to present myself instantly at some distant spot on the globe where he happened to need me was a clause written into my contract. In such emergencies the instructions, however economically worded, were precise and unequivocal, the reason for the summons made apparent to me if to no one else. What file, I fumed! Apart from the correspondence files in the cabinet, there were upwards of thirty locked in his safe. A bad line? Nonsense! Matthew would have taken steps to have it changed for a better one. A cold in his head? He simply didn't catch colds. I could sift no sense out of it except that an order to fly to Kessima must surely signify that any crisis in which he was involved was a personal rather than a national or international one. Which only stirred up a thicker murk of confusion. Matthew invariably solved his personal crises without help from me or anyone else.

My train of thought jerked to a standstill, sped in a new direction. Over the past few weeks the legendary name of Grivas had once again appeared in the newspapers, and reporters had speculated on the outcome of his return to Cyprus and whether the issue of Enosis was once again going to flame across the island. But surely that wasn't sufficient threat to bring Toby back to England!

With Arabella's accident still vividly etched on my mind, I saw him ill, crippled, pain glazing his eyes, and then pulled myself out of what amounted to self-induced hysteria. Toby had his father and mother—neither, if he were ill, would leave his side, let alone entrust him to me. So were they both ill? Had Matthew's reference to Barbie meant that for some reason she was incapable of looking after Toby? Except that it was Connie, the linchpin of the household in Kessima, who looked after the three of them. So had Connie suddenly revolted and walked out? She was more likely to have dropped dead. And if she had, Matthew would have said so. In any case, it was beyond the reach of my wildest imagining to conceive of that small dauntless woman robbed of life.

I racked my brains as to what crisis had taken Matthew to Cyprus on a sudden, unplanned visit in September when we had been due there for a three weeks' stay in mid-October. It being a waste of time to speculate whether it was some twist in the island's politics or a family crisis, I lifted the telephone and asked for the number of the house in Kessima. There was half an hour's delay on the call, during which I slid into and out of a bath, dressed, and gulped a cup of stone-cold coffee. In thirty-five minutes the operator came through to say she was sorry there was no reply. That so early in the morning there should be no one in the house to answer the telephone only served to thicken the fog of bafflement. She offered to try again later, but by now I'd looked up the departure time of the plane: 11.25, which gave me a check-in time of 10.55. It was past nine. I told her not to bother.

After I'd put down the phone, I was suddenly unnerved by daunting pictures of some dire catastrophe out of sight, beyond imagination that, for a moment, utterly demoralised me. Suppose I couldn't cope! The mere suggestion served to kick my wits to life. I was Matthew Grant's third hand simply because I didn't panic in a crisis, but briskly set about resolving it.

While I waited for my call to Launceston, I grabbed my unopened suitcase, sorted through it for any clean, cool garments to take to Cyprus. There weren't any.

No, Diana said, no calls for me. Should there have been? I replied I was just checking and asked after Arabella. She'd had a good night and Tim, Diana's husband, had telephoned to say he'd be able to skip the last day of the engineering conference and be home by Sunday night. So would I please instil into Mother there was no reason to worry. She was banking on me dissuading her from dashing down to Cornwall. Diana, with Tim home, could cope, and didn't need her—didn't need was a polite euphemism for didn't want. I promised to do my best.

I dialed the Epsom number, praying that my father would answer, which would make the operation shorter and less contentious. My father was a man of reason. He accepted that his elder daughter at twenty-four had a right to work for whom she pleased. My mother did not deal in reason but in deep, ineradicable instincts. Her code of morals was assaulted by the nights I slept in the same foreign hotels as Matthew; even more by the working holidays we spent in Kessima in what she regarded as a highly suspect ménage.

My father answered. When I'd explained about catching the plane to Nicosia, he said mildly: "Your mother isn't going to like it. She's counting on your being here for lunch. If you could eat your way through all your favourite dishes, I'd be surprised. And she's worried about Arabella."

"I know. I'm sorry, truly, but Arabella, except for the cast, is fine and Diana's over the shock. Best of all, Tim will be back from his conference tonight, so she won't be alone. Honestly, there's no need for Mother to worry."

"I'll try and stop her, though I'm not making any promises. When do you anticipate getting back?"

"Until I see Matthew I'm not sure. I'd guess fairly soon. I'll write or phone you from Kessima."

My father, as always, accepted with grace a situation he could not alter. "Take care of yourself. No sooner are you air-borne than a plane crashes or, worse, is hijacked. No matter if it's in a different hemisphere your mother is convinced that by some means you've got yourself aboard. So keep your promise, Maria, eh?"

"I will. 'Bye."

As I put down the receiver my mind's eye was flooded by his image. Since his premature retirement from a Lombard Street bank two years ago, he grew a little frailer each time I saw him, as though the flesh, of which he'd never had much, was deserting his bones ounce by ounce. It made his face beautiful, his smile poignantly heart-touching. Last time I'd been home, catching him unawares silhouetted against the light, the ashen tinge to his skin, his deeply bowed shoulders, and the air of serene contemplative acceptance had sent me racing upstairs to catechise my mother, who was sorting out clothes for a Boy Scouts' jumble sale.

"How is he?"

"You can see for yourself. Content. With time to do the things he's wanted to do for a quarter of a century."

"But *can* he do them?"

"Some of them. Enough."

"He's so frail he frightens me."

"Frightens you!" Folding an Arran sweater of mine I couldn't remember parting with, she raised her head and pinned me with a belittling glance, paused before she answered. She was a handsome woman, my mother, fifteen years younger than my father, straight-backed, with the carriage of a girl, and long, nut-brown glossy hair which she had dressed in the same style as long as I could remember.

"Then cultivate enough self-control to keep your fright to yourself. He has the best medical care money can buy. What's more important, he's sensible, paces himself. He could live for years, or he could die in his sleep tonight. He knows that; he knows I know it, but we both of us behave as though he had all the time in the world ahead of him."

"I'm sorry." That my mother, who was a chronic worrier over minor illnesses, foresaw each member of the family fatally involved in an accident every time they left the house, had scaled such heights of fortitude for his sake humbled me.

She gave me a smile that both forgave and admonished, went back to her jumble-sorting. "Just remember not to go picking up everything he drops, and don't leave him not knowing where you are."

I'd promised and kept my promise.

While I waited for the radio cab to take me to Curzon Street and on to Heathrow, I raked frantically through my wardrobe for a couple of cool dresses, underwear, a pair of shorts and a top, added a bikini and rope-soled sandals, enough, I hoped, to see me through a short stay with the temperature in the upper eighties.

When the cab drew up at the entrance to the flat, which was above a row of shops, I checked my watch and found I'd got precisely ten minutes before I must be back in it and on my way to Heathrow.

As I unlocked the outer door, passed through the vestibule, my memory reproduced with perfect recall the scene of myself crossing it to enter for the first time the long, three-windowed room that doubled as sitting-room and office. Matthew's tall, lean form rising from behind his desk, coming towards me with hand outstretched, with that touch, amounting to genius, for gaining the confidence not only of the great and famous, but of a twenty-two-year-old half stupefied by the intensity of her determination to get the job.

With the aid of a journalist girl-friend who worked in Fleet Street, I'd read the cuttings on Matthew Grant in the library of the newspaper on which he'd been a staff foreign correspondent for eight years. When I met him he'd been a free-lance for two. He contributed an astringent current affairs column to one of the Sundays, periodic articles for the American press, appeared on radio and television programmes, mainly those concerned with the Far and Middle East, on which he was accounted an expert. He'd published one book on East Asia, and was completing a second, a history of Israeli-Arab relations over the last fifteen years.

There'd been two pictures which revealed a longish face with a strong jaw, a wide, firmly moulded mouth, slightly jutting flying eyebrows, the whole communicating an air of well-being and self-confidence. What the black and white stills had not prepared me for was the thick, dark blond hair, the tremendously expressive cobalt blue eyes, and the instantly apparent vigour of body and mind.

His smile was relaxed, and even that first one dangerously loaded with charm. "It's nice of you to come and see me, Miss Caron. Try that chair. I think it's about the most comfortable."

During the hour-long interview I was made aware of his incisive mind, and the intuitive courtesy that amounted to the gift of a silver tongue. At noon, when it was over, he opened a bottle of champagne.

"You'd suit me, Maria Caron. What you must decide is whether I'd suit you." His querying glance was level and deadly serious. "You have to bear in mind that roughly a quarter of your time won't be wholly your own, and that can play havoc with your social life." Suddenly he grinned like a boy. The cuttings hadn't told me his age, but I'd have guessed it pretty accurately: thirty-six. "Maybe, I'd be doing you a favour to settle for the splendidly efficient secretary in her middle forties whom I interviewed yesterday?"

Since another of his talents was an ability to pierce any subterfuge, he must have had a shrewd idea of my answer before I gave it to him. It was only as I was leaving, the job meticulously outlined, salary and expenses agreed—there were no hard and fast hours—that he added a footnote, half-humorous, half-serious.

"I give you my permission to hate me as hard as you like, and you assuredly will; at times I'm a very hateable man, most journalists worth their salt are." He paused, holding me with his unflickering blue gaze. "But don't fall in love with me. The moment you start putting flowers on my desk, stirring the sugar in my coffee, we part. Agreed?"

When I could get my breath, I laughed aloud. "You're *that* conceited?"

"On the contrary. I'm a realist, one who's learnt the hard way, by experience. One male and one female in close proximity, available to each other, it wouldn't matter if I were an alcoholic or had a hump on my back, we'd be liable to fall victims to the old boss-secretary syndrome, with all its complications. With me, count me an oddity if you like, work—at least my work—and sex don't mix." The rich smile came back to charm me. "Which in this case is my loss."

"You don't have to worry. It won't happen."

But the warning had come an hour too late. Matthew Grant was a creature of fire and ice; of compassion and sensitivity that counterbalanced the ruthlessness and drive that were a necessary component of his profession. He was blessed—or cursed—with that indefinable quality that generates excitement in others. He could literally, when he chose, enchant people. It was my misfortune to be one of them. There were dark spells when I convinced myself that I hated him; that if only I could steel and hold my resolution, I could walk out of his sight for ever, expend my emotions on nurturing and cherishing love for an equable-tempered, predictable young man, without a single quirk, whose name was Donald Hardwick.

As I turned the knob of the sitting-room door I heard the hard cough of a chronic bronchitic. Damn! I'd caught Gladwin on duty. Duster in hand, he flung me a cold, fishy glance of dislike. Maybe he'd been what he claimed: a gentleman's gentleman moving in exalted circles; maybe not. Matthew insisted that, except for his occasional lapses into alcoholism, he discharged his simple duties of cleaning, valeting, and washing up dishes and glasses faultlessly. His appearance was coldly ascetic. Hang a habit on him and he'd have made a marvellous monk. His iron-grey hair was plastered in separate strands across his skull, his mouth was thin and humourless, his cheeks concave and his eyes, as I've said, a fishy no-colour. To do him justice, he made no pretence of liking females; he merely suffered them, sometimes with grace, sometimes without. He wore the uniform of his trade: black alpaca suit, stiff butterfly collar, and a green baize apron with a bib.

He said instantly to emphasise that my presence was superfluous: "I've forwarded Mr. Grant's mail, including a telegram you sent him from Cornwall."

The trick in prising information out of Gladwin was to imply you knew it already. A direct question was an open invitation to him to prove he was closer to his master's confidence than anyone else. But I'd no time to play games with him this morning. "When did you hear that Mr. Grant had flown to Cyprus?"

"He sent me a telegram."

The "when" ignored. I crossed the room, opened the safe at such an angle that he could not, short of leaning over my shoulder, memorise the combination. "I'm flying to Nicosia this morning. I found a telephone message asking me to go when I got back from Cornwall." I hesitated, and then did my own bit of fishing. "It seems Mr. Grant wants his nephew and maybe his stepsister escorted back to England."

"So I understand."

I glanced over my shoulder and knew by his expression of affront he understood no such thing. If I'd had an hour to spare, he'd still have won a sly satisfaction in denying me any knowledge he possessed about Matthew's switch in plans. Anyway, the chances were that he'd received no more than the terse instruction: "Forward mail to Kessima until further notice."

I flipped through the files, indecision making my fingers clumsy. Which? I was familiar with nine-tenths of them, but there were one or two that contained sheets notated in Matthew's highly personalised system of shorthand. Any relating to the Middle East he'd taken with him to the Lebanon; of those that remained I selected six, opened my suitcase, and rammed them in.

I looked up, caught Gladwin gnawing his bottom lip. He spoke grudgingly, it being wormwood and gall for him to admit his ignorance of Matthew's movements was greater than mine. "When do you expect him back, miss?"

"I'm not sure. Before too long would be my guess." I flipped open his desk calendar. No dates for the current week, but for the following one there was a lunch with an American publisher, a television appearance on Panorama, and one which read: See Gibb about M.

Terence Gibb was a stockbroker. M. stood for Marigold, who'd once been Matthew's wife. She was Mrs. Fairley now and lived in a Manchester suburb, with or without husband and children. Since Matthew spent an hour with Gibb every six months or so, checking over her portfolio of investments, presumably their divorce had been amicable.

Once when Barbie and I were alone, I'd been at pains casually to bring up her name. "Marigold! She's nothing but a tramp. Why Matthew should have a chronic guilt complex about her heaven knows, but he has." She gave me one of her wickeder smiles. "Still some men are addicted to tramps. Or wouldn't you know!"

Occasionally among Matthew's private mail was a handwritten envelope addressed to Mrs. Fairley. That was the sum of my knowledge of the ex-Mrs. Grant: that she and Matthew maintained contact, and that he kept a proprietary eye on her money.

I added what Gladwin had certainly noted: "He's got three dates the week after next, which means he must be back in London by the weekend. If he hasn't been in touch by the time I see him, I'll telephone you."

"Thank you, miss." His fishy glance added: For nothing.

On the way to Heathrow, checking the narrowing margin of time, I was conscious of a nagging feeling that I'd forgotten something. As I paid off the driver, picked up my case, I nailed it down. Money. In the safe there was a packet of one hundred pounds in five-pound notes, its purpose to cover sudden, unanticipated flights in the middle of the night to remote places where feast days closed banks, and where credit cards could turn out to be meaningless oblongs of plastic.

My ticket presented no problem: Matthew ran an account with B.E.A., but after paying the cab driver I was left with a purse of assorted silver and copper and a single five-pound note. With Matthew meeting me at Nicosia airport, I'd no cause either to fume or reproach myself. But I did. Like Gladwin, my professional pride was tender, easily bruised. And here I was breaking Matthew's credo that money bought you out of trouble or, on the rare occasions when it proved ineffective, made it easier to bear. It followed that, stepping aboard any plane, you carried on your person an emergency ration of dollars or sterling.

In the departure lounge, with nothing left to do but wait for my flight number to be called, I opened my shoulder bag intending to take out Mrs. Pratt's message and reread it. It wasn't there. I'd left it behind at the flat.

Small as this second lapse of memory was, it shook me, as though it provided final damning proof that on this particular day I simply could not do a thing right, either through sheer incompetence or because I was being pursued by a malicious little demon of ill-luck.

TWO

On the plane I slept for an hour and woke to discover that sleep had acted as a solvent on my jittery panics and mindless confusion, not at all proud of the girl who'd rushed around like a scalded cat and mislaid half her wits. Matthew would be at the airport and within five minutes every mystifying and bedevilling question would be answered. It was futile to dream up visions of catastrophes affecting Toby and Barbie when, with Matthew in Kessima, I simply could not credit that any irredeemable catastrophe could overtake either of them.

Even with the extra weight of the files my case was light enough to carry through immigration and customs. The plane had only been half full and in my mind's eye, skimming ahead, I had seen the reception area empty. But we had overlapped another plane-load and it was crowded with passengers linking up with relatives and friends.

I did a survey of heads to pinpoint Matthew's, feeling the smile beginning to form on my mouth, the deep rivers of my heart to flood with content. My searching glance was deflected from adult male heads by the rear view of a small boy's flaxen one. Toby! Matthew must have brought him along for the ride.

His name was at the point of flying off my tongue when he turned. Not Toby, but a boy with a round, grinning face, all his front teeth, and sky-blue eyes. Toby's face was oval, no more flesh on it than on the rest of his body, his eyes the same dense blue as his uncle's, and he was missing two front teeth, which made a gap he liked to spit through when no one was looking.

Within fifteen minutes the separate entities in the crowd had sorted themselves out and dispersed. No Matthew. I walked out onto the forecourt, stood under the long awning. Even by the short route over the mountains, Kessima was eighteen miles away, the last five along precipitous corkscrewing roads. Past five o'clock, the sun no longer scorched, but I could feel the heat retained in the ground through the soles of my sandals, and the air I breathed was scented by the fiercely hot day that was dying. Beyond the great plain of the Mesaoria the jagged teeth of the mountains were bathed in the delicate honey light that envelops them in the last hour before sunset.

How far away was he? Probably by now cutting through the city centre to the airport highway. I focused my glance in the direction he must appear, so sure that I sighted Barbie's white Triumph, which Matthew used when he was in Kessima, that twice I raised my arm only to let it fall. He'd come fast, scaling as many seconds as possible off his lateness. Fanatically punctual, deadlines stamped into his head, he'd be furious at not being on time.

My glance was pulled from the road by the sound of my name being called, not by Matthew, but by a voice that even in this moment of stress conjured up dreams that sometimes seemed real; other times no more than fantasies of wish-fulfilment.

Donald Hardwick slammed the door of a car and hurried towards me, hand outstretched. No more than average height, he was blessed with physical grace. His glossy brown hair shone as though it had been burnished, and as he took off his sun glasses I saw the leaping gladness in his hazel eyes, heard the surge of warmth in his voice. I thought simply: At last the day has brought me something good.

"Maria! How marvellous! I'd no idea you were due here. No

one whispered a word." Our two hands touched, held, then fell apart.

"It's a surprise visit. Come to that, I didn't know I should find you here."

For a few seconds, an arm's length between us, we measured one another. His nature, which was more outgiving, confident, optimistic than mine and being single-hearted—if he were—gave him an advantage over me. Even so, in that tiny pause, with the boost of surprise fading, I could sense the old doubts springing back to life in him.

His smile was so shining, so eager that he must have tossed them to the winds. "If I'd travelled out today instead of yesterday we'd have been on the same plane. What I missed! I've driven in to pick up one of Alex's top legal aides." He nodded towards a Mercedes where a middle-aged, thick-set man was hunching his shoulders in petulance at the delay in conveying him to his destination. "So it looks as if I'm to have the treat of giving you a lift to Kessima." He reached for the bag at my feet.

"I'd love it, except that I'm waiting for Matthew. He's picking me up."

"Matthew!" The glad note drained out of his voice. Figuratively he stepped back a pace, yet I couldn't think why he should imagine I'd be in Cyprus without Matthew. "Is he here?"

"Yes." What, I marvelled, had happened to the Kessima grapevine that should have relayed news of Matthew's arrival to the Villa Hesperides, where Donald would be staying!

He asked in a throw-away voice: "And how is the great man these days?"

"I'm not too sure. I'm just back from spending a fortnight in Cornwall with my sister. We're to meet up here."

His glance remained studiously pleasant, but somewhere inside me I heard a tiny knell of despair. Were we, once again, about to beat out the spark that had ignited between us in February when we'd met at a party given by Alex Theocharis and his wife Carima? On the floodlit terrace I'd been convinced it would flare and burn forever. Had he? I'd believed so at the time, then lost all but a sliver of my belief.

Donald and Matthew found no common ground. Once when Barbie had mentioned his name, Matthew had remarked: "Hardwick? Estimable young man, but at bottom I suspect he's a lightweight in that, in a crunch, he'd make sure of being on the winning side."

I heard the echo of Barbie's protest. "What's wrong with that, for heaven's sake. Who wants to be a loser?"

"No one, but Hardwick could be if they don't get the foundations of that hotel laid soon, which may take some doing: upwards of fifty people will have a legitimate claim to that highly valuable tongue of land."

Barbie scoffed: "Alex will fix that. He's a born fixer. Doesn't it all, in the end, come down to money?"

"Not in a peasant community. Over generations people's attachment to a piece of land becomes literally an extension of themselves. Root them out, buy them out, and they'll die. What's more they know it, and naturally they don't want to die, even with money in the bank."

Barbie laughed. "Alex employs a flying squad of top lawyers. He's determined to get that peninsula because it's a gorgeous site for an hotel. And he will get it, and Donald will build a fabulous hotel that will bring in plane-loads of tourists. It'll be famous and so will Donald. You'll see."

Donald Hardwick was an architect, which accounted for his frequent visits to the Villa Hesperides. Its owner, Alex Theocharis, was a member of a consortium that was planning to build a super-luxury hotel on the northern shore. His wife, Carima, ex-film star—or maybe not quite star and not quite ex—when the names of possible architects were being mooted, had suggested Donald Hardwick, who had been a childhood friend.

I hoped that Barbie, whose judgment was non-existent, was right, and Matthew, whose judgment was a finely honed instrument of his trade, was wrong. I didn't want the hotel to founder before it was built, its creator find his beloved brain child stillborn.

I asked: "How are the plans for the hotel shaping up?"

"Slowly, but, fingers crossed, I hope surely. There are still a couple of landowners holding out." He made a backward gesture with his head. "That is why he is here. One of Alex's big legal guns. Cypriot born! Unfortunately as Alex's plane is laid up he had to travel from Athens as a fare-paying passenger. Ruffled his feathers a bit."

"And getting more ruffled by the second. The type to take a poor view of his chauffeur wasting his time by chatting up a girl."

"Ah, but no ordinary girl!" The shining eager light, one that could only belong to a man of good will, returned to his face. "Let's compromise! Why not set out with us and if we pass Matthew on the way, you can swap cars? Wouldn't that be easier on your feet than kicking your heels here?" He glanced at his watch. "Forty-five minutes late. He could have had a puncture or run over a goat and be arguing the toss with the law or a jeep full of United Nations men. What about it?"

"I'd rather wait. We could miss one another. He can't be long now."

"As you please." I knew, with a sigh that, once again, I'd let him down. He half turned away, and then looked back at me, caring still. "But we'll be seeing one another, won't we? How long are you staying in Kessima?"

"Until I see Matthew I honestly don't know."

"Ah, Matthew!"

The scorn was so muted as to be inaudible to any ears but mine; it stung me to retort. "He's my boss. I work for him."

"Indeed you do. *Au revoir*, then. I hope Matthew doesn't keep you waiting too much longer."

"I'm sure he won't."

But I became less sure as the minutes ticked by. When I could no longer see the pinnacles of the mountain peaks, I did what I should have done earlier: telephoned the house. Given half a chance, Toby would answer, but he'd have to be quick or Connie would get ahead of him. The ringing tone continued for so long that it became evident Toby wasn't around, which suggested Matthew was indeed giving him a ride to the airport. Barbie, the instrument within her hand's reach, did not always, unless she was expecting a call, exert herself to answer. Kim was oftener out of the house than in; or he might be at his work-bench in the cellar, where, in the same fashion that some amateur painters daub paint on canvas, he carved hunks of wood into weird gnomelike shapes—and was genuinely baffled that no one wanted to buy them. So it was Connie's brisk, rather shrill voice I was waiting for. I listened to the ringing tone for a full five minutes by my watch, and then hung up, conscious of a chilling sense of dismay. A second later I remembered the widow of an English schoolmaster whom, when the heat of the day tapered off, Connie occasionally visited on Sunday evenings. I counted them off: Matthew and Toby, on their way to the airport, Connie paying a social call, and Kim either amusing himself or busy on one of his ploys to make him rich overnight. That left Barbie. Had some illness or accident befallen that lovely, artless, indolent girl, with lavender eyes and curtains of sovereign gold hair caressing her cheekbones? Barbie was the child of Matthew's father and his second wife. He had been her loving protector since the day she was born. Any hurt to Barbie and indirectly to Toby, and he'd literally move heaven and earth to mend it. Common sense preached that if Barbie were ill Connie wouldn't go gallivanting, and Kim would be on hand, but I was too ridden by fevers of anxiety to be cooled by that line of reasoning. My sole concern was to get to the house as fast as wheels could take me.

It was past six, only the airport lights holding darkness at bay. As the Turkish-Cypriots refused to admit Greek drivers into their territory except under the four-times daily United Nations convoys, and to reach Kessima by the short route involved crossing the "green line" dividing the two communities, I needed a Turkish-Cypriot taxi-driver. It took me ten minutes to locate one, and he was less than enthusiastic about driving over the mountains after dark. Eventually he shrugged philosophically, with that air all Cypriots have of indulging the freakish whims of foreigners.

I explained that a friend should have met me, but he'd been delayed. If I saw his car ahead, I'd warn him, so that he could stop and I'd change over.

"Okay." He was a giant of a man with a placid, unsmiling face. He was also a fast—on occasions a reckless—driver, honking his way through the snarled traffic in the Turkish villages we passed with their coffee shops strung with ribbons of coloured lights. Once on the straight road over the plain of the Mescaria, he put his foot down hard. The darkness beyond the headlights was only broken by road signs, one spelling out repeatedly: No Overtaking of United Nations Convoys. Presently he broke the silence by enquiring if I knew the village of Kessima. When I said yes, he remarked: "Very small village, not many foreigners visit it."

"A few live there permanently."

He gave a sly chuckle. "Because they not like English taxes, live cheaper in Cyprus."

The headlights as we swung round corner after corner picked out the vibrant green of the conifers and the deep gold of the apricot earth. Through the open window flowed the aromatic scent of herbs that had been dried by the fierce summer heat into twigs and skeleton flowers that crumbled to dust in the hand. Surfacing through the skin of my anxiety was a suppressed delight at the landscape to which I should wake in the morning in The House By Itself.

Above and parallel to Kyrenia, I saw the far-off glow of the flood-lit Venetian ramparts of the castle. In the spring Matthew, Toby, Giselle, and I had climbed them one cool afternoon, gazed entranced from their heights at the picture-postcard harbour and cast our eyes over the blue sea as smooth as stretched silk to the mountains of Turkey. When we came down two amiable American archaeological students had allowed Toby to help them wash their shards and broken pots with a hose-pipe. He'd dripped all the way home.

On the last stretch of the main road we met little traffic to fire my dwindling hope of sighting Matthew in Barbie's white Triumph. On the narrower mountain road leading to the village of Liphos, below Kessima, we passed not a single vehicle. Noting the reckless wide swings with which, horn honking, the driver took the bends, I remarked: "You seem to know the road."

"I had brother once who lived in Kessima. I visit him. Now he does not live there."

A brother who had most likely owned one of the now empty cube houses in the lowest alley in the village. They had belonged to a small Turkish-Cypriot minority in a predominantly Greek-Cypriot community who had moved away during the four years of the Troubles that had preceded the birth of the Republic. In Kessima itself there had been no outright violence, no midnight snipings between the two races, but the Turkish-Cypriots had chosen to abandon their homes and their cemetery under the olive trees and not to return to them after the settlement.

Toby and I, stumbling across the Turkish cemetery one day, had walked soberly through a series of mounds of earth supported by rough boards, some short, some long, and one so tiny it could only be a baby's grave. There'd been one splendid one, its marble headstone engraved with the star and crescent, but most had no more than an upright shaft of wood, the roughly painted name scorched out by the sun. The urns and pots that had held flowers had been kicked to pieces by goats, or maybe tumbled by birds preying on the flower seeds. A sad, abandoned little grove of death.

As we walked back to the road that would lead us home, Toby remarked gravely: "I like goats. I wouldn't mind them keeping me company when I'm dead. I wonder how old the baby was." Provided neither his parents nor Connie was within earshot, he quizzed every new person he met about their age. I wondered if he'd outgrown that compulsion, what had replaced it, and above all whether he'd be peacefully asleep when I reached the house.

As we circled the great plateau of rock that guarded the entrance to Kessima, I automatically glanced right. The terrace lights of the Villa Hesperides fanned out into the darkness, and as I made out human figures reduced by distance to blurred matchsticks, moving between the columns, it flashed through my mind to query the accuracy of Mrs. Pratt's note. Was it possible on a bad line she'd misheard the day? If it had been Monday, not Sunday, Matthew, Kim, and Barbie might well be drinking on that lighted terrace. Ah, but not Connie and not Toby.

In so far as the village possessed a focal point, it was a sandy oblong through which all incoming and outgoing traffic had to pass. In the tavern on the south side, immediately opposite the tiny white-domed Greek Orthodox church, the heads of men drinking swivelled slowly to chart the direction of the car. When we turned left down the cobweb of narrow streets, they guessed our destination—some may even have recognised me. If we'd turned right they'd have known we were bound for the Villa Hesperides.

The driver asked: "Is it to the house that belonged to the German that you go?"

"Julius Mannheim? Yes. It's on the far side of the ravine. But if you'd rather not cross the bridge, you can put me down on this side and I'll walk to the house."

"I drive you to house. Friends, relations belonging to you buy Mannheim's house when he kill himself?"

"He bequeathed it in his will to the man for whom I work. Matthew Grant."

When I'd asked Matthew how he came to own a house in Cyprus, he'd said: "It dropped into my lap one morning in a hotel in Saigon when I received a letter from a solicitor in Nicosia saying it had been left to me by someone called Julius Mannheim. Since the name meant nothing to me, at first I assumed there'd been some mixup, and it should have been sent to some other Matthew Grant. I was about to write back when I remembered that we had met once, when I'd been covering the Civil War: for half an hour over a drink in the bar of the Ledra Hotel. He accidentally knocked a glass out of my hand, and when I came to look at him I realised he was half out of his mind with either rage or grief, rather like a case of shell-shock. He turned out to be a German who, because his wife was a Jewess, had left Berlin in 1938 and settled in Cyprus. Their only child, a boy of nineteen, had elected to stay behind, and died in a concentration camp. Six months before I met Mannheim his wife developed lung cancer, and the previous day he'd been told by her doctors that her heart was too weak to stand an operation and that without it, at her age, the chance of recovery was practically nil. He refused to accept the verdict. Apparently he'd heard of someone who'd been successfully treated for lung cancer at the Middlesex Hospital and was totally obsessed with the idea that if only he could get his wife flown to London her life would be saved. By this time Mrs.

Mannheim was so weak she could only travel in a plane equipped to carry a stretcher. And, at the height of the emergency, he could find no authority who would provide one. By nature he was autocratic and overbearing and it was obvious to me that he would demand as a right what he should have sought as a favour. It was only later I learned that he'd already got one strike against him, which probably accounted for his horny cantankerousness. He was an experienced amateur archaeologist, and when, after the war, foreign teams began excavating various sites on the island, he offered his services and was accepted. A few months later he was caught red-handed with some gold buttons he'd stolen from one of the tombs. He wasn't prosecuted but inevitably the theft became public knowledge and he was ostracised.

"So far as getting his wife to England, all it amounted to was knowing the right people to approach. I managed to persuade the Army to fly her to Lineham, where an ambulance met her and took her to the Middlesex. Having done that, I admit I never gave either of them another thought. I learned later that Mrs. Mannheim died three months after she reached London. Mannheim returned to his house in Kessima, barricaded himself in, and became a recluse. Two days before he killed himself he took a bus into Nicosia and made a will leaving me the house."

"What's it like?"

"It was eighteen months before I could get to see it. I'd pictured it as a typical Cypriot village house, four whitewashed mud-brick walls under a flat roof, jammed between its neighbours. Instead, it's a sizable three-storey property, outside the village, standing alone, hence its Cypriot name, which means The House By Itself. Mannheim had allowed it to rot and collapse around him, but its bone structure was sound enough. Exactly one year later I slept for the first time in my life under a roof I owned, the plans I'd roughed out on paper three-dimensional around me. It would have taken twice as long, cost three times as much if Giselle hadn't been willing to undertake the supervision, bullying and cajoling of builders, plumbers and painters while I was in Vietnam and, later, in Washington."

"I daresay she quite enjoyed doing the job for you."

"Could be. She has enormous wells of creative talent, but I'm nonetheless grateful that she expended nearly a year's quota on my house."

A labour of love! His perceptions were too highly tuned for him to remain unaware that Giselle Nash was in love with him. It followed that, for reasons of his own, he chose not to acknowledge it . . . or not to me. I thought sometimes to be loved too much by too many people is almost as bad as being unloved. You took love for granted, accepted it as a right, and an awful lot of people loved Matthew Grant.

The driver murmured: "It is unlucky house. Whoever lives there someone dies." I must have shaken my head in disclaimer because he insisted: "It is true. The family who own it before it belong to the German thief, the father he fall and break his back on the mountain one night and no one find him until he is dead. You do not believe that there is evil spirit which lives in some houses?"

"Mr. Mannheim died of grief and loneliness."

"In another house, not so far from neighbours, he would not have taken a gun and killed himself. Maybe it was bad spirit in the house that turned him into a thief. I'm sorry pretty young lady like you go and stay there."

"I'll be fine." I spoke absently, leaning forward to catch the first glimpse of light through the slits in the shutters. I had to wait until we'd circled a second rock bastion that guarded the village from the mountain. As we travelled over the wooden planks of the bridge that spanned the ravine, my face was pressed to the windscreen. The glow of the last street lamp was left behind, and I stared into unrelieved darkness. So fierce was my disbelief that I closed my eyes while I counted ten, but when I opened them the house was as dark as the night that framed it.

"No one home," the driver said. "Maybe they not expect you to come."

I did not answer. The parking ground over which the headlights swept was an empty space of golden rock ground down into hard-packed sand. Out of the whirling conjectures that fought one another like wolves in my head, the least alarming won. This silent and mystifying end to my headlong journey could only be the result of some stupid blunder of mine. Somewhere along the line I should have reacted differently. Why, for instance, hadn't I waited until I could get a call through to Matthew?

The driver repeated louder: "I say no one at home."

"I must have arrived first. They'll be home soon."

I tumbled out of the car. He followed, carrying my suitcase, dogging my footsteps as far as the heavy outer door. The bolt slotted through the central panel was padlocked.

"You have the key?"

If I lied, said yes, he'd wait until I produced it. "No, but I can get in by the outside staircase and through a window in my room." I pressed the five-pound note in his hand, seized the case he'd put on the ground. "Thank you. Good night."

He loomed over me, a huge, immovable, protective presence I did not need or want. "When I drive away you will have no light. I stay till you are safe in house."

There was a raging impatience in me to be rid of him. Until I was alone, undistracted by his well-meaning but hampering solicitude, I wouldn't have a hope of resolving a situation that seemed insoluble. There were perfectly rational explanations for Matthew's non-arrival at the airport and for the empty house. At the moment they eluded me, but once inside I would find them.

I dug into my shoulder-bag, produced a pocket torch, pressed the button. He dismissed the miserable beam of light. "I wait here until you are safe in house. Young English lady at night should not be left alone, locked out of the house of her friends."

"But I shan't be. If I can't get in, I've other friends in the village. I shall go and spend the night with them." I began to run, calling good night, repeating thanks over my shoulder, to the gate that led into the garden. I hurried along the vine-arbour, at the end of which the old, original outside staircase mounted the wall as high as the second storey. In February the latch on one of the two pairs of shutters to my room had been broken, and the window catch itself was hanging by a single screw. I'd reported both to Kim. He'd promised to get busy on them. But though he had an extravagantly equipped work-bench in the cellar, it was a pretty safe bet he'd never got around to such a piffling minor repair. If he'd confounded me by getting busy with hammer and screwdriver, I'd have no means of entry into the house, and no option but to descend into the over-protective arms of the taxi-driver, make good my promise by begging a night's shelter from the Villa Hesperides or from Giselle Nash. Neither appealed to me.

Climbing the deep, uneven steps, I heard a ghost whisper behind me. I turned, lowered the beam of the torch, and sent five midget cats flying from me in terror. Barbie's cats: Minnow, her darling, a pale silver grey, and her progeny of four, a black and white and three tabbies. When I began climbing again, Minnow plucked up enough courage to slink at my heels.

Kim had run true to form. The shutters were unlatched, and the catch on the window was loose enough to pry apart. My relief as I climbed into the room made me breathless.

The taxi-driver who had followed me, called from the bottom of the staircase: "You okay, miss?"

I switched on the light, came back to the window, and leaned out. "Everything's fine. Thank you for all your trouble and for being so kind. Good night."

He remained for what seemed an age, deliberating whether or not to take my word, maybe, for all I knew, questioning my right to break and enter, before with a slow, heavy tread he returned to his cab. I waited by the window until I heard it rumble over the wooden bridge, and then I turned round to examine Matthew's house, which should have been alive with the sounds made by four adults and a child, but which was as silent as a grave.

THREE

My eyes found a guest room unready for a guest, with pillows and blankets, covered by a quilt, arranged in a neat mound on the bed. Athena, who came to clean four mornings a week, ever-protective of her employer's possessions, had rounded up oddments, paperbacks and a couple of side-lamps, stacked them on the dressing-table, and covered them with a length of butter-muslin, behind which they became ghosts of themselves. The rugs were rolled up and tied with string.

I stared at the categorical proof that I was not expected to be where I was, then walked out onto the second-floor landing, where I was faced with three closed doors: Connie's room, Toby's room, and a bathroom. I left them unopened and ran up the inner stone staircase that climbed the wall to Matthew's quarters. The top storey of the house was smaller in dimension than the ones below, encircled by a wide parapet that made a natural observation platform for a series of panoramas over mountains, sea, and village. Matthew had scrawled "Crow's Nest" on the rough plans he'd sketched for the conversion of a series of nondescript rooms into a magnificent sitting-room-study, a bedroom no bigger than a monk's cell, and a bathroom.

The name had stuck. It had been on the Crow's Nest that Giselle had lavished pains, energy, taste, and a talent for accepting nothing short of perfection, plus her knowledge of Matthew. The Crow's Nest was virtually a gift that no one else could have given him.

Here, too, Athena had been at work. Every movable object was collected and tidily stacked on the massive walnut table, shrouded in the ectoplasm-like butter-muslin. She'd even wrapped up my typewriter. Only the solid wall of books had defeated her. The olive-green and pearl-grey bathroom was as stripped and immaculate as if it had been a show piece in a furniture store. The narrow bedroom was in the same state of unpreparedness as mine a floor below. I sucked the air into my lungs and persuaded myself I caught a whiff of tobacco smoke, but it was so faint I could not catch it a second time.

Looking into a void for inspiration, I turned my mind back to the white paper covered in scarlet writing that, for a whole night, had tumbled unread about my sitting-room. Mrs. Pratt had said Matthew had telephoned from Cyprus. But had he? Was that no more than an assumption on her part? It could be that he'd telephoned from Beirut before he caught a plane to Nicosia—and for some reason missed it. Why hadn't I asked Gladwin where Matthew had dispatched the cable from to order his mail to be forwarded to Kessima? Because, I thought with a nip of shame, Gladwin and I played idiotic games like a couple of jealous children intent on scoring off one another.

Mail! I raced down the stone slabs to the ground floor. There was no letter-box, no chink of opening in the massive blue outer door. Connie, when she came downstairs in the morning, opened it, and, unless the house were left empty, it stayed open until nightfall. The postman crossed the courtyard, booby-trapped by painted oil and petrol tins containing Connie's plants, and put his letters and packages on a table inside the sitting-room.

Three letters for Barbie, one for Connie, six for Toby—answers to advertisements he'd cut from English newspapers inviting applications for information on the armed services, language courses, and trial samples of patent medicines. He didn't always bother to read the literature that arrived; the thrill was to be the recipient of letters addressed to Tobias Matthew Mitchell, Esq. Under the table were three balls of screwed-up bills addressed to Kim.

The tidiness of the room was proof that neither Barbie nor Kim had entered it since Athena had cleaned it on Saturday morning. I bent, fingered the ashes of the blood-red carob wood in the open grate. Cold. What else did I expect with the heat of summer lasting beyond darkness!

I felt a gentle but forceful weaving round my ankles. Minnow intimating that she and her grown-up family were on the verge of starvation. She'd been born without vocal cords, which made her silent pleas irresistible.

Four tins of cat-food and a clean dish stood on the draining board in the kitchen. Only Barbie would have put them there. Connie, since Minnow had nipped into the courtyard carrying a squirming live snake to feed to her litter of kittens, had banned them from the house. Thereafter Connie never ventured off a hard path until she'd given it a thorough thrashing with a stick. By the door stood her "snake-boots," a pair of ancient white plastic overshoes into which she burrowed her feet before she stepped into the garden.

Minnow and her brood ate two tins at speed, ears pricked, half-terrified at being fed indoors, as though expecting their arch-enemy to appear and boot them out. The last mouthful gulped, they sidled towards the door that led to the garden. I unchained it, and they vanished in the direction of the straw bed Barbie had made for them under the lemon tree.

No point in looking for clues in the kitchen; it was in the clean scrubbed state in which Athena always left it. I climbed back to the first floor.

In Barbie's pseudo film-star bedroom where, above the bed, silk swags fell from the clasp of a gilded cherub, I opened the fitted wardrobes, ran my hands over the racks of clothes, my nostrils catching a drift of her favourite Dior perfume. Not, like the other two, an abandoned bedroom, in that its occupants could enter it, drop their clothes on the floor—as they invariably did—and dive into bed. In the bathroom there were drips of moisture in the basin, the soap was wet, and in Kim's dressing-room a sweater and a dirty shirt were slung over a chair. The remaining room on the first floor acted as an overflow store-room for the clothes Barbie could not cram into her wardrobes.

On the second floor I found Toby's bed made up under its Indian striped blanket. His books on the side table, which ranged from the Bible to any encyclopaedia on which he could lay hands, were gone, proof that he was away for the night. But his glass bottle of snails was still on the window sill, the pictures of his current heroes: Chay Blyth, Graham Hill, and a variety of astronauts were pinned to the wall. Proof that his absence would be of fairly short duration, otherwise snails and pin-ups would have gone with him.

The photograph of his super-hero, which merited a mock-leather frame, stood on the table by his bed. It was a press photograph. Caught unawares, not particularly pleased, but tolerant of a fellow newspaperman doing his job, there was a quirk to Matthew's mouth. It had been snapped in fierce sunlight that streamed across his dark blond head, narrowed his eyes. I wondered what a stranger seeing it for the first time would make of it, except to recognise it as the photograph of a handsome, forceful man who looked as though he knew precisely where he was going. But had he known on Friday?

I crossed to Connie's room, which was alongside mine. The triple mirror was directly opposite the door, so that the note she'd sticky-taped to the centre panel collided with my glance as I opened it. On it she'd printed: "Address until 16th. September, Miss Constance Tollard, 51, Dewmount Crescent, Surbiton, Surrey. Water courtyard plants every day from well, a can to each. Indoor plants every other day."

Relief was so great that a shaky laugh exploded in my throat. Connie's absence explained. No melodrama. No mystery. She was spending her annual fortnight's vacation with her widowed sister in Surbiton, doing the rounds of the West End theatres, indulging herself in shopping sprees at Bentall's and Marks & Spencer's. The summer holiday, plus a week at Christmas, had been written into the contract Matthew had made with her when, returning to England after a term in the Middle East, he'd found Kim jobless, Toby, at four, wan and asthmatic, and Barbie too dispirited to cope. Kessima, with its mountain air, mild winters, the house free of the last painter and plumber, was the solution. But to move them, provide for their wellbeing necessitated a combined cook, housekeeper, and nanny. Whether Connie had been an old acquaintance or a name on the lists of an employment agency, I'd no idea. Only that she was the perfect candidate for the job. The agreement between Matthew and Connie had twelve months to run, until Toby was eight and went to a preparatory school in Sussex.

To picture Connie in Surbiton with her feet up, half a pound of milk chocolate brazils within reach, watching Sunday night television, released me from the wildly spinning conjectures that had teased my brain numb.

With Connie's absence explained, it was simple to place the others. Barbie and Kim at the Villa Hesperides and, with Connie on holiday, Toby spending the night with Giselle Nash, who after school on two afternoons a week tutored him in English history, geography and introduced him to the novels of Walter Scott and Charles Dickens. Matthew? The guest room that had not been prepared for me? A mind dulled by fatigue could provide only one answer. Mrs. Pratt *had* misheard the day . . . I whispered Sunday, then Monday over and over to myself. On a bad line one word could easily have been mistaken for the other.

The telephone was in the sitting-room on the ground floor, with one extension in Barbie's bedroom and a second for Matthew in the Crow's Nest. From any of them I could have called Giselle and confirmed that Toby was asleep under her roof. A second call to the Villa Hesperides and I'd have learned whether or not Barbie and Kim were there. No more than five minutes' effort, and yet I could not bring myself to lift the receiver. After a day of being bounced from one small shock to another, I preferred belief without confirmation rather than run the marginal risk of having that precious belief snatched away.

I made coffee, drank it hot and strong sitting in a low chair by the dead fire. I told myself I'd only to remain where I was and they'd all come home.

I saw Barbie's sweet, languorous smile, Toby's gap-toothed solemn one, Kim's over-brightly feigning a welcome, feigned because he knew I checked Matthew's bank statements, which demolished the façade he maintained that he was the sole supporter of his wife and child.

Matthew was there too. Relief, gladness burning away his exasperation at schedules that had failed to dovetail, telephone lines that had substituted one day of the week for another. In my head I saw their lips move, but strangely I couldn't hear a word they said. It was as though I'd been smitten with deafness. Presently the silent tableau lulled me to sleep.

I was woken by the sound of a car being driven into the parking space, followed by the slamming of doors and, after an interval, the scratching noise of a key being inserted into the padlock on the outer door.

I stood rigid, hand braced on the arm of a chair, telling myself that an end to my miseries of uncertainty was only seconds away. The great door parted, folded back. The side-lamp I'd lit was not powerful enough to throw its radiance beyond the threshold of the sitting-room, but a moon must have been rising or waning to provide a twilight background against which were silhouetted the figures of two men who stood transfixed and speechless at the sight of me illuminated in a ring of light.

In the soundless spell they put on me, or I on them, my eyes detected a glimmer of white gold, and I cried: "Kim!"

Without uttering a word he moved forward, leaving his companion to close the outer door, his footsteps slow, dragging, as though he needed to spin out time before he was forced to speak. When he reached the big room, he switched on the main light. He blinked, drew a sharp audible breath, and made an ineffectual effort to cloak his stupefaction with a smile of natural astonishment, while I stared at the ugly purple-red bruise that stretched from the corner of his left eyelid down to his jaw. In one place the skin was broken and a dribble of blood had dried into a dark scribble on his cheek.

Before either of us found our tongue, my eye-corner caught a movement in the shadowy courtyard. The second man was big, he limped, and his name was Heller. I was unprepared for the heave of revulsion in my stomach, the crawling sensation over my flesh. In the six months that had passed since I'd glimpsed the other half of Heller's personality, a sadist with a dead heart who did not recognise other people as people but only as objects to satisfy his desire, I'd persuaded myself I'd forgotten the nauseating episode. Heaven knows, I'd wanted to. Now I discovered every sequence was separately alive in my memory.

"Maria!" Kim shouted. "Where the devil have you sprung from?"

"Matthew sent for me."

He came a couple of steps nearer, asked in blank incredibility: "Why should Matthew want you in Cyprus now for God's sake?"

"He didn't say. He was to meet me at the airport this afternoon, but he didn't turn up. I assumed he was here. Isn't he?"

The space between the two men closed up until they stood abreast. Heller's black head topped Kim's by an inch; he was a bulky and immensely solid man. Under the thinnish hair, carefully brushed to a quiff over his forehead, his face was chubby, as rosy-cheeked as a country child's. His mouth was a brilliant, glistening red, as though he were forever licking his lips—though I'd never caught him at it—and aligned in a permanent smile. He shaped his visible image into that of everyone's friend or favourite uncle—depending on their ages. He was a glad-hander and a free-spender. His conceit was so overweening he existed inside a bubble of delusion that he was irresistible to women, that he'd only to spread the flattery thick enough, hand out enough expensive presents, and they'd throw themselves at his feet. The weirdest part was that there were women who did just that. Equally there were others who dubbed him a detestable loud-mouth.

Kim's glance flicked sideways, but Heller did not choose to pick it up. Instead, out of the grotesque clown's mask, he continued to stare at me with eyes narrowed by the little bolsters of fat on his eyelids, which gave a lie to the grin, the rumbling chuckle. They were as cold and remorseless as a winter sea. His memories of that February afternoon were as ineradicable as mine. It was reasonable to suppose, as he was a vain man and vain men don't like botching a job, that the sight of me was as hateful to him as he was to me. But no one looking at him would have suspected it.

Kim said positively: "For once you two must have got your

wires crossed." He appeared so utterly at a loss that my confusion deepened. "Matthew left here on Friday night. He's been and gone. You've missed one another. Planes that pass in the night!" He smiled at his own weak joke, turned to Heller. "Isn't that so? I mentioned to you yesterday when I was over at your place that Matthew had paid us a flying visit."

The focus of Heller's glance did not shift—by now he'd probably got my dress off, and was down to my bra and pants—but he concurred affably: "That's right. According to you he came Thursday, left Friday evening."

Kim nodded. "On Thursday about midday he telephoned me from Beirut and ordered me to pick him up at the airport, ferry him here. Which, like a good boy, I did."

"What made him come to Kessima three weeks earlier than he planned? Was it for personal reasons, or because of the political situation, the rumours flying around?"

"Rumours!" He shrugged his shoulders derisively. "There are always rumours, but who listens to them! Presumably some sort of crisis blew up—then the big man's life is littered with crises! Or maybe he fancied a twenty-four-hour break. He didn't confide in me. In fact, I hardly set eyes on him; he was up in the Crow's Nest working—or resting—anyway, incommunicado. Late on Friday afternoon, he called for his private chauffeur to drive him to the airport, and I again obeyed his command."

"That's where you left him, at the airport?"

"No. Not to let his left hand know what his right is up to is so engrained in our dear Matthew he can't help acting as though he's an undercover man for M.I.5. Maybe he is."

My expression must have warned him to cut the wisecracks. He went on: "We left here around 6.15. When we were approaching Nicosia, he looked at his watch, said he'd got time in hand, and would I drop him in Metaxas Square as there was a friend he wanted to see. I wouldn't have expected him to tell me the name of his buddy, and he didn't. He said, very gracious of him, that I needn't hang around; he'd pick up a cab to take him on to the airport. So, chauffeur dismissed!"

"Did he actually tell you he was catching a plane to Heathrow?"

He gave a groan of intense exasperation. "My dear Maria, I

repeat, he told me nothing about where he was going or why. Then he never does."

I pressed: "Nothing to suggest he might be returning to Kessima today?"

"I keep telling you, not a word."

Heller gave his avuncular chuckle, shook his head in feigned sympathy. "Dear, oh dear! Quite a little mystery for you to solve, Miss Maria. You say he wrote and asked you to meet him at Nicosia airport today?"

I gritted my teeth at the ridiculous name by which he addressed me—an affectation that amused some women but infuriated me. He knew I'd said nothing about a letter; he'd been listening too hard. "He didn't write; he telephoned."

Kim blinked, his mouth opened and shut once, before he demanded: "When? Where from? What did he say?"

"On Friday morning, from here. I wasn't in the flat and his message was taken down by the woman who cleans for me."

There was a moment's silence in which the cold grey eyes wedged between their rolls of fat, and Kim's startled blue ones, fastened on me. Kim said slowly: "What time on Friday morning."

"Around eleven."

Heller suggested amiably: "But when you got the message you telephoned him back, didn't you?"

"I'd been staying with my sister in Cornwall and I didn't read it until this morning. When I phoned through here I couldn't get any reply."

Kim tore his glance from me, turned it on Heller, said draggingly: "Sounds to me that char of yours is deaf or a bit slow in the uptake. Either that or she got her dates wrong. Why should Matthew ask you to fly out here when he was flying to London?"

I countered: "Why should he cable Gladwin to forward his mail to Cyprus if he didn't intend to stay long enough to collect it?"

Heller slapped his thigh in self-congratulation. "I've got it. Only one answer. Matthew must have sent you another message cancelling out the first, and it's snarled up in the pipeline or lost. It's happened to me a million times. The inefficiency drives you crazy, but try complaining, and it gets you nowhere."

Ignoring him, I asked Kim: "Where are Barbie and Toby?"

"In Troodos. The heat got Barbie down and Toby caught a summer cold. Also one week without Connie was enough for her. They're due back tomorrow, or rather today."

"Matthew must have telephoned Barbie."

"If he did she didn't mention it when we talked over the phone this morning."

"You told her he'd been here?"

"Would you have fancied telling Matthew's doting little stepsister that he'd flown in and out of the island without as much as bothering to phone hello to her? Not likely!" His tone became as peevish as though I were deliberately harassing him. "Maria, for God's sake, it's after two. I happen to have a damned hard day and at the end of it you drop out of the sky and expect me to play guessing games with you. Well, it's not on. We'll sort out this mess, if mess there is, in the morning." He turned to Heller. "Like to doss down here? You can have Toby's room. Save you the drive home."

Heller declined, gave me the mock bow that like the "Miss Maria" afforded him exquisite pleasure because he knew, with his avuncular image exploded into dust, it enraged me past bearing. "Good night, Miss Maria. Happy dreams. I hope you and your boss catch up with one another real quick, else he'll get all disorganised not having you to look after him. But don't you worry your pretty little head. I'll always be glad to pull a few strings to help you run him to earth. No trouble at all. In fact, it would be a pleasure."

"Night, boy." He clapped Kim's shoulders. "Be seeing you."

I did not thank him. I did not look anywhere near his false clown's face, but I was conscious as he walked away that his limp was more pronounced. At the door he waved his right hand, which had a shiny stump instead of a little finger, chuckled with mockery and malice inaudible to any ears but mine: "Don't forget, any service at any time, Miss Maria."

When I'd paid my first visit to Kessima, Heller was already established in his gaunt, graceless villa that overhung the cliff on the coast road. According to Barbie there'd been a Mrs. Heller, but she'd disappeared years before, and the house was run by a middle-aged English housekeeper. Heller entertained lavishly both there and on his yacht, forever doing favours to curry favour—with an obsessive need to be accepted and liked by the English residents. He won Giselle's heart by procuring six bottles of her father's favourite whisky, a rare blend not normally procurable on the island. Barbie, who wasn't above dropping hints of small—and sometimes large—items for which she hankered, was forever being presented with beribboned packages.

Inevitably there were speculations as to how he'd come by his money, his limp, and his missing finger. A mercenary in the Congo, a trader in illicit arms, a bank robber were some of the more colourful suggestions. Heller's story was that he'd sold his haulage business while still young enough to enjoy a good time in the sun.

Less than a month before, when I'd been clipping and marking newspapers, I'd come across an inch of type with a Nicosia date line. The body of a young man had been washed up on the northern coast. He'd still been wearing a snorkle and was believed to be an Englishman, Bruce Vernon, who'd been visiting friends on the island.

I'd handed it to Matthew. "If it is Bruce, he must have been staying with Heller. He always does. Do you remember him? Kim brought him to the house quite a few times. Curly ginger hair and freckles. He had a terrible line in corny jokes that used to make Barbie hoot with laughter."

"Yes, I do. He was some sort of salesman, wasn't he? Poor devil."

A week later there'd been an equally brief report on the inquest. Death by misadventure. Heller had given evidence that Vernon, an enthusiastic but weak swimmer, had persisted, despite repeated cautions that the sea was treacherous on that section of the coast, in swimming alone. On the last occasion, though Mrs. Bales, his housekeeper, had pointed out that there was less than an hour before sunset, he'd ignored the warning. When he did not return, a boat was launched, a search party organised, but it had failed to find him. He was unmarried and both his parents were dead.

Matthew shook his head. "It was a damned foolhardy thing to do. Those gullies on either side of Heller's villa are death traps for anyone but a swimmer of near Olympic standard. I once tried them and beat a hasty retreat."

"You'd have thought that knowing Bruce had gone into the sea so near dusk, someone would have kept an eye on him."

"Underwater all they'd have had to keep an eye on would have been a snorkle!" He gave me a mildly sardonic grin. "What are you suggesting, foul play? Allowing your dislike of Heller to prejudice you?"

For a moment I wondered how he would react if I told him of that nauseating five minutes. But I was too abysmally ashamed of having been fooled—and, yes, frightened—to breathe a word to anyone. Self-disgust that I'd landed myself in such a corny situation—and had, literally, to fight my way out of it—kept me silent.

"Not foul play, but maybe guilty of just a little callousness. Bruce had been gone an hour and a half before they raised the alarm. Come to that you're not keen on Kim half living in Heller's pocket, and forever turning up with some rich gift for Barbie. So what's the difference?"

"Simple. If someone happens to be under an obligation to you, particularly someone as touchy as Kim, you have to be ultra-scrupulous not to trade on it. For instance, by criticising his choice of friends."

That had been one of the occasions—there weren't many—when I thought: You lean so far backwards to be fair, not to judge any issue without weighing every contributory factor, that you end up going round in blinkers.

As Heller's car drove over the bridge across the ravine, Kim's temper boiled over. "Maria, I'm all in, so for God's sake, don't start another inquisition. I couldn't take it."

He did in truth look so exhausted I wouldn't have been surprised if he'd dropped in his tracks. I wondered what exertion, mental or physical, had brought him to such a state, especially on a Sunday when he hadn't even the excuse of being at "the office."

"What happened to your cheek?" For the first time I noticed his hands: the flesh was ripped back from two nails; the palms were scratched and bruised. "You look as though you've been in a fight." If he had, it would have been one he hadn't been able to duck; otherwise he wouldn't have risked his handsome face, which was part of his stock in trade. Also he had an unmanly aversion to the sight of blood. Even Toby knew better than to ask his father to bandage a skinned knee.

He scowled. "Brawling's hardly my line. I got bumped off the road into a ditch by some maniac who came tearing round a hairpin bend in the middle of the road."

"Would you like me to bathe it? I know Connie keeps witch hazel in one of the kitchen cupboards for Toby's bangs and bashes."

"No, thanks." He turned away, leaving me his unmarred profile. Even tired, as he undoubtedly was, so far as physique went, he was extraordinarily handsome. But looks, an ability to charm until he became bored—which he did quicker than most people —were the sole gift providence had handed out to him. "What I need is a good stiff drink and bed, not a ministering angel."

He was welcome to his drink, and to his bed, but not until I'd asked him one more question that screamed for an answer. "You must have told Matthew that Barbie and Toby were at Troodos and due back tomorrow—no, today—so why didn't he wait and see them? Didn't you find it very odd that he didn't?"

"Since I find half of what Matthew does odd, no. He's by way of being a law unto himself. You should know! Now go to bed, there's a good girl. If you've any more questions, save them until daylight."

I left him pouring a treble whisky, collected sheets and a pillow case from the linen cupboard, and made up my bed. In it, I listened in the dark for Kim to come upstairs. But first, I knew by the tell-tale ping of that instrument by Barbie's bedside immediately below me that he made a telephone call. At 2.30 A.M. who would he be likely to telephone except a man who was abroad as late as himself? Heller.

He had no need to climb higher than the first floor, but he chose to do so. I'd left the door ajar for coolness, and he paused outside it, then eased it open. The dim light filtering up from the floor below must have shown him my apparently sleeping form. After five minutes' heavy breathing, he went down again, twice missing his footing and swearing foully.

If there'd been any laughter in me, I'd have laughed at Kim engaged on an act of petty spying, and, typically, making such an unholy din that the operation defeated itself.

In the darkness I lay trying to fight my way through the confusions and contradictions of the day behind me, and failed. I strained to match fact against conjecture, and was left with a host of flying ends.

Gradually there crept upon me a sense of loneliness that clung to me like a shroud, which for a long while I couldn't rationalise. Then the answer came. I'd never slept in this room without being enfolded in the lovely knowledge that Matthew was sleeping immediately above my head.

FOUR

I was woken, when the sunlight was streaming through both windows in pale golden swathes, by footsteps above me. On the instant certainty flew into my head, stayed there. Matthew had arrived during the night. He was upstairs. I'd only to mount twenty stone slabs and I'd find him, and all the multiplying confusions of yesterday would be reduced to a ridiculous comedy of errors to be laughed out of sight. My heart gone wild with relief, I grabbed my dressing-gown from my open suitcase and, not pausing for slippers, ran up the stairs.

Kim stood at the top, the upper half of his body in shadow, wearing the same blue denims, bright patterned open-neck shirt he'd worn the night before, suggesting he hadn't taken his clothes off before he went to bed. Any face seen from below takes on a different perspective, becomes half strange. His looked wholly so.

I shouted up at him: "Has he come?"

He shouted back, with a different emotion from mine but as high and urgent: "Of course he hasn't. Why should you suppose he had?"

"I thought I heard him."

After a moment of uneasy silence, he jerked out: "There was a rainstorm during the night. Didn't you hear it? The roof's sprung a bit of a leak and I went up to make sure no water had dripped in."

Disappointment robbed me of my voice, but not of my reasoning powers. If Matthew's room had been turned into a swamp, Kim would not have bestirred himself at 7.30 in the morning. After a late night Connie counted herself lucky if she bullied him out of bed by ten o'clock.

He descended to my level, put his arm round my shoulders, and edged me down the stairs, back into my room. His voice feigned kindness, but his eyes flicking over me were tense, edgy. "Not to worry. We'll soon get everything sorted out. Tell you what, I'll give you a treat, bring your breakfast to bed. Hop back in again."

Instead of doing so, I stood by the window that looked south, struggling to come to terms with the cruel back-lash of disappointment. Gradually my eyes and senses absorbed the skin-deep comfort of the absolute quality of the light that revealed, as though it were a magnifying glass, the pink and grey rock of the mountains, bared every separate rib against the cloudless blue sky. I'd forgotten the wonder of the light; I always did. My glance slid down the lower green foothills until it reached the night-cooled garden. Under the pyramid of think glossy leaves three of the little hard green lemons were brushed with streaks of yellow. On their straw bed Minnow and her grown-up kittens were knotted into a variegated quilt of fur. The bougainvillaea spread a stunning cerise cover over the roof of the wooden shed in which Connie kept her gardening tools: the whole an ancient landscape of heat and abundant, never-flagging sun.

The earth in the watering pits round the shrubs and trees was deepened from gold to orange-ochre with the night rain, but already no single drop of moisture was visible. It couldn't have been much of a storm, no more than to release a tangy fragrance into the air. Yet Kim, who should have slept like a log, had bestirred himself about drips! I tried the other window. The shutters were bone dry. I dismissed the leaky roof as an unlikely tale. What had tempted Kim up to the Crow's Nest was the kick he got out of ferreting among other people's possessions, which was why Matthew kept his private papers under lock and key. But since Kim had had months to pry into drawers and cupboards, I could find no purpose for his early-morning search.

The morning glories that ran wild among the brambles choking the ravine were uncrinkling their purple petals before my eyes. Seen from above, the village's network of alleys made a spider's web, coiling at half a dozen different levels about the tightly set white cube houses. Far, far away, there was a point where the blue of the sky merged, without a hair-line mark, into the blue of the sea.

The primary children, satchels swinging against their backs, ran through the slabs of sun and shadow to school. Toby, if he'd been home, would have been among them. I picked out his "best friend", Eugenia, her black hair hanging in two pigtails tied with blue bows. I saw Aristo, who at fourteen was a skilled potter, unlock the door of his father's shop and disappear inside to work at his wheel. I was watching a shepherd coaxing his glossy brown and cream sheep, with their huge swinging tails, across the bridge, when Kim, balancing a tray on one knee, pushed open the door. He'd made coffee, toast, added butter and honey. In the early years of his marriage, before Matthew made them a gift of Connie, presumably in self-defence he'd learned basic cooking. This was the first time I'd seen any evidence of it, and I must have shown my surprise.

He quipped: "You couldn't do better in a four-star hotel, so back to bed and have it like a four-star guest."

I declined, but cleared the bedside table, sat on the edge of the bed. He pulled up a chair opposite, poured out two cups of coffee. His bruised cheek had paled a little during the night; even so it must cause him discomfort, and I couldn't understand why, a born hypochondriac, he wasn't making an unholy fuss about it. Catching me staring at it, he abruptly altered the angle of his chair, so that the discoloured side of his profile was hidden from me—as though it were something shameful he wished to pretend wasn't there. With his high regard for his good looks, he probably did!

Though he'd little reason to appear less jaded than he'd been when, a full hour after I'd left him, he'd gone to bed, he was at pains to be cheerful and conciliatory. If Matthew's telephone call to me had been sparked off by some crisis involving Barbie and Toby, it had not touched him—or so he would have me believe. Still striving to rationalise the events of the previous day, I drank my coffee in silence, left the initiative to him.

He cleared his throat, said in a reasonable, ingratiating way: "Don't you think the quickest way to short-circuit this shambles in communication between you and Matthew would be for you to fly back to London?" When I did not answer, he went on: "The Volvo went into the garage on Saturday to have the front bumper straightened, but Antinou swore he'd have it ready this morning. I could run you to the airport when I pick up Connie. Or earlier, if you like." His glance of enquiry was ingenuously hopeful. Too hopeful! "What do you say?"

"First I'll have to find out whether Matthew is back at the flat. I'll telephone Gladwin around nine o'clock."

"Won't Matthew take a pretty dim view of you hanging about here if he wants you somewhere else?"

"Maybe," I agreed, and added that, since Barbie and Toby were due home today, I might as well stay long enough to see them. I could always catch the night plane.

His conciliatory mood switched to one of sullen resentfulness. It didn't surprise me. The only idolised child of a widowed mother who'd died when he was nineteen, he'd never acclimatised himself to having his will denied. He argued back with some heat: "Heller's right. Can't you see it? Matthew must have sent you a second message cancelling out the first, and it's got lost in the pipeline. Why should he order you to fly out to Nicosia on Sunday when he must have known he wouldn't be here to meet you?"

"I imagine he didn't know."

With a gesture of exasperation at my obduracy he abandoned his breakfast, went to the window, and with hunched shoulders looked up into the mountains. I thought: He wanted me to leave, and now I've refused he's lost his temper, is seething with frustration because he has no power to order me to go. Examining him, I glimpsed some other emotion. Alarm? Unease? I couldn't be sure, only that his nerves were on edge. Because his mind lacked depth and precision it was always a temptation to underestimate Kim. Actually, under pressure, he could be devious and surprisingly shrewd. I wondered if he was under pressure now, and if so who was exerting the pressure; also why he wanted me out of the house before Connie and Barbie arrived home.

I'd looked away while I'd been thinking, and when I glanced back I saw he'd half turned from the window and was staring fixedly at my open suitcase. Tipped into the lid were the files I'd taken out of the safe. I saw him moisten his lips before he asked: "Did Matthew tell you to bring those with you?"

"They're some I picked out in case he happened to need them."

He looked at me sharply, strangely, with an unusual degree of intentness. "But he did *ask* you to bring them when he telephoned?"

I parried a question he'd no right to put. "I exercised my own judgment. Why the sudden interest in Matthew's files?"

He shrugged his shoulders. "I just marvel that he never stops working. He's either writing his head off or snooping round the corridors of power fishing for breath-taking revelations."

His cheap sarcasm rooted in jealousy wasn't worth an acknowledgement. When I didn't speak, he said with a pretence of not caring: "Well, suit yourself, but I'm willing to bet that you'll discover before the day's out that you've been wasting your time. After I've picked up the Volvo, I'll be at the office, and I won't be back until I bring Connie from the airport. Oh, by the way, it's Carima's birthday and Alex has laid on a party for her tonight. If you're still here, I'm sure they'd want you to go along."

So he still maintained the fiction of having an office. When he'd first come to Cyprus, through Matthew's influence he'd got a job as a salesman with Zinia Kattamis, who owned an estate and land agency with branches in Kyrenia, Larnaca, and Famagusta. Presumably she'd gambled on the persuasive powers of a charming, highly presentable Englishman selling his compatriots villas and flats. She'd lost, and fired him shortly before I began working for Matthew. Since then he'd dabbled in a car-hire business, water-ski instruction and now had a cupboard of an office tucked away in a back street behind Kyrenia harbour. He talked airily of land deals, yacht chartering, and other gentlemanly ploys, but I knew, and he must have been aware that I knew, that what he picked up did little more then keep him in cigarettes.

Standing well back so that he couldn't see me, I watched him cross the bridge, pass through the sharp angles of sunlight and shadow down the main street that would lead him to Antinou's garage. He walked with his head bent, like a man oppressed with a mountain of trouble. His moods, like Barbie's, were mercurial: alight with expectation of rich profit one minute, despairing the next. I knew better than to try to make any coherent pattern out of them.

I showered and dressed, then hung up the few clothes I'd brought with me, not one of which would see me through the way-out extravaganza of a party that Alex would lay on for Carima's birthday. Possessed by a deep-down, rumbling uneasiness, I found it paradoxical that I should give a thought to being excluded from what was no more than a routine festive occasion. Ah, but if I were honest, it wasn't missing the party I minded, but missing seeing Donald Hardwick. By now I longed desperately for a decision to make itself between us. For the emotional fire we'd lit in one another, and which still flickered, to blaze or fall into dead ashes. Simply, to know one way or the other.

I closed the wardrobe door and climbed up to the Crow's Nest. Sitting at Matthew's great table, I asked for the number of the Curzon Street flat. The operator reported there was no reply. That in itself was an answer. If he'd arrived there, Matthew certainly wouldn't be abroad at 9 A.M. And with his master absent Gladwin was having a long lie in.

Next I tried every airline with an office in Nicosia. None of them had a record of Matthew Grant boarding a plane on Friday or Saturday. Alex wasn't the only owner of a private plane on the island. Among others, there was a jockey, whom Matthew knew, who used one to fly him to race meetings. I was racking my brains to remember his name when, through the window, I saw a familiar figure coming across the bridge. A black kerchief hid her face; a black cotton dress with a gathered skirt reached to her ankles. Athena! If Matthew had been in the house on Friday morning Athena would have seen and talked to him. Then I remembered there were two weekdays she didn't come, and I wasn't sure which days they were.

When I met her in the courtyard, she pressed her palms together, the loose black sleeves falling back to reveal her sticklike arms. Her face, the colour and texture of crumpled brown paper, glowed with pleasure within. She wished me good morning, making a weird sound of my name, and then her hands flew apart, and she pointed up the staircase. "Master?"

When I said no, a pained, worried look screwed up her face, and she moved her head from side to side in distress, talking rapidly in Greek, the words bursting in quick spurts from her mouth, her sloe-black, lustrous eyes beseeching me to understand.

Before I'd visited Kessima for the first time Matthew had suggested I learn the Greek alphabet, simple phrases, and above all, the words for please and thank you. "How would you like to be a waiter or a shopkeeper and find that people who've lived in your country for twenty or more years don't have sufficient regard for you to learn how to thank you for a service in your own language?"

I'd learnt the alphabet, strings of common phrases, but they'd grown rusty from disuse. Every Cypriot I met spoke some English and was determined to practise it. Even Athena liked you to wish her good morning in English so that she could reply with the only phrase she knew of a foreign tongue. The result was that in a crisis we had not enough common words between us for me to ask the questions I wanted her to answer. Apart from Matthew, Toby was the only one in the household who could conduct a conversation with her. Connie and she communicated in a vigorous sign language. Barbie said: "Hello, Athena," and left her to Connie. Kim mouthed key words, like coffee, as though she were a deaf imbecile.

In the end even her inexhaustible patience broke, and she beckoned me upstairs, looking behind her all the way until we reached the Crow's Nest. She was nimbler than I was, less out of breath when she ran to the opposite end of the walnut table from the telephone, swished aside the butter-muslin, and held out to me in her palms a crystal ash-tray that was broken in two. It had been a birthday present to Matthew from Giselle last February. Watching him unwrap it, acknowledging the perfection of the exquisite simple design, I'd wondered how she'd known the date; she could only have asked Barbie.

And now Athena was riven by distress because she'd broken it, as though harm to an employer's possession was a sin past forgiveness. I took it from her, smiled, and comforted her, hoping that the tone if not the words would communicate to her that no one, certainly not Matthew, would blame her. It was a clean break, and I put the two pieces together to suggest, perhaps, it could be repaired. She stopped protesting, and with a sad hopelessness closing on her face, left me and went downstairs. I laid the two pieces of crystal on the table. When Toby was back I'd ask him to tell Athena she wasn't to worry about the breakage.

Alone, I found myself involuntarily going through a little ritual of substitution that only the lonely and the bereaved perform to lace threads of comfort into their empty hearts: touching with my fingertips the articles of his trade. Matthew's hand had gripped the ruler, his forefingers closed upon the pen, his elbow had rubbed the leather of the blotter. It was a ritual that filled my ears and eyes with beautifully precise images of him: his smile that enchanted, his natural air of grandeur, his rich, buoyant laugh, his look of brooding aloofness that contrasted with his gay humour, and his burning fervency for a cause or a purpose but never, at least in my sight, for a person other than Toby and Barbie. And all the while my fingers touched I longed with my whole being to reach a state of mind where I could exist without the support of such a pitiful, shameful prop.

I set each piece in its place, the last one a fading snapshot in a leather frame of a youngish woman which he kept on the third bookshelf. She had the merriest, brightest eyes and a mop of undisciplined dark curly hair. Her arm was curved round the shoulders of a boy. Both of them were barefooted, his shorts and her skirt blown awry by the strong wind that rolled in from the sea behind them. She was Annie, who had married Matthew's widowed father when Matthew was ten years old. "Never believe," he said when I first saw the picture, "all the tales you hear about hard-hearted stepmothers. I drew a winner, a woman with a great big loving heart and a head that was incapable of containing a mean or jealous thought." Barbie's mother, who with her husband had been killed in a coach crash when Barbie was seventeen. The wells of love Matthew had left over from Annie he lavished on her daughter, including that most precious by-product of love: illimitable patience.

When I'd finished, I frowned at an empty space. His anglepoise desk lamp was missing. It wasn't anywhere in the room; maybe Kim or Barbie had borrowed it. I'd ask them.

A corner of an envelope projected from one of the sidecovers of the blotter. I opened the flap to tidy it away. On it Matthew had written two and a half words: "Miss Giselle Na . . ." The envelope was empty. It could have been written and abandoned in February—or two days ago. I held it to the light. Was the ink faded? I couldn't decide, but what it decided for me was how I should spend the next hour.

The friendship between Giselle and Matthew stemmed from before I knew him. His house was almost an extension of her own; after all she'd been its overlord when it was reduced to a skeleton, supervising the laying on of the flesh of new plaster and paint. Sometimes I suspected—maybe unfairly—that she was Barbie's friend solely on account of Barbie's kinship with Matthew. The relationship between Matthew and Giselle obsessed me because I had never managed accurately to gauge its depth and quality, which was why I had not run early in the morning down the spider's web of alleys to question Giselle. Before seeing her I had to put on my best face, not with the hope of matching her perfection but of narrowing the gap.

I changed shorts and top for a sleeveless blue linen dress, brushed my hair, letting it lie about my shoulders before, remembering the mounting heat outside, I pinned it up on the crown of my head.

For all my efforts, the self that stared back at me from the mirror was about my worst: mouth too tense, deadly dull grey eyes grown a size too large by the pressure of anxiety, and light brown hair that needed a month of sun to streak it with gold. With all the merciless truth of a thirteen-year-old, Diana had commented when I was fourteen: "You look like some awful Little Orphan Annie until you smile, and then you're not half bad." And Matthew, nearly a decade later, had remarked: "It's extraordinary, you only have to be happy to become a raving beauty. You should make a habit of it, being happy, I mean." As though my happiness were no concern of his!

I'd written my letter home and was on the threshold of the courtyard when I saw Carima's mini-moke turn in. Donald Hardwick jumped out. His glance, as he whipped off his sun glasses, was warm and glad, brushed with hope or excitement. A blessedly uncomplicated man, he seemed to possess the knack of throwing off his grudges in the night, maybe because he preferred to be happy, to have happy people about him. Then, given the choice, who didn't! His deep hazel glance was open and direct, with a marvellous clarity, almost a sweetness, that stirred my heart.

He stood smiling at me. "Are you coming in or going out?"

"Going out, but there's no rush."

"Fine! All the way here I've been warning myself that I might find you incarcerated in Matthew's eyrie. How is he this morning?"

"I'm still waiting for him to arrive."

Under the shock of surprise some of the gladness left his face. "You mean he didn't turn up at the airport?"

"No. I took a cab." Athena had opened the side-door that led through to the garden where the vine rambled over its high supports to provide shade except where the sun penetrated the leaves to speckle the garden furniture with gold. "Shall we stay outside? It's still cool. What'll you have? Coffee? A drink?"

"Nothing, thanks." His voice was abstracted, and, following at my heels, he asked: "When *do* you expect him?"

"I'm not absolutely sure. Any time, I guess."

He did not speak until the table was between us. "Somehow I imagined you two never lost touch. To an outsider it almost seems as though a sort of extra-sensory perception operates between you."

I laughed because I wanted to make him laugh, for him to be made happy again. "It's news to me, and if anything as kinky as that did exist, it's definitely on the blink now. At this moment I simply haven't a clue where he is or when he will arrive."

He didn't laugh, but he watched me laughing, and I watched the tension easing out of him. "So I'm in luck, or I hope I am. I was to have spent this morning at the site with Alex, but a crisis blew up in one of his other companies, and the trip's postponed until four this afternoon." There was a tiny pause before he said very quickly: "What would you say to the idea of an early lunch at one of the hotels on the coast?"

"I'd love to say yes, but . . ."

A flash of discomforture, almost hurt, crossed his face, as he finished for me: "But you can't. Well, we've covered this ground before, haven't we! Not to worry."

We'd met three times since February. We'd had two dinners together and once danced half the night away at a discotheque. We'd shared a Sunday lunch and lingered so long over it that, since I'd promised to spend the afternoon at home, he'd driven me to Esher, suffered with grace one of my mother's stodgy Sunday teas. She'd telephoned me next day to award him her stamp of approval. Wryly, but not minding too much, I'd seen her shaking out the Brussels lace bridal veil, a family heirloom, which had graced her head and Diana's on their wedding days.

The fourth time he'd telephoned to make a date for the evening, I'd been within an hour of leaving for Paris with Matthew, and on the fifth due to work through half the night researching background for a slot Matthew was filling on I.T.V. Thereafter there'd been no contact between us until we'd met at the airport, but I knew with a knowledge that hums down the senses that, if the relationship had not been interrupted, in one way or another, most likely in the orthodox way—some at least of his senior partners might have frowned on one of their rising juniors entering into a union unblessed by state or church—we would have belonged to each other.

I said, to take the hurt off his face that he was struggling to hide: "It's not Matthew. I want to be here when Barbie and Toby get back from Troodos. It's a long, hot ride and Barbie will be all in. Connie's been on holiday in England and isn't due until early evening. Don't you see, I can't not be here. I must do something about supper for them."

His face cleared of the suspicion that had darkened it. "Except for Connie and Toby, you don't have to do a thing about supper. A gargantuan one is already laid on for Carima's birthday party: champagne, caviar, not to mention fireworks which I've rather rashly undertaken to stage-manage. Everything but roast swan and troops of Hussars! Carima sent me with a message that she'll never forgive you and Matthew if you don't turn up. And she means it."

"I'm sure she does." But it was Matthew she wanted, not me. "But I didn't come equipped for a super-party. To use the oldest chiché in the world, I've nothing to wear."

He half-laughed, half-sighed, and I knew whatever had threatened us was outdistanced. "My reply to that is another equally old cliché: come as you are. Honestly, it couldn't matter less what you wear. There are to be upwards of two hundred guests and some of them are bound to be weirdies in chain-mail or fake yak hides." He paused, then openly pleaded, his face grave under a tyranny of hope: "Come because I want you to so very much."

Was it at that moment, when tenderness brimmed in me, that I sentenced my old love to death? If so it was because he seemed to promise me light, escape from the dark loneliness to which two years ago I'd condemned myself.

"Maybe I can borrow something of Barbie's. I'll ask her when she arrives."

He said simply: "Just come, that's all that matters." He looked up the garden where English flowers that Connie bullied into staying alive in a temperature that could rise to a hundred degrees were sick or dying, then with open supplication at me. "Will you promise me you'll come?"

I promised. He said: "I'll be waiting for you," and left quickly as though to linger might threaten that promise. Like me he was searching hungrily, sometimes in hope, sometimes in despair, but unlike me he had no crippling burden of the heart to discharge.

FIVE

As I descended the gritty tangle of streets lined with shutters closed against the sun, smiles and greetings were heaped on me. Andreas—the signboard of his shop announced "Merchant Tailor"—came running to shake my hand between his two podgy ones, and the smallest of Aristo's sisters shyly offered me a zinnia minus its stalk.

The only shopkeeper who did not demean himself by recognising my existence was the butcher hacking at his haunches of meat and unspeakable bunches of entrails suspended from hooks in his cavernlike shop. It wasn't to be expected that he'd bestow a smile on anyone who lived under the same roof as his traducer. Connie was forever flaying him with words he didn't understand—but in a tone he did—on his filthy, unhygienic habits. Scraggy goat and tasteless lamb! Until Kim revolted, Connie fed them on hashed corned beef and tinned ham to an accompaniment of blood-curdling predictions of epidemics of food-poisoning that never happened.

Having descended to the level of the square, I posted my letter home and climbed up a flight of uneven steps to a street even narrower than most that ended in a cul-de-sac. Giselle's house only differed from its fellows in that the cube was so dazzlingly white the paint might have been wet. Inside there were two rooms and a kitchen downstairs; upstairs two bedrooms and a bathroom. A ten-year-old baby Fiat that I'd never seen other than shining and dust-free fitted like a painted sardine into a tiny drive-in at the side of the house.

Two terra-cotta urns of tumbling white geraniums guarded the door—not for Giselle the old petrol and paint cans that most people, including Connie, put into service as plant pots. The knocker was a bronze dolphin. I knocked and when there was no reply, pushed against the half-open door and stood on the threshold of a cool, dimmed room that was functional, restful, and, in a modest way, beautiful. There were silken rugs on the stone floor, which glowed with a grey-gold patina, an antique clock with a gentle tick, a faded walnut desk, chairs and stools and a low table on which lay an atlas and a copy of *Barnaby Rudge* with, drawn up to it, a small chair for Toby. Bookshelves took up one wall and on the opposite one, where the light favoured it, hung an oil painting of Colonel Nash, and below it a specially designed frame for his medals. He had a wide-sweeping ink-black moustache, a hawklike glance, and an autocratic tilt to his head.

From the smaller room a querulous voice croaked: "Who is it? Who are you? What do you want?"

The sparse remnants of Colonel Nash's ebony hair were snow-white and wispy, the moustache yellowy-grey, but he still retained the autocratic tilt to his head, and as imperious a manner as when he'd commanded a battalion in the Indian Army, even though his glance was milky and practically sightless. His knotted hands, stained with brown patches, plucked irascibly at the fringe of a shawl wrapped round his knees. "Who are you?" he repeated before I could answer. "Coming in here, without so much as a by-your-leave!"

"I beg your pardon, Colonel. I did knock. I'm Maria Caron and I work for Matthew Grant. I came to see Giselle. Is she anywhere about?"

"You'll find her picking the olives. I trust you haven't come to beg any favours from her. She does too many. People take advantage of her kindness. And I'd be obliged if you would refrain from smoking either inside or outside in the garden. Last time she visited us, Mr. Grant's housekeeper had the impertinence to smoke and the house reeked of the loathsome weed for weeks. You understand me?"

"Actually, I don't smoke. May I go and find Giselle?"

"Provided you remember that her time is fully occupied and she has none to spare to run errands for Mr. Grant. He exploits her, and you are at liberty to tell him so from me."

With eyes that could only see me as a blur he watched me as closely as if my intention were to steal the silver. He hadn't married until he was middle-aged. Soon after his daughter was born he'd lost his wife and, somewhere along the road, most of his money. When I first met Giselle they'd been living in Cyprus for eight or nine years. Two weekday afternoons she spent balancing the accounts of a citrus farmer; on another two she tutored Toby, and on the remaining two she acted in a care-taking capacity for a dozen villas whose occupants were only in residence for short periods of the year. The name of Giselle Nash was a by-word in Kessima: a sort of magic wand people waved when they needed an instant solution to a problem.

I walked through the kitchen and the open door into a garden that ascended in a gentle gradient towards the foothills. No fetish here for the English annuals and biennials over which Connie fretted and fumed. Just the apricot earth snaking through the shining-leaved lemon and pomegranate trees, a great mound of passion flowers, a rosemary hedge, tumbling coral and purple bougainvillaea, and well-watered beds of cucumbers and tomatoes. Over my head the ripening bunches of grapes on the vine were enclosed in muslin bags to protect them from the ravages of wasps.

Outside the back door were the twin domes of Giselle's Greek sealed ovens. In one she baked bread, in the other meat. There seemed no art to which Giselle couldn't turn her hand from exquisite flower arrangements to water divining. Her competency, resource, ability to cram twice as much as the normal person into twenty-four hours, made you suspect that, if the whole world exploded in flames and only one human survived, that human being would be Giselle Nash.

In the garden where the burned grasses shimmered in the sun, I saw her rhythmically shaking the silver-leaved branches to send the olives cascading onto the white sheets she'd spread. Satan, his upper lip curling back from his great ugly teeth, gave me a wicked leer. All the donkeys I'd known had been docile, appealing animals. Not so Satan. If anyone but his mistress came within reach of his vicious heels, he kicked out and more than often reached his target. Witches were supposed to have cats as familiars. Giselle had a vile-tempered donkey, but, to be fair, no one but me would have dreamt of associating Giselle with Witchcraft. She was universally prized as a counsellor, friend, and comforter in times of trouble.

"Maria!" Her pellucid green eyes widened in surprise and quickening delight. "What a lovely surprise! I didn't think you and Matthew were due until next month."

Giselle Nash was an inch less than my height, which was average, blade slim, with short, gleaming bronze hair that curled at the tips. Her face, tanned to a glowing amber, with high cheekbones and a finely chiselled jaw, was, in profile, a perfect cameo. Full-face it lost its perfection. The chiselling was too sharp, the beat of her inexhaustible fund of physical and mental energy too apparent. It was the type of face that is virtually ageless, but since she'd been more or less adult when Colonel Nash settled in Cyprus, she couldn't be far short of thirty.

Her glance flew over my shoulder seeking Matthew.

"There's only me."

It said much for her self-control that her look stayed friendly. "Wait a minute while I clear up and then we'll go back to the house and have a cold drink. Anyway, I ought to be taking a look at Dadda. He gets the miseries if I leave him too long, poor darling." She looked down at the olives. "It's such a wretched crop this year, it's hardly worth picking."

I helped her tip the contents of the sheets into one of the two panniers on Satan's back. When there weren't enough to fill two, she took both panniers off, gave him a fond slap on the rump. His response was to kick his back heels high, show off his silver-white belly.

She led the way with a light stride, each physical movement

full of grace and purpose, her beige twill slacks, white cotton shirt, seeming to possess some magnetism in reverse that repelled dust and dirt. She pulled a chair deeper into the shade of the vine, and in less time than it would have taken most people, returned with two glasses of chilled pomegranate juice. "I remember you liked it." Her memory for detail was phenomenal. She nodded her head backwards, said fondly: "Dadda's dropped off, so if you don't mind, we'll keep our voices down. He sleeps so badly at night he needs to nap during the day."

Above the peach-coloured liquid, her green eyes questioned me. As clearly as though it were my own, I could feel her surge of happiness. In two years, a vestige of Matthew's talent for seeing inside people's heads had rubbed off on me.

As I spoke I kept her sharp triangular face under close guard. "I looked in to ask you whether Matthew called to see you on Friday, or telephoned you?"

She looked as bemused as though I'd addressed her in a foreign language. "On Friday? No. But can't you ask him? Isn't he here?"

"He's not here now, but he was on Friday. Kim met him at the airport on Thursday evening. He stayed twenty-four hours and then left, after telephoning me on Friday morning in London. I wasn't in the flat but he left a message with my charwoman that I was to fly to Nicosia on Sunday and he'd meet me. He didn't."

Her face, clenched with shock and bewilderment, told me what I knew already. She could not believe, flatly refused to believe, that Matthew had spent a day and a night in Kessima without making any effort to see her. She said on a gasp she tried but failed to suppress: "But where did he fly to? Where is he now?"

"I've no idea."

"Why haven't you?" She remembered her manners. "Sorry. What I mean is that it's all so extraordinary, completely out of character. Matthew vanishing, leaving you not knowing where he is, when normally his plans are charted out weeks ahead. That is what you're saying, isn't it?"

"Yes."

She stayed silent while her agile brain went into action to

solve a problem that defeated me. It was a challenge to which she reacted with immediacy and zest. "Well, first, who did see him, talk to him while he was here?"

"Kim. No one else that I can discover, unless Athena did on Friday morning."

"She couldn't have. Friday is her laundry day at home." It was typical that she was *au fait* with every domestic detail of Matthew's house. "What did Kim have to say?"

I told her.

"You believed him?"

"Why not?"

She pondered, then shrugged her shoulders. "He lies when it suits him, or sometimes just to be perverse, but I can't see why he should over this. What did Matthew say in the message he left for you?"

I could have given her the full text, but so much of it was guesswork there seemed little point. "That he'd meet my plane, that's about all."

"The airlines could help. They'd have a record if Matthew flew out of Nicosia on Friday night or Saturday morning."

"They haven't. I've tried them all."

"A yacht? Heller's for instance. Or a private plane?"

"Could be," I conceded. "Though yachts are too slow for Matthew, and Heller hadn't been in touch with him. I know because Kim brought him to the house last night. And Alex's plane is laid up."

"There are others."

"I know. There's a jockey with one who once gave Matthew a lift from Athens, but I can't remember his name."

"Simon Kerslake," she said promptly. "I'll get on to him." She stared deep into the olive grove, her face sealed in the stillness of absolute concentration until her glance flashed back at me. "Someone is bound to have seen him arriving and leaving the village. Haven't you asked around?"

The belittling note in her voice sharpened my response. "I've not had time." But even as I spoke part of my mind was compiling a list of six or seven likely friends Matthew might have called on in Nicosia, to any of whom he could have entrusted a message to be telephoned to me. The majority were newspaper men who, as a tribe, never lack alibis for broken promises. My ears began to be haunted by phantom telephone bells. I wanted to race back to the house.

Giselle leaned forward. She had pushed below the surface any chagrin or pain she had suffered, was now motivated solely by a determination to run to earth an explanation of a mystery that eluded me. "Why don't I make the enquiries for you? When I've got Dadda settled for his afternoon rest, I'll go down to the tavern and have a word with Evangelos. He's the best bet. No one can slip in or out of the village without his knowing."

She had a point. Evangelos would tell her more than he would me. Except there was surely nothing to tell except that Matthew had been seen driving into the village on Thursday and out of it on Friday! I took up her offer but added that by this afternoon Matthew would probably be in touch with me. Then I thanked her for the drink. At the door the eyes, which were a true brilliant green, narrowly examined my face as it emerged from shade into the unshadowed sunlight. For a second she frowned as though touched by a flash of anxiety. Then she smiled, a serene, almost catlike smile. "There must be some perfectly simple explanation. I'm positive you don't have any reason to worry. There isn't a man alive better at looking after himself than Matthew!"

"Oh, I'm not worried, just puzzled." I smiled too. She wasn't reassuring me so much as herself. "By the way, are you going to Carima's birthday party tonight?"

"I'd love to, but Dadda so hates me leaving him in the evening. If I get any news about Matthew, as I probably will, I'll telephone."

Not only a dutiful daughter but a fond one. She honestly loved that emaciated old despot. For a moment before we parted we silently weighed one another up. What she saw in me, I'll never know. What I saw in her was a girl who, while not conventionally beautiful, was uniquely attractive, with a wide assortment of talents, illimitable energy and resource, plus a quality of dauntlessness. All of which made her a pretty rare girl, maybe an irresistible one.

Not for the first time, I allowed myself to speculate miserably whether she was or had been Matthew's mistress. Twice a year she travelled to London to visit Colonel Nash's sister, an eighty-year-old rich widow in poor health. Since these visits entailed the removal of Colonel Nash to an hotel which he fiercely resented, it seemed probable that Giselle was the old lady's heir. Lady Connerby retired early and Giselle's late evenings and nights were her own. Matthew took her to theatres and out to dine and, for all I knew, they slept together in the Curzon Street flat, all signs of her presence whisked away before I arrived in the morning. For a moment while my heart hammered the breath out of my lungs, I saw them laughing behind my back.

"Giselle, where are you? Who are you talking to?"

"Coming, Dadda," she sang. "Just coming."

Athena had closed but not locked the outer door. As I climbed the stairs to the Crow's Nest, I heard the telephone ringing. I knew it was Matthew. Relief, anticipation of the sound of his voice, put wings on my feet. As I picked up the receiver, I cried out his name.

"Matthew!" a woman's voice echoed. "Have I got the wrong number? I wish to speak to Mrs. Mitchell."

It was Eileen Towers, one of Barbie's girl-friends checking that she'd be back from Troodos in time to go to Carima's party.

To fall off a pinnacle of hope leaves you bruised, just as realisation of your own foolishness rouses a slow burn of anger. It smouldered for three quarters of an hour during which I telephoned six of Matthew's friends who lived on the island. None had seen or spoken to him since early March. There was one number from which I could get no reply; that of David Squires, a novelist who had a house in Lapithos. A free agent, addicted to travel, he might be anywhere in the Western Hemisphere, or the Eastern come to that. I crossed his name off my list. Finally, I rang the Curzon Street flat. Gladwin answered. No, he'd had no word from his master. When I asked him to leave a note for Mr. Grant to ring me at the Kessima number, in his waspish way he got very hot and bothered. Why this, why that? And where was Mr. Grant if he wasn't in Kessima? What about the mail? I soothed him down with non-committal answers. Or rather, I hoped I did.

At a dead end I sat with my head in my hands willing the smouldering anger to blaze and consume every other emotion. In his presence it wasn't easy to sustain anger against Matthew; a reasoned, fluent tongue doused the flames before they got a hold. One ringing laugh and I was laughing with him. But when he was disarmed by distance, then anger could be stoked to a white heat. I scoffed: a bright, high-flying bird, borne on wings of his own brilliance, for once tripped by his split-second time-tables, his sixth sense of sniffing out a crisis ahead of everyone else! I let the anger blaze until it became a furnace that destroyed the last fragment of guilt that I was responsible for the misunderstandings. Mrs. Pratt was neither deaf nor muddleheaded. I'd obeyed an order he'd either forgotten to cancel or entrusted to some incompetent to pass on. So, no more frenzied inquests on what I'd done or omitted to do. From now on I'd play a waiting game.

As though I'd passed through a crisis and needed fresh air, I stepped out onto the parapet. In the heat haze of midday the far-away hair-line between sea and sky was no longer visible, and the spider's web of alleyways was so empty of life that the world within sight seemed to belong wholly to me. I walked round the parapet to stare at the ascending ribs of limestone veined with sandstone and dolomite where, above the carobs and firs, the peaks were as bare as tusks. I persuaded myself that I could see the castle the crusaders had built, now a ruin through which the winds whistled, where Matthew had taken Toby and me one bright, warm February day. But it was built into the mountains of mountain rock, and its masterly camouflage defeated my eyes. Anyway, I had no wish to remember that day.

I was on the point of descending to eat the cold lunch Athena had left me, letting my glance slide down to the green foothills when it came to a halt, trapped by a girl who, poised on a ridge of stones immediately beyond the garden, was examining the house through a pair of binoculars.

Her clothes were comically inappropriate to temperature and terrain: a scarlet woolly cap that hid her hair and half covered her ears, and a transparent plastic mac that was shorter than the wide-skirted dress she wore underneath. My first reaction was that she must be slowly steaming to death. If she'd been pointing a camera, I'd not have given her a second thought, but she was focussing binoculars and pretty powerful ones, judging from the case slung round her neck. For serious climbers, or strenuous walkers, there was a path that circled the garden, wound up through the foothills to the mountains. In the tourist season you'd see plenty of them, sturdily shod, small knapsacks on their backs. The girl certainly didn't fit into their category, so what, from the vantage point she'd picked, was worth looking at? From that angle the house formed a blind against the view, so the answer was blank walls and closed shutters. I waited in a slice of shadow until she returned the binoculars to their case, picked up the outsize leather handbag that must have weighed a good few pounds, and walked gingerly along the contour of rock leading her to a path that would bring her out on our side of the ravine.

I stood inside shielded from sight by the shutters. In ten minutes she emerged to scramble down a wall of crumbling earth and lumps of stone. Near the bottom she tipped forward and fell headlong. When she'd picked herself up, brushed herself down, and once more retrieved the outsize handbag, I saw why: she was wearing thin-strapped pink sandals with heels! She was lucky to have got away with nothing worse than the two skinned knees she was dabbing with a handkerchief.

A tourist? There was little in Kessima to attract them, though some of the more venturesome with an itch to get off the coach trails drove their rented cars as far as the square and, for half an hour, wandered round the village clicking their cameras. But it was a pretty odd tourist who turned her back on a spectacular view and stared at the blank walls of a shuttered house.

In case she was in need of first aid I stayed to watch her cross the bridge over the ravine. She walked with no visible limp, rather with a fast, purposeful stride which made no concession to the heat. I was about to go downstairs when, in the shade thrown by the rock bastion, she turned about and stared fixedly at the front of the house, this time without binoculars.

It flashed through my head that she might be one of Kim's discarded girl-friends, except that she didn't look the type—her face was nondescript to the point of plainness. Then whose wouldn't be under that woolly cap in the fierce heat of midday! Kim preferred girls with some distinctive quality that caught and held the eye, plus a generous coating of sophistication that entailed less risk of them making a public fuss when his enthusiasm waned. Or were the woolly cap, the plastic mac, and pink sandals a form of disguise?

In the end, when she disappeared into the maze of village streets, I was left with two alternatives. Either she was a compulsive Peeping Tom, a bit of a crackpot, or she had a specific reason for spying on Matthew's house—more likely, on someone who lived in it.

SIX

Toby, string-thin, natural fair hair bleached to near white, his blue eyes seeming to possess a wider than normal vision, caught sight of me and was out of the car before his mother had cut off the ignition.

Delight almost beyond containment suffused the sharp brown triangle of his face. Racing at full pelt, he collided with me and, at the moment of impact, shouted at the top of his lungs: "Uncle Matthew!" As he ran for the stairs and the Crow's Nest, I grabbed him. "Toby, Uncle Matthew's not here yet."

"Not here!" he echoed in a stunned voice. "But you're here. Why are you here if he isn't?"

"He's been delayed."

The uncompromising penetrating glance of a seven-year-old tested me for truth. "But he *is* coming, isn't he?"

"Yes, he's coming."

"When?"

"Toby, I don't know exactly. Soon."

He was a reserved, stoical child who rarely cried; when he did it was in secret. His thin legs, which shamed Connie when seen beside the sleek, chubby limbs of Cypriot children—anyone would think I starved him, she complained—slowly mounted the high steps to his room. Barbie, her soft round features and long, sovereign-coloured hair as wet as though she'd emerged from under a shower, her sleeveless cotton top clinging to her like a second skin, collapsed on a chair inside the courtyard. She closed her eyes, murmured: "My idea of hell is driving all that way in this fiendish heat. God, the dust! I'm choking with it."

Barbara Mitchell was a perfectly healthy young woman except that she appeared to operate on fifty per cent less energy than the norm. It took comparatively small doses of activity to exhaust her. I fetched her a glass of iced fresh lemon.

She drank it at a gulp, then gave me her dreamy, seraphic smile. "But at the end, what do I get, a gorgeous surprise bonus. Where is he?"

Standing before her in the shadowed courtyard, I had an overwhelming sense of Barbie's and Toby's love for Matthew, his for them, a love so committed it would endure as long as any of them breathed.

"Maria, wake up. I asked you where he was."

"He's not here yet. I arrived first."

The shock of disappointment, added to fatigue, turned her normally sweet-tempered voice into a querulous wail. "But when is he coming?"

"Look, I know it sounds crazy, but I can't tell you. Somehow we've got our lines crossed. He was here for twenty-four hours from Thursday evening. On Friday morning, before I got back from seeing my sister in Cornwall, he telephoned the flat and asked me to catch the Sunday-morning plane to Nicosia where he'd meet me. He didn't. Kim drove him to the airport on Friday evening." I remembered he'd dropped him off in Metaxas Square, but I didn't correct myself and add to her confusion. "So far, I haven't been able to track down where he went or where he is now."

She exploded in a blind rage of incredulity: "Matthew was actually in Kessima on Friday and didn't telephone me! I don't believe it. I simply don't believe it."

"I'm sorry, it's true."

"You're a big help!" Tears welled up in her mauve-blue eyes

and slid down her cheeks. After a moment she gave a sniff of contrition. "Maria, I didn't mean to snarl, but you don't know what it did to me, being certain when I saw you that Matthew was here, and then finding he isn't. You see for the last two months I've been . . ." She gulped the rest of the sentence back, brushed the tears away with her knuckles, her mood reverting to one of peevish hectoring. "Wherever he's gone to, I want him back. You're supposed to be so smart and clever. Matthew's forever saying so. Find out where he is, and tell him to get here, because I need him."

She pulled herself to her feet. "I'm beat. I'm going to have a shower and lie down." As a shadow came slinking in from the garden, she crooned: "Oh, there's my angel cat!" She picked up the little silver-grey body, held it under her chin, felt its rib cage. "I bet," she said savagely, "Athena's been pinching all the tins of cat food I left out for them."

"I doubt it, knowing Athena. There were four tins left after I'd fed them two last night, and I made them a huge dish of bread and milk for their breakfast."

Singing a sort of lullaby, she fed and petted the five of them before she climbed the stairs.

I went to collect the bags she'd left in the car. I'd got two of them out of the boot when behind me Toby said: "That one's mine. I better carry it. It's got my presents in. There's one for Athena, one for Eugenia, one for Connie, one for Miss Nash and one for Daddy. If I'd known you were going to be here, I'd have borrowed my next week's pocket money and bought you one too."

"That makes us quits. I had to leave London in such a hurry I didn't have time to buy you a present either."

"It doesn't matter in the least." He was, at his best, a polite and naturally considerate child. "You sent me that book of bird pictures for my birthday." Walking alongside me, he tilted his face to test my sincerity. "Of course, if you particularly wanted to, you could buy me a present here. But you don't have to."

"I'd like to." I suddenly remembered I'd no money to buy anyone a present. But I would have when Matthew arrived. I was proud that my resolve not to fume and panic stayed firm.

When I came down from leaving Barbie's cases on the first-floor landing, Toby had dug out five packages from his. He carefully unwound them from their brown tissue paper, laid them on a table in the sitting-room: a picture book of Disney's Snow White and the Seven Dwarfs, a garish red and blue pottery ash-tray, a snake-skin purse, a handkerchief embroidered with a map of Cyprus in gilt thread, and a packet of cigarettes.

"If you like," he offered, "you can guess who each present is for."

"The book for Eugenia." They were inseparable. "Why is he always with a girl?" Kim thundered. "At his age he should be running round with a bunch of boys." Barbie countered: "Oh, don't fuss. In another year he will be."

"And . . ." I paused as if faced with a puzzle. "The cigarettes for Daddy, the purse for Miss Nash (it was the most expensive present), the handkerchief for Athena and the ash-tray for Connie . . . or is it the other way round?"

He said with his brand of logic that could be devastating: "It would be silly to give the ash-tray to Athena, wouldn't it? She doesn't smoke. Connie does, like a chimney. Uncle Matthew says she'll die of lung cancer."

He had the normal small boy's ghoulish streak. "Not will," I corrected. "Just that she runs a risk."

"No," he said flatly. "Uncle Matthew said will."

I knew better than to enter into any argument with Toby about incontrovertible proof of my facts. It could go on for hours. Disappointed that I showed no disposition to fight, he said sedately: "I think I'll take my present to Eugenia now. She'll be home from school. I'll take Athena's too, and Miss Nash's. I like it best when Colonel Nash is asleep and he often is in the afternoon. Do you know he never calls me by my name, just 'Boy,' and every time I see him he asks me if I've been caned at school. Do I have to change my shirt?"

"I should. And wash your hands. While you're doing it, I'll get you a glass of milk. Biscuits?"

"No, thank you. Eugenia's mother will want me to eat some of her cakes and if I'm full up and can't, she'll think I'm being rude."

When he came down, spruce and tidy except for his hair, which was a thick, unmanageable mat, so long over his forehead that he peered through his fringe like a blue-eyed Yorkshire terrier, I remembered Matthew's ash-tray and Athena's distress. "When you see Athena do you think you could give her a message from me?"

He pondered, the tip of his tongue tucked in the gap in his teeth, not prepared to commit himself. "What is it?"

"One of Uncle Matthew's ash-trays, the crystal one, is broken. I suspect Athena may have dropped it. When I saw her this morning she was very upset, and I couldn't make her understand it didn't matter. Would you explain that to her for me?"

"Why should she think Uncle Matthew would be cross because she's broken something accidentally? When I spilt ink on one of his maps, he wasn't angry with me because he said I hadn't done it on purpose."

"I can't imagine, except that she is very proud of being responsible for other people's possessions, making sure they don't come to any harm while she is cleaning."

"All right." Half-way across the courtyard, he turned round. "Will Uncle Matthew be here tomorrow?"

To lie to Toby, even with the best intention, was, if you were caught out, an invitation to retribution. "Maybe, I hope so."

When he'd gone I sorted out his dirty laundry from his treasures, which included a small telescope, a collection of fossils, six books, and a dead lizard wrapped in a plastic bag, and put his soiled clothes in the overflowing laundry bin.

When Barbie had slept for two hours, I took her a glass of lemon tea. In the shuttered room she was lying awake on one side of the film-star bed, naked except for a cotton wrap. As I put down the tea, she sat up against a great mound of ruched pillows. "What have you done about finding out where Matthew is?"

I eased half open one of the shutters on the shady side of the house so that we would not be one shadow talking to another, told her that I'd tapped every source of information I could think up, and that there was nothing more to be done except to wait for Matthew to arrive or telephone. I gave her the tea, sat down on the end of the bed where I could see her face. It told me she'd spent more of the two hours crying than sleeping.

She wailed: "It isn't like him. Matthew wouldn't do this to me. You know he wouldn't. If he hadn't time to drive to Troodos, he'd only to telephone me and I'd have driven home to see him. He'd know that. Well, wouldn't he?"

I admitted he would.

She glared balefully at me. "So what's happened? Where is he? Even if you don't know you must be able to guess. Why are you making such a state secret of it?"

"I'm not. I'm as much in the dark as you are."

She plainly didn't believe me. "The message he telephoned to your flat. Is that all it said, catch the plane to Nicosia on Sunday morning? Not why?"

I looked at her. Cantankerous, tired, but in the best of health. Toby distributing his presents, nothing ailing him. Neither of them in need of my care and protection. A bad connection with Mrs. Pratt unready to swear to anything except the plane I was to catch and that I was to bring an unspecified file. What point was there in adding to Barbie's confusion? "You know as much as I do."

"Which is precisely nothing."

She was in the mood to pick a quarrel with me, but I wasn't going to let her. "What makes you want to see Matthew so urgently? Has something happened?"

"Yes." She looked over my head. "But it's something only Matthew can sort out." She sipped the tea, then gave a little shrug of her shoulders, as though it had sweetened her temper. "I suppose you might as well know. Toby and I are finally going home for good. I want to see Matthew so that he can fix it up, all the arrangements, I mean."

"Have you told him?"

"How could I? I only decided while I was in Troodos, decided definitely, that is. It's been on the cards for a couple of months."

I wondered how Kim figured in the situation, and asked her.

"I wouldn't know," she said loftily, "and I certainly don't care."

Her soft, rounded features, slightly pouting mouth were set

in a mulish expression. I knew from experience that I'd get no answers to any questions I put to her. She could, when she chose, behave in a comical *grande dame* manner, reduce me in the twinkling of an eye from friend to the paid employee of her stepbrother. Not that I needed her answers. It was crystal clear that I'd arrived in the middle of one of the periodical crises between Barbie and Kim. Her bank account was in the red, somewhere in the house was a spike of unpaid bills, and outside murmuring tradesmen. Kim had been playing around with some girl—to a degree he never stopped and mostly it suited Barbie's indolence to turn a blind eye. But this time he must have stretched her tolerance too far. She wanted Matthew to pay her bills, call Kim to heel, and make her small world shining and cosy. The going-home was no more than a threat. She'd made it before, more than once.

Since, in her present mood, she was unlikely to confide in me, and I could hardly intimate that her troubles to me were an old, well-worn story, I changed the subject.

"I've been invited to Carima's birthday party. It would be fun to go, but I left London in such a frantic rush, I didn't pack anything remotely suitable to wear. Do you think . . ."

All her natural generosity welled up and she didn't even let me finish. "Help yourself. Anything you fancy except the long white jersey. I haven't worn it yet, but I will tonight, if I go."

She'd go. She could never resist any party and certainly not the super kind that Alex laid on for special occasions.

I opened the wardrobe doors, which switched on the interior strip-lights. At a rough guess there were probably well over a hundred assorted garments to choose from. Sartorially Barbie was equipped for a jet-set life she only led spasmodically. I picked out a short lemon chiffon with a belt that would hide the tucks I'd have to stitch in the waist. On Barbie it had been a mini, on me it would be a near midi. I held up the hanger. "Okay if I promise not to let anyone spill any drink on it?"

Normally any mention of clothes fired her interest, set her chatting knowledgeably on fashion trends she absorbed from the V*ogues* and *Harper'ses* that were her twin Bibles. This time her lavender glance was lack-lustre, her voice disinterested. "Keep it. If you don't want it after tonight, throw it away."

I thanked her. But I wasn't looking for hand-outs. Tomorrow morning I'd unpick my tackings, press it, and hang it back in her wardrobe, where it would be lost in dozens of other dresses she'd never wear again.

She asked in a sudden spurt of alarm: "Where's Toby?"

"Out distributing his presents to Eugenia, Athena, and Giselle."

She snatched the last name out of my mouth. "Giselle! She'll know where Matthew is. You bet she will."

"She doesn't. I went to see her this morning."

She laughed in my face. "Then he never came here at all. He's still on his way. He wouldn't be in Kessima for a whole day without seeing Giselle, you know he wouldn't."

"Kim says he was here."

"Kim . . . Kim . . . Kim!" she sing-songed like a petulant child. "Did you ever hear of a sillier name for a grown man! It's a dog's name. Kimberley Mitchell. I bet his sainted mum picked it out of an old-fashioned movie."

"Why on earth should Kim say Matthew was here if he wasn't?"

"His idea of a joke maybe. To fool you, or more important me."

In this capricious mood, when she put forward a totally illogical theory simply because, like Giselle, she didn't choose to admit that Matthew had been in Kessima for twenty-four hours without telephoning her, argument was a waste of breath. She was afloat on a plane that didn't admit reason. Instead, I remarked: "Kim should be back from the airport soon with Connie, and you can ask him."

She gave me a strange half-bitter, half-sad look. "I can ask him, but that doesn't mean he'll answer!"

I hung the dress over my arm. The private games, sometimes malicious, sometimes teasing basted with taunts, that Kim and Barbie played were no concern of mine. I'd no wish, certainly no right, to comment.

Before I reached the door, she called me back, wailed: "Maria, don't be so horrid and huffy." She was leaning forward across the slice of brightness that flowed through the parted shutters, the lavender eyes no longer lavender but dark violet, the pupils dilated. "I know you think I'm a fool, that I put on acts. But not now, Maria, I swear it. Truly, I'm worried to death about Matthew. Suppose something's happened to him!"

"What could have happened?"

"He could be dead."

I shouted: "Are you clean out of your mind? How could he be dead? What do you mean, run over, taken ill, put into a hospital? If he were, we'd know. All the world would know. He carries a wad of identification papers."

I ran out of breath and for a moment we stared speechless at one another in a sort of horror, then I dropped the heap of chiffon on the bed, put my arm round her shoulder. "Oh, Barbie, sometimes you behave as though you were younger than Toby. You know how he loves to scare the living daylights out of himself. You're no better."

She sniffled. I found her a tissue, cajoled: "Matthew would laugh if he could see us, wouldn't he?"

"But he can't." She pulled away from me. "All right, not dead, but suppose he's been kidnapped!"

I laughed hysterically. "I'd like to see anyone try. Anyway, where's the ransom note?"

"They sometimes wait a week, even longer before they send it. Don't you read the newspapers?"

"Barbie!" I smoothed her tangled, still-damp hair. "He's not rich enough to be worth kidnapping. Nor is he a nine-to-five man. Every conceivable sort of emergency rises up to hit him. Heads of state and cabinet ministers can occasionally be coaxed to talk provided it suits them and no names are quoted. It's a highly complex game top people play. It requires a lot of finesse, and no one's got more than Matthew."

Her alarm unabated, she said waspishly: "I don't understand a word you're saying."

"I'm saying that plane tickets can be booked under an assumed name, a car with one-way see-through windows be waiting at an airport, no trudge through customs and immigration. A bit cloak and dagger, but I promise you it happens. It has to Matthew more than once. He's probably out in the desert closeted with an oil sheik. There's one he's been trying to pin down for months."

"Then why don't you know for sure? I thought he told you everything."

"I was two days late in getting back from Cornwall, so I wasn't in the flat to tell." Suddenly I felt totally exhausted, empty of ideas. I'd worked hard at inventing alibis for Matthew as much to convince myself as Barbie.

She plucked disconsolately at the lace on the top sheet. "I keep thinking about Bruce. One day we were all having drinks, and he was making me laugh, and the next he was a lump of dead flesh that had to be fished out of the sea." She gave me a pitiful, genuinely scared look. "People do die, not only when they're old, but when they're young like Bruce."

"Bruce Vernon died," I said firmly, "because he went swimming in the sea after dark."

She nodded. "I suppose you're right, but it's odd the way I can't forget him, as though he sort of haunts me. I can't bear people I know dying." She gave me a soft, appealing glance. "Life must be a whole lot easier if you're sensible, clever and don't fly into panics!"

She little knew! I laughed. "I'd change places with a ravishing blonde with a set of feather brains."

She laughed back, that lovely, low-pitched sound that turned every male head within earshot. "Me!"

"Yes, you. But you won't be a ravishing blonde if you don't haul yourself out of bed and start shampooing and setting your hair."

She wailed: "Where has all the time gone!"

The horror pictures she'd painted in her mind were obliterated. For the next two hours she would be totally absorbed in the complex ritual designed to bring her to the Villa Hesperides in peak form, so lusciously beautiful, so conscious, yet so unvain, of the effect she created, that her path was like a royal progress, lit by adoring smiles.

I loved her, yet at the moment I closed the door of my room my affection was buried under a mountain of resentment. I'd allowed a girl who never used the few brains she had to toss me head-first into an ice-cold panic, to set my pulses thudding.

Dead! Kidnapped! What did she read, kids' comics? No, to do her justice, she read the newspapers of the day where violent death was on every page, and kidnapping the newest and nastiest power game. I borrowed a reel of silk and a fine needle from Connie's work-basket, pinned the tucks in the dress, sewed them with invisible stitches, and hung it up. By then I was sufficiently collected to do what Barbie had driven me to do. But when I reached the bottom of the stone staircase that led up to the Crow's Nest, my legs refused to mount them. I was terrified that, once in the room where his presence was enbalmed, I should become a prey to Barbie's hysterical delusions.

Instead I went downstairs and used the telephone in the sitting-room. None of the four hospitals I rang had a record of a patient named Matthew Grant being admitted. The second I put the receiver down, it rang.

Giselle, having made certain that I hadn't heard from Matthew, gave me a condensed report of her afternoon's work. Simon Kerslake was in Tunis, had been for a week. So if Matthew had flown out of Nicosia in a private plane, it wasn't his. She'd been down to the tavern and talked to Evangelos and some of the regulars. They'd seen Kim drive Matthew through the village on Thursday evening, and he'd waved to them. No one had seen Kim drive him out to the airport. On the other hand Evangelos hadn't been at the tavern between five and seven, as he was visiting his wife, who was in hospital. So far as the friend Matthew had told Kim he wanted to look up in Nicosia was concerned, though she'd contacted newspaper offices, the head barmen at the Ledra, Hilton, and other likely hotels, she'd not been able to trace anyone who'd seen him on Friday evening.

When she paused, I thanked her for all her hard work.

But she hadn't finished. "The most incredible part to me is that normally the first thing Matthew does after he arrives is to go round the village saying hello. It's a sort of ritual. He loves it and the villagers adore him. To stay indoors without setting a foot outside the house for twenty-four hours suggests to me he wasn't well. There simply isn't any other explanation. Did Kim mention anything about him being ill, even off-colour?"

"No, just that he was very busy working up in the Crow's Nest."

"But why," she demanded, and didn't wait for an answer. "I went to see Antinou in case Kim might have stopped for petrol. He didn't, but what he did do on Saturday morning was to take the Volvo in with a dented bumper, collect it this morning. What happened to it?"

"He slid off the road into a ditch, bruised his cheek."

"Going or coming back from Nicosia?"

"I didn't ask him."

"Don't you think someone should? Just in case the whole story is one of his wilder flights of fancy. If he's there, let me talk to him."

"Matthew's telephone call to my flat wasn't a wild flight of fancy! And Kim's not here because he's ferrying Connie from the airport."

"Is Barbie home?"

"Yes. She got in a couple of hours ago."

"How did she react?"

"With a suggestion that Matthew's been kidnapped."

I expected her to laugh. Instead there was a moment's dead silence before she asked: "What gave her that idea?"

"It's a piece of pure Barbie melodrama to account for the fact Matthew didn't telephone her at Troodos. She overlooked one thing: to be worth kidnapping you have to be rich. Matthew isn't."

She rapped back: "But some of the men whose secrets he keeps are multimillionaires."

She was right, though by now I was in no mood to admit it. Robbed of visual effects, her voice on the telephone had a bossy ring that grated on my nerve ends. "Can you see anyone grabbing hold of Matthew in a dark alley and making off with him!"

"There are more sophisticated ways in which it could be done."

"No. The whole idea is crazy."

"No crazier than he should vanish from sight without letting either of us know where he is." I let "either of us" pass without comment and heard her take a calming breath. "If he hasn't been in touch with you by the morning, I think you should go to the police."

"And lose my job!"

I braced myself to hear her say: "If you won't, then I will." She said something quite different. "If you're scared of going to the police, then I think you should consult Alex. With his contacts he could make enquiries so discreetly that not even Matthew would be embarrassed."

I promised if Matthew hadn't phoned by the morning, to consider it. But the thought of throwing myself on Alex Theocharis's mercy made no appeal. To me he seemed a man with as many contrasting sides to his character as a prism, consequently I could never make a firm and lasting judgment of him. She'd rung off, but my hand was still holding the receiver when Kim, with Connie beside him, drove into the car park. He carried her suitcase into the courtyard, leaving her to follow with an assortment of hand-luggage.

He nodded at the telephone. "Matthew?"

"No. I'm no wiser than I was when you left this morning."

"Cheer up! Even Matthew can't prolong a disappearing act beyond a couple of days. I still say it would be simpler to track him down from the London end, but, there, that's your job, not mine." The bruise on his cheek was fading nicely, and though he had difficulty meeting my eye, rather as though we'd been through a quarrel we both wanted to forget, he was less outwardly contentious than when we'd parted over breakfast. "I see Barbie and Toby are back."

"They got in a couple of hours ago."

"Where is he?"

"On a round of visits distributing his presents. He promised to be back before six." I added as though he'd asked: "Barbie's upstairs."

"Then I'd better mix us some martinis. What about you?"

I declined. As he reached for the gin, I said: "That accident when you bashed your face, did it happen when you were driving Matthew to the airport?"

He turned in slow motion, as though all his limbs were rigid, shouted: "What damned business is it of yours where it happened?"

"It's my business if Matthew was in the car with you."

"Well, he wasn't. I was on my way home."

He swung round, toppled half a bottle of gin into the martini jug.

I went out to help Connie with the assortment of bundles and bags she was hauling out of the car. Seeing me, she gave a snort of pleasure, and her round, very bright brown eyes radiated joy. "Well, there's a nice surprise to come home to! I didn't think we were to have the pleasure of your company for another three weeks."

Pleased as punch was how she would have described herself. Having kitted herself out for the winter at Marks & Spencers, she was wearing an emerald fake-fur cap on her black, newly permed hair, a red leather jacket, and a tartan skirt. Snappy dresser she might be, but it sometimes crossed my mind to wonder if she were colour blind. She was short, broad, not with fat but with muscle and bone, her whole form stuffed tight with energy. Her face was round and plump with a high colour and a chin that proclaimed her obstinate, combative spirit to the world. If you were in her good books you could do no wrong. If you fell out of them you could do no right.

"Mind that," she cautioned, as I reached for an overflowing plastic bag. "There's a box of cream buns at the top for Toby, and I haven't carried it thousands of miles to have it squeezed to pulp. He sent me a nicely written postcard from Troodos, promising they'd be back before me. Where are they?"

"Barbie's washing her hair, and Toby's taking his presents round."

Inside the courtyard, her glance flew round the paint and petrol cans. She dropped her bags and poked her finger into a container of flagging carnations. "I thought as much. Dry as a bone." When Minnow, who'd probably been having a nap in Barbie's room, slunk past, she gave another of her snorts, fiercer this time. "And the whole house crawling with cats; into the beds I shouldn't wonder."

But she was too happy to sustain her displeasure. She beamed on me. "If he's working, I won't disturb him. He'll have heard me come, and he won't be long before he's down to say hello."

"Matthew's not here, not yet."

She was a keen-witted, highly perceptive woman. I swear her astonished gaze that searched my face picked up the alarm of which I'd so recently rid myself, and of which I refused to be reminded. For a second her mouth hung agape, then she said: "You here and not him! That's funny! When's he due?"

A stupefying ennui overcame me. I'd told my story only three times, but I felt as weary of it as if I'd repeated it a hundred. I simply could not put it into words again.

"I'm not sure, but it should be quite soon."

"The sooner the better," she snapped. "The way things are round here, I nearly didn't go on my . . ."

The sound of her name being jubilantly called deflected her attention from me to the small figure running towards her. She met him half-way, tweaked the collar of his shirt straight, smoothed his hair. He put his hand in hers, and his upturned face and her down-bent one mirrored a comfortable contentment in one another. As a home-coming present she'd cook him his favourite supper: sausage and chips, topped off with cream buns she'd bought expressly for him over 2,300 miles away.

In my own room Barbie's and Kim's voices—though not their words—floated up to me through the windows that were wide open now that the sun was slipping into the sea and darkness was creeping through the village. Not shouting, as they did when they brawled, but in clipped hard tones, laced with silences. Presently they died away, and there was only an occasional clink of glasses. They could, with the party ahead, have called a truce or, as often happened, become so tired of wrangling they'd achieved a sort of peace that, with luck, would last for a couple of days.

SEVEN

On party nights you could see the brilliantly illuminated Villa Hesperides from the village square. The small pink palace was one of the three homes between which Carima and Alex Theocharis divided their year. The others were in Athens and Paris. Outside it had a semi-comic pretentiousness; inside, bathed in luxury and dreamlike comfort, you forgot, or forgave, the fake plaster turrets and cupolas.

The main rooms were on the first floor, opening on to wide pillared balconies. Although we were over an hour late, Alex and Carima were still greeting their guests. Carima's mahogany-red hair hung in a glossy curtain over the gold-embroidered caftan that was kind to her slightly thickening figure. At seventeen she'd won a sex-kitten role in a Hollywood film that had printed her name on screens across the world. Thereafter, either her talent had flickered out or the fickle tides of cinema fashion had run against her. She'd played a long list of supporting roles—I'd seen her on television in a rerun of an American crime series—but the name Carima Selby rang no bell with current film-goers. Even so she was forever on the brink of starring in some epic to be shot in Rome, Elstree, Dublin, or

Hollywood; and somewhere adrift among the guests was bound to be a producer or a contact man for a producer. Carima threw her net wide, the hospitality at the villa was fabulous, and Alex could afford to indulge his wife's whims though not, it would seem, to the extent of financing a film guaranteeing her the star role.

Barbie, in white jersey, with pearls laced into the gleaming sovereign curls, had produced her favourite self: a dewy English rose. She kissed Carima. "Happy birthday, darling, and a little present for a girl who's got everything." She dropped a beribboned package on a laden table.

"From me, as well," Kim said. "Which means I get a kiss too."

There were exclamations of dismay from Alex and Carima at his bruised, sore cheek, but he brushed them determinedly aside.

Carima grasped their hands in a charming gesture of welcome, as candidly pleased as a child. "Thank you, my loves. Tonight I feel as though I have got everything, or I would have if Matthew were here." Her glance found me. "Where is he? I thought he took you everywhere with him. Donald was so exasperatingly vague. Isn't he coming?"

"He's still on his way." Carima was basically kind, but it cost her an effort to hide her pique. She doted on Matthew, not only for himself, but because she cherished an illusion that a free-lance writer with a stake in the communications media might, on some occasion, be coaxed into giving her a puff. Suppose, for instance, he were asked whom he considered the three most beautiful women in the world and put Carima Selby's name at the top! Carima's naïveté was part of her appeal.

Alex kissed Barbie on the cheek, raised my hand to his lips. Carima was his second wife. By his first he had two handsome grown-up sons who were occasionally to be seen around the villa. He was short, thick-set, his hair thin and greying, with a set of gaunt features that combined to form a fascinating ugliness. Swimming in his pool or playing tennis on the hard court hewn out of mountain rock, he looked as virile as a man of forty, but in close-up his satyr face was old and wise, and his eyes, so deep a brown they looked like black sloes, shrewd and wily. I neither liked nor disliked him; perhaps because I had no standards by which to judge him. He was a self-made millionaire who moved in rarefied spheres of power and had a reputation for rapacity and unorthodox practices. I suspected he served no ends but his own, a suspicion which tended to destroy trust. Socially he was a charmer, a natural protector of any woman irrespective of age. The eyes, which never missed a trick, consoled me. "You must be a lonely girl without Matthew."

I denied it. Donald had promised he would be waiting, but I couldn't catch a glimpse of him in the crowd of guests. Granted we were late, but surely not so late that he'd given me up!

Alex cupped my elbow in his palm. "Even so we must find someone special to take care of you."

The escort presented himself, with a low bow of the head and almost but not quite a click of the heels. "Miss Caron, what a pleasure it is to meet you again."

His name was Hans Schreiber and he was serving with the Austrian contingent of the United Nations peace-keeping force. As he led me to the set-piece cold buffet which spread across one side of the dining-room, I had a faint sense of *déjà vue* in that on the same date a year ago he'd been my supper escort.

"Why," Matthew enquired on the way home, "did you spend the major part of the evening glued to the side of a single Austrian member of the U.N.?"

"I like Austria."

"And all Austrians? He looked a singularly dull young man to me."

"He was born in St. Jacob, a village in the Tyrol I know. I was quite happy to listen to him talking about it. He's homesick."

He was still homesick, but less so in that his term of duty was coming to an end, and at Christmas he was going home to marry his Lisl.

Followed by a waiter with our plates and glasses, we found a table on the terrace. As we sat down, Hans, whose father was a bank manager, remarked judicially: "I think Mr. Theocharis is a very rich man to provide such delicious and expensive imported food for his guests." Money, the acquisition and nurturing of it, fascinated him. I hoped his Lisl was thrifty. A band playing in one corner of the terrace, its beat subdued by the weight of human voices and laughter, did not make for easy conversation. When nearly at the end of the meal I missed a remark, he enquired huffily: "You look for someone?"

"No. The band distracted me. Did I miss something you said?"

"It is of no importance. But someone seems to be looking for you."

It was not Donald's face I saw, but the round, beaming one of Geoff Dawson. With his wife he owned a private hotel, the Windsor Court, about a mile inland from the coast, which catered for vegetarians and nature lovers. They were a couple of enthusiastic amateurs who, with insufficient capital, took a pride in the improvisation and stratagems by which they kept the hotel afloat and a roof over their heads.

He wore an old-fashioned dinner jacket, shiny and an inch too tight across his chest. "Dear Maria, how are you, and what a splendiferous occasion!" He brandished a glass of orangeade, and I introduced Hans, who, with a definite click of his heels, excused himself. Geoff looked dismayed. "I hope I haven't broken up a pleasant tête-à-tête!"

I told him he hadn't and, reassured, he glanced around, starry-eyed, elated as a boy. "Doris would have given her eye-teeth to be here, but we have a guest arriving late tonight so one of us had to remain on duty; we make it a cardinal rule never to leave our guests to be greeted by domestic help. So we tossed for it and I won."

I was conscious while he was chattering of a girl lurking—that is the only word—behind him. Now he pulled her forward. "So I brought Lois with me. Maria Caron, may I present Lois Brown, who's staying with us."

A girl of medium height in her late twenties, or maybe a little older, wearing a boldly patterned Ban-Lon dress that was too tight across her heavy bust, lank, dark hair that fell to her shoulders, and a face that was disfigured with bright ridges of sunburn. She had intent dark eyes and a small, stiff mouth that did not smile as, parrotlike, she said how-do-you-do.

I asked: "Are you making a long stay at the Windsor Court?"

"As long as I like."

To jolly her along, Geoff gave her arm a good-natured squeeze. Both he and Doris were addicted to lame ducks. "The longer the better for us. The first thing we've got to teach her is not to go walking in the heat of the day without a hat."

But she *had* worn a hat, a red woolly cap into which she'd stuffed her hair, which was why it looked such a mess. He went on: "Lois is a great dancer. That's where we're bound for, the dance floor. Maybe, later, you'll give me the pleasure of a dance, Maria?"

I said I'd love to, and they edged their way to the salon, its sliding doors opening on to the wide verandahs, where guests were dancing. She was burdened with the same outsize handbag that she'd picked up from the dusty track when she'd fallen off the wall.

As I abandoned the dining-room for the cool scented garden, I pondered: A girl who didn't consider it necessary to smile when introduced to another, didn't trade in social conventions. All right, a shy girl, a bit lost in a high-flying party at which she knew no one but Geoff. It was a plausible explanation except for that curiously intent, unflickering stare she'd directed at me as though she were trying to pry through my flesh to my bones. The same stare she'd pinned on the house. It left me with a prickly feeling, a sensation of unease.

I'd have gone on pondering if my glance hadn't been caught by three men standing at the top of the double curve of steps that led from the first-floor balcony to the garden. Donald was bending over the parapet, searching through the varying patterns of light and shadow, sandwiched between the sour-faced man he'd met at the airport and Heller, who had his hand on Donald's shoulder. Revulsion of which I was ashamed but over which I had no control struck, and I turned my back on the trio.

But the movement had betrayed me. Donald called my name, and, lifting two tulip glasses of champagne from a passing waiter, and balancing them in either hand nearly on a level with his head, came down the steps towards me.

He held out a glass. "A peace offering. The bubbles are still there but I can't promise it's chilled. I wanted, I intended to be waiting for you the instant you arrived, but I got shanghaied into a session with Stephanides. He's flying back to Athens at the crack of dawn. Fifteen minutes, he swore. He took four times as long. I begrudge him every one of them. Will you forgive me?"

"A session with Stephanides and Heller?"

He looked baffled. "Heller, no. He's not involved in the hotel, at least not to my knowledge. And I should know. He merely joined us on the balcony when I was frantically looking for you." He paused, examined my face. "What's up? What's gone wrong? Are you mad at me?"

"No." I made myself laugh. "I have a bit of a thing about Heller. He always sets my teeth on edge."

"Forget him. I've already wasted too big a slice of our evening."

But I couldn't forget him because his avenger's stare was still focussed on me.

Oblivious, Donald said with a throb of excitement: "One of the perks of being a house-guest is that you get to know corners that ordinary party guests don't know exist. There's one I want to show you. What I can only describe as a midget folly, below the tennis court. By daylight it's hideously phoney, but when it's lit by Chinese lanterns and a shower of moonlight . . . well, it can charm the eye." He held out his hand. "Willing to chance it?"

"A fake ruin in an archaeologists's paradise!"

"I know. Crazy! Presumably one of the landscape gardeners who laid the place out for Alex conceived this little extravaganza." Somehow he managed to carry the two glasses in one hand, hold out the other to me.

In silence, wrapped around in the scents of the night, with the music and voices dying out behind us, we went along a maze of paths where low-powered spotlights picked out in a twilight glow the angles and steps. Beyond the hard tennis court, behind a tamarisk hedge that undulated with every whisper of breeze, overlooking a tiny artificial lake, was a scaled-down model of a Greek temple.

"There," he exclaimed. "Even the moon is obliging."

It had, with its fake broken columns, a stagelike effect: a touch of a switch and it would disappear, be no more than a couple of flats to be folded away. His hand opened and closed on my elbow and I felt, like a current flowing through me, his hope and pounding excitement, and my own rising to meet them.

"How do you know it will be empty?"

"I don't. I'm just keeping my fingers crossed. It's too far from the band, the food, and the drink to appeal to the bulk of Alex's guests."

But he'd crossed his fingers to no effect. A Chinese lantern suspended from a pole, its four sides shaped into dragon masks, threw a vapour of light over two figures half-lying on a marble seat, rapt, insensible to the sound of our voices, our feet approaching. But what sound hadn't accomplished silence did, and, as if jerked on puppet strings, the mouths parted, the two heads turned in unison.

"I do beg your pardon," Donald said, and with an arm round my shoulder drew me away.

I stumbled and he grabbed my arm to steady me. "Not to worry, I've a reserve up my sleeve. At the top of those steps on the left there's an arbour dripping with jasmine."

This time, the hideout was empty except for three garden chairs. He pulled two of them close, exclaimed in surprise: "You're shivering . . . shaking . . ." In fact my teeth were chattering and when he put the glass of champagne to my lips it was a moment before I could drink.

It was tepid and flat, but I gulped it down, my mind blocked by one outraged glance that had spewed hatred at me, and another so coldly disdainful that in the distorted shadows it had been a sneer.

"Should it give you such a shock? Isn't Kim a perennial playboy as far as dolly birds are concerned?"

The shock was not Kim absorbed in a preamble to the act of love, but a terrible foreboding that overwhelmed me: I had been guilty of one misjudgment, why not another?

I said as steadily as I could: "I wouldn't have described Maxime Lennings as a dolly bird." Maxime was a highly intelligent, strikingly good-looking young widow who had a job on the production side of the American Forces Network. She was lithe as a panther, with an eye-catching face, brains, panache, a salary to provide her with a high-powered sports car and an expensive flat. What could Kim Mitchell give her? It was a silly question, because I'd seen the answer with my own eyes. And if she wanted him for keeps, she'd get him.

"Maybe you're right," he conceded. "She's a bright, ambitious young woman. But it's not the first time Kim has run a girl-friend and a wife simultaneously, is it? Barbie may not know, or she may know and not care."

Apparently this time she both knew and cared; hence her s.o.s. to Matthew to "fix it" to move her and Toby back to England.

When I did not answer, he said with a faintly despairing note: "Are you *that* closely involved with them? Barbie, with her looks, wouldn't go more than a few months without attracting a queue of men outside her door. And what's Toby? Seven? In ten years' time he will be going his own way, doing his own thing. And meanwhile he has a loving mother, a splendid, sensible nanny, and a doting uncle." He groaned. "Blast! I swore that tonight I'd keep clear of Matthew Grant and all his clan. This was to be our night. And look at it! First Stephanides gets a strangle hold over me, and then we bust in on Kim Mitchell having a heavy petting session with his latest girl-friend that for some reason upsets you."

I breathed out the remnants of shock. As the tension eased out of my bones, I became conscious of the two of us in the near-darkness; again that sense of theatre, as though we were waiting for a curtain to rise, each of us possessed by a fear that our tongues, which were so treacherous to one another, might use the wrong words.

"It was silly of me to panic. I can't think why I did. I should know Kim well enough by now not to be surprised by his amours. They're harmless in that they run their course, and then he toes the line until the next girl catches his eye. For heaven's sake, let's forget him. Give me the latest news on the hotel. Are you going to be able to start building soon?" In the shadow I caught his look, querying, uneasy with the suspicion that I was fighting him off. "I'm not making polite chat. I really want to know. Are you still bogged down in all the hold-ups about the land?"

"To a certain extent. It's the pace that gets me down. Snails in slow motion!" He gave a rueful half laugh. "My senior partner suspects I'm dragging my feet and earning myself a series of free holidays in the sun. Actually, I have very short spells of free time. But one of them is coming up tomorrow. I've got to check on a couple of queries one of the survey team has suddenly raised." He took a cigarette from a packet in his hand, lighted it, as though he needed a pause to brace his courage. "Will you come with me? Alex's chef would provide us with a picnic lunch, and we could eat it on the island."

There it was. His final throw. A gauntlet flung down for me to pick up . . . or not. If I refused or even qualified my acceptance by a proviso about Matthew's possible arrival in Kessima, he'd relinquish me. As though it were a physical act, I pushed Matthew's name out of my skull. "I'd adore it. What time do you want to pick me up?"

For a second he was silent, as though testing the echo of my words in his ears, then I heard him snatch his breath on a sigh. "That's marvellous; how marvellous you'll never know." In the scented jasmine cave, where the air was so soft it seemed to stroke my skin, he took my hand and laid it against his cheek. My palm folded over his jawbone moved my heart, and when the moment of tenderness passed, my mind at peace, I gazed down a path that was wide and peaceful, with no hidden pits, no dead ends, no craving for what I couldn't have that made little hells of my days.

As I withdrew my hand, he kissed each fingertip. "Ten o'clock. We'll have the whole day, a lovely long wonderful day all to ourselves."

Trumpets, slightly off-key, rang a clarion call that ripped through the silence that enclosed us.

He groaned, "That's the prearranged signal for the ceremonial cutting of the cake on the stroke of midnight. We could stay lost. How about it!"

"A bit rude?" I queried. "Carima might be hurt." Donald was a person of special significance to her. They'd known one another as children, met again when they'd both travelled a long way in time and distance from their home town in Suffolk. I'd never heard any reference to her parents. They could be dead; she could have slothed them off. Whichever it was, Donald was her substitute for family, and she wasn't above exploiting a situation in which he stood to gain money and prestige from her husband's patronage. I didn't think she'd stand for him being lost.

"Maybe you're right. I did promise Alex I'd act as stage-manager for the fireworks, make sure the hoses are on hand in case one of the garden boys lets off a rocket in the wrong direction and sets half a mountain alight. With everything dried up there's a hell of a fire hazard."

As the three Greek trumpeters in national costume were repeating their clarion call for the third time, Carima was despatching servants to bring Donald to her side. Her radiant birthday glance skimmed over me disapprovingly, as though I'd been guilty of borrowing one of her prized possessions and been tardy in returning it. Alex, sensitive to every nuance of emotion affecting anyone within his field of vision, made room for me by his side, patted my hand. His intuitive kindness was such that I found it odd that my instinct was to keep my guard up, my trust on a leash.

When the waiters had distributed the last snippet of cake, at some prearranged signal the first firework gushed into the black velvet sky. Fireworks, since Diana and I had outgrown the fun of letting off sparklers and bangers in the back garden, had passed me by, and I found an hypnotic fascination in watching the rockets shoot, expand into complicated flame-dripping designs—one even spelled out the name Carima—then, their magnificence spent, die in drips of coloured rain as the next one zoomed for the moon.

I watched the Greek dancing that followed with an American photographer, now living in Rome, who'd flown in to take still pictures of Carima. "Honey," he said, when the stage cleared, "I'd like to ask you to dance, but if I stood up I'd fall down." He had an endearing grin. "Not drink, sheer exhaustion."

I told him not to worry, I didn't want to dance either, and began looking round for Barbie. She wasn't in sight, but coming briskly towards me was Geoff, his face as rosy-pink and beaming as though he'd been drinking champagne all night instead of orangeade.

"Would it be too much to drag you away and have that dance you promised me?"

The photographer whose name was Al something, made a generously expansive gesture. "Help yourself, buddy, if the girl is willing."

Geoff said: "It's only fair to warn you I'm no great shakes, but if there's a tune that sounds remotely like a fox trot, I shouldn't tread too hard on your toes. I've never got the hang of these modern dances . . . so it's asking a big favour."

"I expect you're better than you think you are. Let's have a go."

We stayed out on the terrace. He danced in the same style as my father, but clutching me so hard round the waist and fixing my head in a sort of lock under his chin that the whole exercise was exhausting, and I wasn't sorry when the band stopped.

He dipped his body from the waist, pressed his hand to his heart. "Dear girl, that was a perfect finale to an evening I'm not likely to forget." He looked round marvelling. "I'm beginning to feel guilty at winning the toss from Doris. She should have been here; it would have been the experience of a lifetime for her."

"Knowing Doris, she'll get far more of a kick at you having an evening out than having one herself."

"You're so right." His nice, lumpy face softened to tenderness. "Never a day passes but I thank God for Doris." He coughed, looked momentarily embarrassed. "And now I must find Lois. She can lie in in the morning, but I have to be up with the birds to get the chores out of the way. Can you see her anywhere?"

"She's standing at the buffet with Mr. Heller."

They stood face to face, too far away for me to hear what

they were saying. Heller's red-lipped, utterly meaningless smile was pinned to his lips. Her chin was thrust forward belligerently and there were two dark crimson patches on her cheeks that weren't sunburn. A string of words exploded from her throat with such fury that they distorted her profile. He let her finish, then he shrugged his shoulders insultingly, turned his back on her as though she was an impudent and importuning beggar.

I said quickly, because I'd only a few seconds before Geoff would give her a summoning wave: "Who is she? Why is she in Cyprus?"

"Who, Lois? She's on holiday. Poor girl, I gather she's getting over some sort of family trouble. Doris had tried, very tactfully of course, to persuade her to confide in us, but it would seem she doesn't care to."

"What does she do with herself?"

"She likes walking. She goes off for half a day, sometimes a whole day. By herself, when the best medicine to take her mind off whatever's troubling her would be cheerful company. I've made one or two attempts to get her to team up with some of the other guests, but with no success. Still, I shall go on trying. That's why, at Doris's suggestion, I asked Mrs. Theocharis's permission to bring her with me tonight. We both hoped that at a splendid party like this, she'd relax, forget whatever's troubling her."

Without Geoff giving her a summoning wave, Lois Brown had spotted him, and was peremptorily thrusting a path through the clusters of guests. "I'm ready to go if you are." She stood uncompromisingly in front of him, her cheeks aflame, this time not wasting half a glance on me.

I called good night to her, but she did not reply. I thought: Maybe the simplest explanation is that she is a natural solitary, unable to communicate with anyone but herself. But the unease remained. How was it she knew Heller sufficiently well to have a blazing row with him in public?

Barbie materialised before me. One of the strings of pearls she'd threaded through her hair dangled over an ear, otherwise the English rose image was unblemished. She was the only woman I'd ever met on whom, in its initial stages, drink had a beautifying effect. The Mona Lisa smile that never expanded and never died made her face as serene as an angel's; every languorous movement took on an extra grace, as though she was floating.

"Maria! I've been looking everywhere for you. Kim's sent for the car. All right with you?"

"Fine." At the Villa Hesperides you were relieved of the chore of parking your car. On arrival a uniformed servant drove it to some rear quarters and magically presented it to you when you were ready to leave. "But first I must find Carima and say good night."

"She's downstairs. Alex, too." She pressed into my hand a napkin wrapped round something soft and mushy. "Cake for Toby and Connie. You'd better carry it or I'll be sure to sit on it in the car." She giggled to herself. "I don't eat cake even at birthday parties, only bread!"

She sat in the front of the car with Kim, resting her head on his shoulder. I sat in the back. He'd taken care that our glances hadn't met, but he was humming to himself, a habit of his when he was irked or frustrated. This time it was because he'd been caught out. By now the shock of that moment in the folly, the thrust of doubt it had evoked, had died away. I was tired, and the sight of Barbie nuzzling his ear, and of him lifting a hand from the wheel to stroke her chin, was proof—if I needed it—of the capricious, highly volatile quality of their relationship. I laid the squashy package of cake on the seat beside me, closed my eyes, and thought of tomorrow.

But the pattern of light and shade on my lids wasn't right, the turns the car made were not the ones that would lead us back to the house. When I opened my eyes we were passing Geoff's and Doris's private hotel, which was two miles in the opposite direction.

I leaned forward. "Why aren't we going home?"

"Because Heller invited us for a night-cap," Kim snapped.

Barbie turned round, gave me her seraphic smile. "Wasn't it sweet of him? He knows I hate going straight home after a party."

Even above the car engine you could hear the sea, swirling in a roaring tumult up the narrow gullies that hemmed in two sides of the house. The third boundary was a tumble of rocks that lurched over the cliff. The fourth, at the end of a track from the road, was a high stone wall into which was set an equally high gate. It was opened by Bengy, a young muscle-man who crewed on Heller's yacht and acted as chauffeur and barman. He was a handsome, tough, completely brainless blond who looked as if he'd been in the fight game.

Heller, whose arrival could only have preceded ours by minutes, was waiting ceremonially at the front door.

The exterior, except for its spectacular views, was of nondescript design, its walls a dirty pebble-dash. The inside was surprisingly spacious, with furniture and fittings that ranged from opulent to dingy second-rate, as though Heller, or someone deputed by him to do the job, had indulged in wild spending splurges and had then got bored or run short of money.

He kissed Barbie's cheek and slapped Kim's shoulders, before with feigned solemnity he reached for my hand, pressed it between both of his. "Dear Miss Maria. Such a pleasure, a treat, you might say, for me to entertain you."

As though it were the first time I'd been under his roof; that February afternoon had never been.

With genial aplomb he ushered us into his main room, where a picture window overlooked the sea, now filled with a sky in which a full moon floated.

There were three other guests ahead of us, two of whom had come on from Carima's party, an attractive blonde with an electric smile and magnificent teeth, and her husband, a less forceful personality with a nervous glance that never stayed still. The third guest was a corpulent middle-aged man with a thin face that didn't match his body. It appeared he was there to discuss the possibilities of chartering Heller's yacht for a month's cruise.

Temporarily behind the bar until Bengy took over was Heller's housekeeper, Mrs. Bales, a pallid, grey-haired woman with a timid, ladylike mien. With his back to it the middle-aged man whose name I do not remember gazed as visibly entranced at Barbie as though she were some divine being descended to earth solely for his delight. You couldn't blame him: her serene smile beamed good will on the world, with just a little extra measure for him. Kim and the young couple picked up a conversation they'd apparently started at the villa on the merits of different gambling casinos. Heller turned his attention on me, and with an expansive wave of his hand invited me to name my drink. I chose tonic water.

His fat clown's face mimed horror. "On top of champagne! If your boss was here, he would read you a lecture a yard long on mixing your drinks!" The slit eyes between their swollen lids derided me. "A great man for lecturing you is Mr. Grant. One of the world's do-gooders. But since he isn't here, I shall take it upon myself to bring you another glass of champagne."

"Tonic," I said, "please." Since I didn't intend to drink any more, it didn't matter what was in my glass, which made my stubborn insistence pretty silly.

While Mrs. Bales caught Heller's attention to report she needed a fresh supply of scotch, I went and sat down on a sofa at the end of the room. I was perfectly aware that I was behaving childishly. With Barbie and Kim there, plus three other guests, it wasn't remotely possible that Heller could repeat February's nauseous little episode.

On the next but last day of our stay Matthew had been lunching with David Strange in Lapithous. In mid-afternoon Bruce Vernon had arrived to invite Barbie and me to a bathing session on Heller's private beach. My reaction had been to decline, but Barbie, bored, had coaxed and pleaded. She wanted to go, but if I wouldn't, then she wouldn't either.

The party had consisted of Heller, Bengy, Bruce, and the two of us. Wading out of the water, I'd cut my foot on a knife-edged rock. Mrs. Bales, who had brought tea down to the beach, took me back to the villa to an upstairs bathroom where there was iodine and sticking plaster. When the telephone rang, I thanked her and said I could finish the job.

Five minutes later I'd emerged on to a shadowy landing, to be grabbed by Heller and thrust into a dim alcove. His loathsome body pressed against mine. One of his hands pinioned my wrists behind my back, the other, minus a finger, searched for my breasts and all the while his slimy mouth sucked at mine. I could not breathe; I could not shout. For a small eternity we writhed and struggled with deadly ferocity in total silence.

Release came when Barbie, anxious about the depth of the cut, called from the lower hall: "Maria, are you okay? Need any help?"

He leaned back, his swollen red face, the manic glint in his eyes so horrible, I shut my own. One of his hands slid round my throat, pressed. "Say, yes. Better say yes, quick, Miss Maria."

I croaked that I was all right. Wordlessly he let me go, ambled downstairs as I stumbled back into the bathroom to be sick. In the sitting-room, with Bengy serving drinks, Bruce operating the record player, and Heller dancing with Barbie, I was crippled by a total sense of incredibility. It hadn't happened; it could not have happened unless Heller were subject to seizures of psychotic lunacy. Then, over Barbie's gilt crown, the red clown's mouth smiled at me, and I couldn't think why I hadn't screamed the house down. It took me a long time to work out why I hadn't. Sickening self-disgust plus fear—not of being raped, that had never entered my mind—but of being strangled.

Watching him advance towards me, I wondered how many others were aware of the sadist who lived and breathed and waited behind the jovial kind-uncle mask. There must be some, but if so they didn't live in Kessima. Only the eyes, half hidden between the little bolsters of fat were a give-away: vicious, so utterly callous, they were as good as dead.

He set the glass of tonic before me, made a mock bow. "What the little lady ordered!"

"Thank you."

He peered at me with smiling malice. "What a cross, glum girl you are tonight!"

"Not cross. Only curious."

He laughed. Though he chuckled continuously he rarely laughed outright. The chuckles were audible backing to his image; paradoxically the laugh, which should have been hearty and rollicking, was thin and empty. The glance he darted at me was slyly speculative. "Little girls are born curious; they stay that way until they die."

"I'm curious about someone called Lois Brown. Do you know her?"

The massive shoulders in the white dinner jacket shrugged disinterest. "You expect me to remember the name of every girl I've met? I've lived too long! Who is she?"

"The girl you were talking to at the buffet after the fireworks."

"That girl!" The slits of eyes summed me up. "What about her?"

"She was furious with you. As furious as if you'd slapped her face."

He chuckled, then focussed his hateful stare on my mouth, said very slowly: "Or kissed her maybe when she wasn't in the mood for being kissed." He paused, and the moist red grin widened. "Could it be that all these months Miss Maria has been waiting for an apology because I stole one little kiss from her!"

"You must be out of your mind! And for the last time don't call me by that ridiculous name."

"Why not! It suits you. You're an old-fashioned girl, as straitlaced, as uppity as a Southern belle . . ." In a split second the mask slipped, exposed pride ravaged, the myth of irresistibility laid waste, as his chest heaved, and then in a low tone that nevertheless was as keen as a whip-lash, he went on: "But armed with teeth to bite and a cat's claw to scratch, a vixen who needs to be taught a lesson. It was a pity that for once, little Miss Maria lost her pretty manners." The grin partially returned. "It leaves me with a score to settle, and I'm a man who's very particular about settling old scores."

Across the length of the room, I heard Barbie laugh. Its tone alerted me, brought me to my feet. It was no longer sweetly giggly, and she was fiercely batting aside Kim's hand that was raised to prevent her passing her glass to Bengy, who was now behind the bar. She'd by-passed the second harmless maudlin stage of intoxication, was well into the third, teetering on the brink of brawling drunkenness. It was the moment for anyone who loved her to get her home . . . fast.

I put my arm round her waist. "Barbie, I'm dying on my feet. I'd love to go home. Are you coming?"

In the moment I deflected her attention, Kim snatched the glass out of her hand. "That's what I call a good idea. Let's all go home."

The rose colour in her cheeks became two ugly splotches of scarlet. "Then why don't you two poor tired little dears keep one another company! Heller will pour me another drink, won't you, Heller darling, and see me home? As far as I'm concerned you two can take off any time you want."

Heller made a curt signal to Bengy, who handed Barbie half a glass of champagne. We watched her drink it. That was our mistake. The middle-aged man looked aghast at his fallen angel; the young couple were pop-eyed and hard-put to it to hide their amusement. Heller stood rocking slightly on his heels, the smile a painted gash across his face. Bengy was openly sniggering. Kim and I stood sick and apprehensive.

She lifted her arm high and as the glass splintered on the floor, she seemed to disintegrate before our eyes, and the sound that came from her throat was an ugly high-pitched screech. "Go on, stare, turn up your noses. I should care!" She shuddered convulsively, but when Kim tried to seize her wrist, she fought him off. "You wouldn't dare gang up on me if Matthew were here. He wouldn't let you." The tears that should have subdued her rage poured in a torrent down her cheeks, but she still went on screeching. "He'd never come to Kessima without seeing me. Never . . . Never. It was a lie, a cruel lie. Either that . . ." She whirled about, her wild glance pivoting on each of us in turn. ". . . or one of you, maybe the lot of you, have been up to something!" She wrung her hands, washing them frenziedly one within the other, then swivelled again, vented her highest fury on me. "You pretend to care. You're his precious, clever little girl, but what do you do when he can't be found, when he could be hurt, or dead, or kidnapped? I'll tell you: damn all." She caught her breath, then hurled it at us. "All right, stand there like a lot of dummies. I'm drunk. Okay, I'm drunk but not so drunk that I don't know you're a bunch of lying bastards." She smiled a mad smile at Kim, then laughed in his face. "And you're not nearly so smart as you think. For months you've been hiding some nasty little secret up your sleeve, scared to death I'll find out what it is. Okay, if you won't tell me where Matthew is, I'll go to the police, and they'll shake the truth out of you. First thing in the morning, that's what I'm going to do."

Rage, fear, love had drained the last dregs of coherence out of her. She swayed once before she collapsed into Kim's arms. Appalled, the three guests edged backwards, figuratively holding their skirts. Heller snapped his fingers at Bengy. For once the clown's smile wasn't in place. His face was as wooden as his stance, as though the gesture of command to Bengy was the limit of his mobility.

Kim and Bengy carried her, a fallen, bedraggled angel to the car and, when we arrived at the house, bore her limp, unconscious body upstairs.

When she lay beneath the silk drapes suspended from the dimpled hands of the cherub, Kim rounded on us. His eyes were driven deep into his skull, and the only colour left in his face was the mottled bruise. His voice had the hard menace of one making a threat he was prepared to carry out. "When she wakes in the morning, she won't remember a thing. Do you understand, not a word she said. And if either of you repeat any of it to her or anyone else, you'll have me to deal with. Go on, swear, and then get the hell out of here, both of you."

"Hey, steady, boy . . ." Bengy protested.

"Swear, you great oaf."

When Bengy had sworn, the remorseless, hate-ridden stare turned on me. "Now you."

I promised, and a small part of me that was not appalled by the ugliness of the scene of which I'd been a part queried whether it was concern for Barbie or a paralysis of fright that had transformed Kim from a play-boy into a man of stone.

On the other side of the door Kim had slammed and locked, Bengy, who'd revelled in every minute of the drama, rolled his eyes. "Seems that the show is over for tonight. But, oh boy, what a show! Someone's sure going to pay for it."

EIGHT

Sleep was so light that my consciousness recorded every external sound: Connie going downstairs, a cock crowing, a baby crying, and a donkey or a mule setting the boards of the bridge across the ravine rumbling. Half-asleep my subconscious was tormented by rearing peaks of doubt. I wanted to ignore them: to lie and draw close all that lay within the perimeter of the day that was just beginning.

It was a light sound, one I recognised instantly, that brought me upright, reaching for my dressing-gown: the pat-pat of small bare feet climbing the steep stairs leading to the Crow's Nest.

In pyjamas that were a size too big for him and rucked about his ankles, Toby was staring trancelike at the big walnut table. His head, under its thatch of straw-coloured hair that made it appear too large for his slight body, swivelled. His voice had a joyful lilt and there was a brilliant sparkle in his blue eyes. "You've put his books and pens out, and his blotter. That means he's coming today, doesn't it?"

"I hope he is, but I haven't had definite news. He could be here when you get home from school, but you might have to wait another day."

I moved to stand beside him, but he turned away so that I couldn't spy on his sickness of disappointment. A natural stoic, he only accepted comfort from four people: Matthew, Eugenia, Connie, and his mother. In that order.

When he spoke it was in an unnaturally high-pitched voice. "I had a dream about Uncle Matthew." His head came up and now, though I was outside the privileged quartet, his eyes sought reassurance. "He was terribly sick in bed, so sick his eyes were closed. I kept asking him to open them and talk to me but he wouldn't."

I actually felt my teeth grit together. In league with his mother to put the fear of God in me, to turn my flesh clammy, to rouse pain in the pit of my stomach.

I put out my hand and for once he slotted his small one into it, proof of the depth of his fear. "Listen, I'll make you a promise. Cross my heart. If Uncle Matthew were ill, no matter where, someone—a doctor or a nurse—would telephone us. Even if he was too sick to tell them who he was, where we are, they'd find his passport, all the other identification papers he carries in his pockets."

"But suppose a gangster stole his passport and his papers, then the doctor and nurses wouldn't know."

"Do you honestly believe that Uncle Matthew isn't equal to coping with a gangster! He's been in wars, earthquakes, every kind of terrible disaster. He's an expert at taking care of himself. Don't worry, he'd get the better of any gangster."

He nodded, trying hard to smile but not managing it. "Suppose there was more than one gangster, lots of them, with guns?"

"Suppose," I joked, "you stop frightening yourself silly! That's what Uncle Matthew would say if he could hear you. Not trusting him to look after himself!"

He gave me a wan, half-convinced look, and I could summon no more words of comfort to give him as I listened to the slippered feet ascending the stairs.

Connie, still wearing her pink hair net to protect her new perm, exclaimed: "So this is where you've got to, is it! Up those cold slabs and no shoes on your feet! It's past time you were getting dressed. Come on, look sharp. You don't want to keep Eugenia waiting, do you?"

As he passed her, she ran her hand over his head, and when she heard his bedroom door close, she scolded me. "It upsets him your being here and not his uncle. I had a rare old job getting him to sleep last night." Her shrewd boot-button bright eyes combed my face. "Did you enjoy yourself at the party?"

"Yes. All very splendid." I saw Alex's unreadable satyr-face, the glance of hate Kim had thrown me from the little folly. I saw Barbie degraded into a drunk, half-manic woman, and Heller's face robbed of its permanent smile made naked and ugly. And Kim's like petrified flesh the moment before he'd slammed and locked the door in my face.

She sniffed scorn. "I imagine Miss Lennings was there!"

"She was around."

"Around Master Kim, I'll be bound."

"Could be, but since he wouldn't have enough money to keep her in lipstick, do you have to worry?"

"You're out of date. Nowadays Kim's rolling." Seeing my look of incredulity, she repeated as solemnly as though she were taking an oath, her palm on a Bible: "Rolling."

I found it hard to credit, unless he'd backed a winner. One fact was beyond dispute: if he was in the money, it wouldn't last.

"Where's it coming from?"

"He's not telling. Proof that it's from some dirty little racket he daren't boast about. That's why the sooner Matthew gets here to sort him out, the easier I'll be in my mind." She gave me an uncharacteristic beseeching look—Connie considered begging for a favour demeaning. "You find him, there's a good girl. Tell him to get his skates on. Something going on, and I don't mean Kim playing lover-boy to that radio girl, and Matthew is the only one who can ferret out what it is, drag him out of it, and make him behave."

Where Barbie's and Toby's interests were concerned Connie was devoid of inhibiting principles. She'd count it her duty to listen at doors, read any letters left lying around, and even, if she were desperate, pick a simple lock.

"You must have some idea what kind of racket he's mixed up in."

"I haven't," she said with sour disappointment. "You'd be surprised how cunning he's grown."

Connie, the peccadilloes of eavesdropping, letter-reading aside, was trustworthy to the core. "I wasn't home when Matthew telephoned to ask me to fly out here. My charwoman took the message. The line was a bad one but she said Matthew said something about me flying to Nicosia so that I could take Toby back to England."

She blinked at me, mortally affronted. "It's news to me. Whatever for? If he wanted taking anywhere there was his mother or me to take him. Matthew knew the date when I was due back. And why should Toby go to England when he's not booked into his school until next year?" Without waiting for an answer, she closed the issue. "Your char must have got hold of the wrong end of the stick."

"Maybe. It didn't make sense to me."

"And not knowing where Matthew is when he said he'd be here doesn't make sense to me," she retorted tartly. "It's not like him. Punctual, never putting anyone out, a more considerate man never breathed. And if you used the brains you're supposed to have, you'd know that as well as I do, and do something about it."

"I've already done all that can be done. I've left urgent messages with all his contacts in Cyprus, at hotels in the Middle East, and at his London flat for him to get in touch with me here. There are simply no more steps I can take, only wait."

"Miss Nash telephoned while you were all at the party last night, and she's worried stiff I can tell you. She's not one to sit and wait for things to happen. It's her opinion that if we haven't heard from him by midday, someone should go to the police. And I reckon if you won't, she will."

She was deliberately goading me. When I did not speak, there was a long pause during which she obviously debated what further methods she could use to pressure me into action, and, failing to find any, she changed the subject. "Did Kim tell you how he came to damage his pretty face?"

"He ran the car into a ditch, hit it on the steering wheel!"

She gave a whoop of laughter at my naïveté. "Not on your life. He ran into a nice left hook. I've seen bruises like that when we lived in Walworth, dozens of them every Sunday morning. What I want to know is who did it; they deserve a medal."

"If you're right, I wouldn't know."

When she'd gone, at war with myself, I stood staring at the morning light sliding down the mountains. A child's bad dream. Barbie drunk and hysterical. And now Connie telling me how to do my job. All because Matthew was the pillar of strength that supported the three of them. He'd only to be out of contact for a couple of days and they were undermined, demoralised.

Matthew wasn't a bank manager with a work schedule that ran on tram-lines. He was an expert in a profession where his only task-master was a dead-line on television or in a newspaper. When a crisis blew up in a country on which he had made himself an authority, planes had often to be boarded only seconds before they were air-borne. I'd dinned the explanation for his absence into my head so many times that it repeated itself parrot-fashion. When he'd telephoned me to cancel his first message, either late on Friday night or during Saturday, there'd been no one at the flat. So, under relentless pressure to get to his destination, he'd entrusted the task to a colleague or a hall porter to relay, and they, too, had got no answer from my flat.

It was simple, irrefutable logic that made nonsense of Barbie's hysteria, Connie's reproaches, and Giselle's trumpet calls for action. I was a junior partner in his professional life, knew its rigours. They didn't.

Tonight or tomorrow Matthew would surface, either in Kessima or London. We'd pick up where we'd left off; me a martyr to hope—no, not hope, to a prayer that would never be answered. A girl who still retained sufficient rags of sanity to recognise that, if I didn't stiffen my will to break loose, I'd stay Matthew Grant's third arm until I was old and greyheaded, when he'd pension me off—handsomely.

I was going to spend the whole day with a man who was prepared to love me, and whom I was prepared to love. A day that belonged to Donald and to me, and into which no one, not even Matthew, was to be allowed to poke an intruding finger.

Barbie was sitting on the dressing-stool in my bedroom, leaning forward towards the mirror. When our reflections overlapped, she wailed: "If you'd just met me, how old would you guess I was?"

I tweaked a dangling hair-piece from her crown. "With last night's make-up on and your hair like a bird's nest, you can't expect to look eighteen."

She stroked the hair-piece then, through smudged lashes appealed, her voice shaking with dread: "Tell me the truth, did I fall flat on my face last night?"

"Nowhere near it. You got tight, put on your slow-motion Grande Dame act. Very queenly."

"Honest?"

"Honest."

She gave a shudder. "As long as I didn't make a scene at Carima's party. If I had and someone had told Matthew, I couldn't have borne it."

"You left Carima's party under your own steam, after gracious thanks all round." The truth, except I'd omitted the last act. Partly to protect Barbie's pride, partly because of that chilling aftermath in her bedroom.

She reached up, ran a finger down my cheek. "You're a dear, sweet, comforting angel, Maria. If I've ever been mean to you, I want you to forgive me. I've been worrying myself sick since I woke up. I'd got this hideous sort of smudgy picture of me shouting my head off, screaming, smashing things. If it had been real, I think I would have died."

"It wasn't." I unpinned two more false curls from her hair, brushed out her own. "Where's Kim?"

"Down in his private dungeon."

At eight, it astonished me that he was out of bed. "Carving gnomes at this hour!"

"I doubt it. I think he's given them up. He's got a new powerful radio he keeps down there. My guess would be that he's got his feet up on the work-bench. He's had a lock put on the door and carries the key around with him."

"Why?"

"I don't know, and what's more, I don't care. Don't you remember I told you that Kim and I are through? *Fini!*" Suddenly she smiled at herself in the mirror. "I've a feeling in my bones that Matthew will telephone or arrive today." She twisted her face towards me, coaxed: "Well, that makes sense, doesn't it? Friday evening to Tuesday! If he was caught up in an emergency like you said, it must be over by now, or if it was just some silly mix-up, he'll have discovered you're not in London, and phone you to board the first plant out of Nicosia for Heathrow."

"If he telephones after ten, you'll have to take a message for me. Donald's spending the day at the hotel site, and I'm going with him. We're taking a picnic lunch and I imagine I'll be back around five."

"Good for Donald!" She was incorrigibly interested in other girls' affairs. "I knew he fancied you, but last time you were here you never gave him a sniff of encouragement. All right, if Matthew phones I promise I won't let on you're out jaunting for the day with Donald Hardwick."

"There's no earthly reason why you shouldn't."

She widened her eyes to feign astonished horror. "I wouldn't like to be the one to break it to him that you'd gone off picnicking on a private beach with Donald Hardwick."

I accused, furious with her: "You're crazy!"

"Okay, I'm crazy. Or you are! Want to borrow something fetching to wear?"

"No, thanks. A bikini under a top and shorts is all I need and I've got them."

She stretched, examined herself once more in the mirror, grimaced. "I'll go and scrub myself clean and then we'll have breakfast under the vine. I'll ask Connie to make us a double ration of coffee. Maybe that will do something for me."

When she'd gone, I reminded myself that Barbie's judgment of people and situations was, to say the least, unreliable. And she loved to tease. That was all there was to it. I drew a blind over her remarks, and kept it down.

From the balcony I saw Toby, his satchel swinging on his back, run across the bridge to meet Eugenia, who was waiting for him on the other side. Fleetingly, I pondered on the quality in one human being that acted like a magnet on another, formed a link so powerful only death could dissolve it. Toby and Eugenia. Me and . . .

NINE

I was waiting in the courtyard by the well when Donald drove in. I called goodbye to Connie and reached Alex's Alfa Romeo as Donald jumped out. He was happy, excited, almost exultant, as he cried: "Don't let's waste a second." Yet he did, to say with a sort of loving pride: "You look gorgeous! Straight off a *Vogue* cover."

"A model girl, forever going places, is that your fancy?"

"No. Just a girl who, on suitable occasions, looks like one."

The sound of the telephone ringing cut like a saw through the intervening space to burst in my ears. Simultaneously Connie appeared, shouting through cupped hands. "Maria! Telephone."

I stood motionless and so did he, the skin on his knuckles holding the door handle strained tight. The pride in him kept his smile in place, but his body was so stiff he hardly seemed to breathe. Connie went on shouting as though the house were empty, as though she and Barbie and Kim were incapable of answering a telephone. As though it had to be Matthew when it could as well be any one of twenty or thirty friends, acquaintances, or tradesmen calling. I reached out and pushed the door wide, got into the car. As he closed it on me, I saw the tension ease out of him.

He pulled the starter. "Whew! I've just learned the precise meaning of having your heart in your mouth! If that had been Matthew staking a claim to you, I'd have lost my day."

I had to wait until the shaking inside me had ceased. "It's my day too, and I'm not losing it or giving it away." With a deliberate act of will power I shut out the echo of the telephone ringing inside my head.

At the end of the village, where the high bastion of rock narrowed the road, we were brought to a halt by a flock of skipping, jumping goats, and then slowed to a crawl to allow three stragglers to be rounded up. Another car, coming uphill, was forced to slow down, and when we drew level I saw a policeman at the wheel and in the back a man in civilian clothes with a girl in a red woollen cap beside him. As our eyes met I automatically smiled, half waved my hand. Her hand did not move, nor did her small mouth deviate from its set, hard line.

When Donald put his foot down on the accelerator, I said: "The girl in the car that just passed us was Lois Brown. She's staying at the Windsor Court. Geoff brought her to Carima's party last night. Did you happen to meet her?"

"No. Being dragooned by Stephanides and then roped in to make sure that none of the gardeners blew themselves up with the fireworks, I didn't meet anyone fresh. She seemed to give you a pretty cold brush-off."

"Maybe she's short-sighted. Why should one of Geoff's cosseted guests be riding round in a police car?"

"Search me. She's probably lost her handbag or camera. If she has the police will spend the next couple of days combing the island for it. And if it's to be found, present it to her with enormous pride."

"I know. I once forgot to pick up sixpence change in a shop and the next time I went in it was waiting for me."

I doubted whether Lois Brown had lost her handbag or her binoculars. The impression of her spying act on the house was deeply impregnated on my memory, but on this day I had not even a minute to waste on rationalising the odd behaviour of a surly-tempered girl in a ridiculous red woolly cap.

When we reached the coast road where a pure azure sea licked and relicked the golden sands, we had another half-hour's drive sandwiched between mountains and sea before we reached the site. We turned off the road and parked the car under the shade of a clump of silver-leaved olives, and then, with Donald carrying the picnic basket, we walked in single file along a narrow, twisting track hemmed in by pigmy evergreens that clung like grim death to whatever meagre nourishment supported them, and giant thistles, the blue heads that I'd touched in the spring, dried to glittering sunbursts with hearts of thick gold velvet.

The path ended abruptly in a smooth glade of sand out of which hundreds of white candlelike flowers sprang straight from the earth, ghostlike and eerily beautiful, the only flowers blooming in a burnt-out landscape.

I pulled off one of the tiny flowerlets: it was not, as I'd thought, pure white. It had a green eye, lemon stamens. I turned to Donald, who had paused with me. "Do you know what they are?"

"I haven't a clue." He hazarded a guess to humour me. "White delphiniums."

I laughed. I'm no gardener, but assorted scraps of my mother's knowledge had rubbed off on me. "No leaves! They're either bulbs or corms. Look, you can see them poking out of the sand."

"We could pick one on the way back, find someone who's not forgotten their botany. I know, Giselle!"

I shook my head. "It's not that important." But when we reached the shore, I glanced back. A golden grove, arid and unwatered as a desert, lit with ranks of white ghost flowers, as straight and tall as altar candles.

We climbed down over rocks that were like petrified sponges, jumped gullies filled with tiny transparent minnows that thrust in and out of the changing patterns of the swaying ribbons of seaweed, and fish that looked like marine versions of the lizards that, with the speed of sound, darted from beneath one dried mat of rock plants to disappear under another.

Where the sea gouged an inlet we had to retreat to a path

running alongside a screen of bamboo that had laid a raft of dead wood beneath our feet.

Beyond lay the perfect shell of the beach, combed by lapping waves, as empty as if the world were brand new. At one end, separated by a stone causeway over which the sea laid a thin, ever-moving coverlet of water, was the island, like a surfacing whale, a golden whale, on its summit a ruined hut built of stone torn out of the ground.

I'd seen it once before; Donald probably dozens of times, but by tacit consent we stood motionless and silent to gaze our fill. His glance sought mine, and he said with soft exaltation: "How precious perfection is. It's so damned hard to find, and getting scarcer every day."

I smiled at him. "Don't you ever feel a pang of guilt at what you want to do to it?"

For a second he looked hurt, then he said positively: "No. At least only for a short interim period when part of it will suffer a tidal wave of bulldozers." He pointed in two directions. "But it will soon recede and when it has, there'll be a long, low stone building that merges into the landscape, and on the island a garden playground and a restaurant practically floating in the sea. A hell of a lot of money is going to be spent on cheating and charming the eye. Do you think I should feel guilty?"

I shook my head, smiled into his hazel anxious eyes. I wondered if, because they were his living, bricks and mortar, the hard-top surfaces that a hundred cars demanded, were beautiful to him simply because they were his creation. If so, with my senses entranced, my mind made indolent by the sun, and my heart waiting, there was no contentiousness in me.

As we walked over sands that were unmarked by any footprint but our own, we seemed to be enclosed in a magic ring of emptiness. But we had been deceived. Figures that had been invisible at a distance defined themselves. A shepherd and a boy had driven a flock of sheep into the sea on our side of the causeway and were trying to entice them back to shore.

"Nature's sheep-dip!" He laughed with rich glee. "I've heard tales that they wash them in the sea, but I've never actually seen it done. Let's sit down and wait. There's not room for all of us." He pointed. "See, he's got the leader out? Hear his bell? Now the rest will follow."

They did, reduced to skeletons of themselves, their glossy coats matted and dripping, each huge tail as thin as a cat's. When the boy at the head of the flock and the shepherd at the rear rounding up the stragglers drove them ten yards from us, I called good morning. Neither shepherd nor boy as much as lifted his head. Which was almost beyond belief in an island where courtesy to strangers was endemic.

I protested: "They couldn't both be deaf, surely! They wouldn't even look at us."

The lightness went out of his face. "I'm afraid I'm the culprit. The shepherd must have recognised me. He was busy praying to the Almighty that I'll venture too far from the beach and conveniently sink like a stone." He looked at the half-ruined barn on the summit of the island. "That belongs to him. His great-grandfather built it for storing carob beans. He's either holding out for a ransom, or he's genuinely not interested in selling; what's more, he's keeping everyone guessing. And before he can sell, if he intends to, he has to get permission from his three sons and, for all I know, a dozen grandchildren apart from the boy who's his grandson."

"And if he was genuinely uninterested in the price, could he prevent the sale of the land?"

"For a time, maybe as long as he lives. Fortunately his eldest son, who owns a run-down garage in Lakonica that could be made into a paying proposition by an infusion of capital, is an extremely ambitious young man. He also has a young and pretty wife who, according to Alex's spies, is devoted to money. The pair of them may well be inclined to exert a little pressure."

"Would it matter terribly to you if the deal was held up, or even fell through?"

"Yes." He spoke explosively, without equivocation. "I'm the most junior of four partners, what you might call a king's messenger sent overseas to report on a site, the creditworthiness of the client. But this project is my own baby." He looked challengingly at me. "So the answer is yes. It does matter to me."

From far away I heard an echo of a voice saying: "They don't want to die even with money in the bank," and shut my ears to it.

He unstrapped the picnic basket and lifted out a metal cylinder of plans. "I'll show them to you, but you'd get the hang of them better from the island."

Carrying our espadrilles, we walked across the causeway with shoals of minute fish swimming across our feet. We scrambled in the blazing sun up a steep escarpment and lay down in the shade cast by a ruined wall on a mat of silver aromatic herbs, their tiny flowers made everlasting by the oven heat of summer.

We lay side by side, flesh not an inch apart, the beat of awareness, of passionate conjecture throbbing in my pulses. When I turned my head, he'd taken off his sun glasses, and his clear hazel eyes were so close I could see every variation of tint in the irises. The whites were as pure and brilliant as a child's. I had only to stir, to form my mouth into the right shape, and he would kiss me. In the end, I didn't even have to make that small effort.

The kiss was a burn of love that released a stream of sweetness to the senses. He freed my hair from its ribbon band and combed it with his fingers. A rich and beautiful promise of love shone in his eyes, yet all he said was: "We have a decision to make: whether we swim before lunch or after."

We swam before, for half an hour diving from a peak of rock that formed a natural diving board, floating on tranquil blue cushions of water. It was like being miraculously relieved of every care. We climbed back to the ruined hut hand in hand. "Are you happy?" he whispered. "As happy as I am?"

"I'm happy."

He laughed. "And hungry?"

"Ravenous."

It was more like a banquet for two than a beach picnic: caviar, lobster tails, chicken breasts, rolls that were still warm, a shaker of martinis, a bottle of hock, three sorts of cheese, a vacuum flask of lemon sorbet, another of coffee.

I gasped at the spread. "Nice to be rich enough to forget the hard-boiled eggs, lettuce hearts and feed your guests on rare delicacies to eat in the sun."

His look was openly speculative. "Would you like to be rich? So rich that you could fulfil every ambition you ever had?"

"I've never given it a serious thought." Riches didn't run in our family, any more than overdrafts, unpaid bills, or hankering after luxuries you couldn't afford. "Would you?"

He poured the martinis before he answered. "To the extent that I want to be successful at my job and money would be concrete proof that I'd won success, yes. I'd like to have sufficient money to travel for pleasure . . . long spells of it, later on. I think that's a fair summing-up." He handed me a martini. The corners of his mouth began to smile, and suddenly his eyes were suffused with longing. "Shall we drink a toast to my powers of persuasion?"

I laughed. "An ambiguous toast if ever I heard one! But yes. Here's to your powers of persuasion."

While we ate he talked, for the first time, about his family; his mother, who was alive, and his father, a doctor, who was dead; his sister, who was a nurse in a London teaching hospital, and his brother, an engineer, who had immigrated to Australia. I recognised it as an overture to what was to come, almost an act of trust. His family meant a great deal to him.

He divided the last of the hock between us, and as we drank both of us turned away from the sea, looked inland where the mountains were sheathed in a heat haze, ghostlike, a merging of grey and green and gold, as though the colours on a palette had run. There was no sound but the sea at our backs, pushing its way lazily, eternally up the sand.

The picnic basket replaced, he unrolled the plans, picked out the line and wash impression of the hotel, weighted each corner with a stone. It was, as he'd claimed, as unobtrusive as skill could make it, but the hut against which we leant would become a plate-glass restaurant, and no shepherd would wash his flocks in the sea. And in place of the stout-hearted little herbs clinging to their rock fissures would be brilliant gardens with sprinklers playing all day to keep them alive. Only the mountains the Crusaders had climbed, and the sea that had been there when the earth had been born, would be undisturbed.

I made the right responses; I meant them. But it was an interlude, and we both knew it. His arms folded about me, flesh clung to flesh and pulse spoke to pulse, our senses leaping, surging. We drew back a fraction, still so close that our breaths mingled, and smiled happiness at one another. I kissed him and his face was radiant and beautiful to me. He had a gift of gentleness that was like being wrapped in silk. I whispered: "We're visible for miles."

"I doubt it," he whispered back. "But if we were, would you care?"

"Yes."

He kissed me again, a harder, more demanding kiss in which I tasted doubt. "An excuse? A let-out?"

"You know it isn't."

He leaned away from me, and it was cold without his flesh pressed to mine. Only our eyes clung together. I saw the gladness leave his, the cords in his neck tighten, as though he'd suffered a recoil of the emotions, a sudden shrinking back. His voice was abrupt, a kind of dread behind it. "If you love someone you gain a third eye, but sometimes it plays you false, deceives you, and you get confused, uncertain. Will you tell me something?"

"What?"

"Are you Matthew Grant's girl?" He touched my cheek gently with a finger. "Don't look so scared. Maybe it's not an easy question for you to answer with a yes or no."

"Why do you have to ask it?"

"It is a primitive urge common to all men to know if the girl you love belongs to another man. *I* need to know because I'm not very good at fighting battles that are lost before they are begun. So what does that make me . . . a moral coward!" He forced a smile that didn't reach his eyes. "You know the old adage, be cruel to be kind. So tell me, however hard it is."

It was as if I had to summon all my will and physical strength to jump a chasm, arrive safely on the other side. "It's a fair question. You're not the only one who gets confused, comes up with the wrong answer. I work for Matthew. It's not a run-of-the-mill job with set hours. Days overlap nights; there aren't any fixed rules, but basically, it's a job like any other paid job."

I paused, with a sensation of being suspended in mid-air. "Matthew is not in love with me, and I don't belong to him."

My reward was the hope that flooded back into his face, the bounteous loving in his eyes, an exultancy in his voice. "I believe you, because I love you." He laughed with that special joy that remembers sadness only a step behind. "That's not news to you, is it? Women always know. More than anything on earth, I want you to love me. Could you try? Could you try very hard?"

I promised, and we lay together enclosed in love, as contentedly exhausted as though we'd had a long hard battle to reach where we were, until the shadows began to lengthen. Then we crossed the causeway, and he left me by a honeycomb of rocks where the fish were lifted out of one pool into another by the ceaseless rise and fall of the sea. I succumbed to the mesmeric effect, relaxed, suffused with quiet joy until he came back, the roll of plans tucked under his arm, the absorption leaving his face the instant our glances met.

It was nearly five, the air about us cooling as we walked along the narrow twisting path through the lichens and spiky silver scrub. By now all the lizards had gone to bed.

It pounced without warning as we were crossing the grove lit with the white candles of the ghost flowers, a sense of calamity that stilled the heart, rooted me to the ground, so that his hand dragged mine, and the only feeling in me was the race of tears down my cheeks. It was as though voluntarily I had given my life away . . . that I was dying.

Though a mist I saw the horror come alive in his eyes, a rage of concern possess him. "Maria, my love, what is it? Are you hurt? You are hurt. Tell me . . ."

The anguish that had struck me out of the blue was so constricting that I could not speak; all that I was aware of was his face riven with a terrible anxiety and around me swaying in dreamlike slow motion the tall white flowers, like spectres nodding their heads at me. His arms were wrapped about me, but I could not feel them. I could feel nothing except the thunder of my heart-beats and when, at last, they slackened, I had to wait until the nightmare of inner darkness dissolved. Only then had I strength to push away the handkerchief with which he was wiping away my tears. "I'm sorry. I feel an absolute fool, but I'm all . . ." My voice gave out.

"What was it? What happened to you? Try and tell me."

Say an agony of the heart, an exposure to myself of the girl who was Maria Caron, an exposure I could not put into words, that I could not bear to admit?

At last my voice answered to my command. "Too much wine, too many lobster tails, and too much sun." The racking anxiety in his eyes put some warmth into my chilled flesh. I wanted desperately to reassure him. "Some sort of queasy spasm, that's the only way I can describe it. Indigestion, a touch of the sun . . . maybe a combination of both. But it's over." I laid my hand on his cheek. "So stop looking worried out of your mind."

"I must worry. To love someone is to worry about them interminably. Don't you know that!" He smoothed away the last tear. "You frightened me. You looked bereft, as if you'd lost everything." He slipped an arm round me. "Darling, do you think you can make it back to the car? I can't bring it any nearer, but I could carry you."

"I'm as right as rain. I could walk a mile." That was the strangest part: when the inner darkness lifted it left behind no physical effect, only a beating urgency to leave forever the scene where I'd suffered it. As I moved forward, he pulled me into his arms, held me crushed against his shoulder. I could hear the great beats of his heart, so that when he spoke his words came in breathless bursts. "I love you so much, I couldn't bear to lose you."

"You'll never have to. What makes you think I want to lose you?"

That was the true climax to the day. The cataclysm that had overtaken me in the grove of ghost flowers had no more significance than a nightmare that had pounced and possessed me in full daylight.

When Connie heard us pull in, wearing her snake-boots, watering can in hand, she came cantering down the garden. As soon as she was within shouting distance, she called: "At last Matthew got round to phoning. Kim's got a message for you."

My heart jumped. The ringing telephone to which I'd closed my ears and mind!

I cried: "When? What did he say?"

She came as far as the courtyard to draw water from the well. "About noon. Neither Barbie nor I was in. Kim spoke to him. He'll tell you all about it." She looked at Donald. "Mr. Theocharis telephoned half an hour ago and said he'd be obliged if you could get back to the villa as soon as it's convenient. It seems he's got someone there he wants you to meet."

TEN

He came with me into the sitting-room, where the shutters were folded back, the windows open to the dusk. A pool of light sharply illumined Heller on a sofa with Giselle beside him, her face angled up at his, laughing at a joke he'd made, a ribboned box on her knee, her cool firmly back in place. Barbie was lying in a chair with her feet on a stool, wearing what Matthew called her Mona Lisa smile, seemingly mystically enigmatic, but actually a sign that her attention had drifted miles away. Kim was at the drinks table squirting soda into a glass of scotch. A happy gathering of bosom friends, miraculously infused with a lightness of heart, all released from fright and hysteria by a telephone call.

I looked at Kim. "Connie says Matthew telephoned."

"Indeed he did." He paused, mouth pursed, to tantalise me. "So you can sweep all your worries under the carpet and stop looking like a mother hen who's lost her only chick." He paused a second time while my impatience seethed. "He phoned from Cairo airport, within minutes of catching a plane to Alexandria. Either tomorrow or Thursday he'll be in London and that's where he wants you. I tried to reserve you a seat on the morning plane to Heathrow but it was fully booked, but I got you one on the afternoon flight."

Relief was overwhelming, but there were still great quagmires of mystification. "What's been happening? Why is he in Egypt? Why didn't he get a message to me?" I became aware of four pairs of eyes regarding me with varying degrees of speculation. I was guilty of interrupting a celebration of forgiving and forgetting put on to blot last night's ugliness from memory. I quietened my voice, insisted: "He must have given you some sort of explanation."

"No, he didn't." He went back to his drink pouring. "And I know my place better than to ask for one. Like the good boy I am, I accepted that my function was to relay the message to you. So, mission completed!"

I was determined to get one basic fact clear. "But he did know I was here in Kessima?"

"Since he telephoned and asked for you he must have, mustn't he?"

So there'd been no second message to cancel out the first one to the flat, and all my confident rationalisation had been a wild misjudgment. "Did he leave a telephone number for me to reach him?"

"No."

"Did you tell him we'd all been worried?"

He gave me a long-suffering look. "Now what would have been the point! It's all water under the bridge. By Thursday at the latest, you can grill him yourself. What about a drink? Donald?"

Even taking into account the streak of contrariness in Kim that exploited any scrap of power that fell by chance into his hands, to accept that Matthew had left me without news of his whereabouts for two days was simply not credible, which meant that Kim, out of puckish spite, was deliberately withholding information.

Behind me I heard Donald answer: "Nothing for me, thanks. Alex wants me back at the villa."

Suddenly I needed desperately to turn and look at him, even to make sure he existed and, if it were possible, to touch him. But when I did so I found he was standing in deep shadow and all I had was his voice that had a strange neutral ring. "If you like I'll drive you to the airport tomorrow. Will it be all right if I collect you at two?"

"Suppose Alex wants you?"

"I'll fix it so that he doesn't."

He said good night and went out through the courtyard. Unsure of what I wanted to make sure, I followed him. Connie was calling Toby in from the garden. He came, dragging his feet, Eugenia by his side. When they reached the light I saw she was crying. Disobeying Connie's insistence that he must come inside that instant, Toby walked with her to the edge of the car park. The seconds I'd spent on observing Eugenia's small, tear-sodden face meant that, by the time I reached the Alfa, Donald was behind the wheel with the door closed.

He gave me a smile of pure kindness. "There," he said as though I needed comfort, "you don't have to fret any longer." I searched his eyes. They were steady, calm, love still there. What had vanished was the joy. My mouth was dry. I was conscious of pain, but not where it was, nor why it was there. I blurted out: "Thank you for today . . ."

He made a sound that was half a laugh, half a protest. "Thank you for thanking me!" His glance hung on my face. The light was not sharp enough for me to read it. "Make me a promise. An easy one. When you wake in the morning remember today, not just the sun and the scenic bits, but all the rest, and go on remembering it until I see you."

"I couldn't forget if I tried."

"At two I'll be here for you." I thought he was going to add something else, but instead he switched on the ignition.

And when his car had reached the bridge I went to collect Toby, who was still loitering on the edge of the car park. "Connie wants you." As we walked towards the courtyard I asked: "What made Eugenia cry?"

"Her father's angry with Niko. He's had his pocket money confiscated for a month, and he's never going to be allowed to go and see his uncle again, the one who works at the monastery. We said hello to him in the garden when Uncle Matthew took us to see it. Don't you remember?"

"Yes, I remember." Niko, I worked out, was the elder of

Eugenia's two brothers, and the uncle, a lay member of a religious order, a gardener in the monastery set high in a spur of the mountains. "What did Niko do?"

"On his way back from the monastery he lost his water flask and rucksack. Only he didn't lose them, not really. A man shouted at him. Or it might have been a ghost. Niko was frightened, and he ran so fast he dropped them. He didn't remember them until he got nearly home. He couldn't go back to look for them because it was getting dark and he was frightened of the man or the ghost who shouted at him."

"It might have been a man who was hurt, in need of help!"

"But he couldn't see him. He was hiding somewhere in the rocks waiting to pounce on him. It was where you and Uncle Matthew and I stopped the day we went to the castle and the monastery. That's where Niko's uncle was shot and killed, in the big cave there. If it wasn't his ghost, Niko thought some man was playing a trick on him, so that he'd climb near enough for him to shoot him."

"Niko's old enough to know better. The shooting was years ago. Long before you came to live in Cyprus."

"I know it was. But it could start all over again. Niko says it could."

School-children playing exciting war-games, or repeating their parents' talk? It could be either.

"It's not likely," I said firmly, "not with the United Nations peace-keeping force here."

"Niko remembers his father and uncles bringing his uncle's body down the mountain. He had a hole right through his head, and you could see his brains, and he didn't . . ."

I stopped him. In the lighted car park, with Connie, his mother, and me on call, he could rattle on glibly about corpses and spilling brains, but alone in bed, in the dark, the ghoulishness backfired into nightmares from which he woke screaming like a banshee.

"Maybe we can do something about Niko's pocket money. Or better still, buy him a new rucksack and flask. I'll get them in the village tomorrow morning, and you can give them to Eugenia for Niko." Except, I remembered, I had no money.

I remembered something else. "Did you tell Athena not to worry about the ash-tray she broke?"

"She didn't break it. She found it in two pieces on the floor underneath the bookshelves. And she couldn't find Uncle Matthew's lamp anywhere. That worried her too because he'd brought it specially from England." On the threshold of the kitchen, he asked dolefully: "He's not coming, is he?"

"Not until October when he promised you he would be here. It's only three weeks away."

"But if he wasn't coming, why did you come?"

"There was a muddle."

Scowling, he answered back: "Uncle Matthew never makes muddles. You know he doesn't, so you shouldn't say he does."

Connie, her last thread of patience snapped, forcibly dragged him in to his supper.

I stared down at the skeins of light in the village below. The fears I'd never allowed myself to admit were vapour on the wind. In their place was a certainty of something awry, just out of sight. Toby was right. Matthew, trained as a newspaper man, not only possessed an inborn sense of timing, but was a master of meticulous planning. No loose ends were left hanging, and certainly no one under his orders left stranded at an airport at which he wouldn't be arriving.

I heard light footsteps behind me. Giselle said: "I must get back to Dadda. It looks as if those two men are embarking on a night's serious drinking. Barbie has gone up to her room. She left a message with me asking you to go up and see her."

She was a study in soft shadowy colours: pale brown slacks, a beige silk shirt, gold skin-tones. The only vivid note was her deep emerald eyes. She said with a happy and unrepentant lift of her shoulders: "So all's well! You were right, and I was wrong; to panic, I mean." In a long, level stare the cool green eyes examined me. "You don't look particularly overjoyed!"

"I know where Matthew is now, but I still don't know why I'm here in Kessima."

"Ah," she said, openly mocking me. "But you would have if you'd been here when he telephoned. Did you and Donald have a good day?"

That had pleased her . . . a suitor, a possible husband to

remove me from the arena. "A marvellous day," I said, and saw us at noon lying on the island, surrounded by a blue and golden world we had to ourselves. But the picture in my mind's eye was tiny and remote, as though I saw it through an immense distance of time, and, however hard I strove to bring it close, it remained far off and long ago. Relaxed, she said kindly, if a shade patronisingly: "At least it took your mind off Matthew. It looks now as if there'll be no chance of seeing him in Kessima until October. Still, that's only another three weeks. The thirteenth, that's when you were due to arrive, wasn't it?"

"The thirteenth, if he hasn't changed his plans."

"Why should he?"

"I've no idea. I won't have until I see him and discover what's been going on."

Her delicate triangular face was gripped by dismay, all because I'd put a question mark on a starred date in her calendar. She recovered herself. "If he's not coming, he'll let me know. In any case I'm due to pay Aunt Violet a visit in November, so I shall see him then. Meanwhile, give him my love."

I lost her when she left the area of the car park. Her light tread made no sound as she crossed the wooden bridge. And then, as she passed under a village street lamp, I saw her again, head high, her buoyant, graceful carriage making it easy to pick her out in a crowd. Two women who witness one another in love with the same man play nasty games with one another. I'd put a doubt into her mind about the October visit. For the first time she'd used me as a messenger to take her love to Matthew.

I went to find Kim. He and Heller had moved out under the vine. At my step their heads moved in unison. I caught a flare of wariness in Kim's and saw Heller's fat cheeks tighten. Kim waved an affable hand in the direction of the drinks. "Change your mind?"

"No, thanks." I got down to a piece of business I found distasteful. "I left London in such a rush after arriving back from Cornwall that I only brought with me sufficient money for the outward journey. If you could lend me enough to get me back to London, I'll give you a receipt and Matthew will refund it to you."

"Why, sure." He took a fat wallet out of his pocket, counted fifteen five-pound notes off a wad. "Enough? You can have more if you want!"

"More than enough. I'll let you have a receipt in the morning." I'd not missed the pride, transparent as a child's, he'd taken in making a hand-out of seventy-five pounds, nor the notes left behind in the wallet. Kim, who needed all the cash he could scrounge to keep himself afloat, with maybe a hundred pounds in his pocket. I wondered what his latest fiddle was, and found part of the answer in Heller's barely repressed glance of fury at Kim's ostentatious display. It probably wasn't Kim's money I held in my hand; more likely Heller's, paid to Kim for a service, or as a bribe to keep his mouth shut about one of Heller's dirty rackets.

As I turned to go, Kim said: "Hey, wait a moment, Heller's brought you a present."

Heller got up and ostentatiously lifted from a table in the sitting-room a box tied with pink ribbon. It contained sugared almonds, the delicious Greek variety sold in a village shop near Paphos, the nuts encased in thick soft fondant. He held it out to me. "To cheer you up, Miss Maria. That's what it seemed to me you needed, cheering up."

"Thank you," I said without looking anywhere near his face, and left him holding the ribboned box.

Barbie was lying back against the ruffled pillows, smiling at the gilded cherub smiling down at her.

She dropped her glance to find me. "I've been thinking, hard, trying to work something out. I've finally decided I don't like Heller."

"I've never been able to stand him."

"Ah, but you're a clever, decisive girl who knows her own mind, is never rocked by a doubt. Me, I'm more complicated." She sounded proud of the fact. "When I was with him he could mesmerise me into liking him, and you must admit he could be rather sweet and generous, and terribly useful." She looked ruefully at the sugared almonds on the bedside table as though already beginning to regret her decision. "Then when he wasn't there, I'd begin . . . well, to have second thoughts. Isn't there a special word for not knowing your own mind for two minutes together?"

"Ambivalence?"

"Could be." She went back to staring at the cherub. "What I've been lying here working out is that I never felt quite the same about him after Bruce died. It made, oh, I don't know, a sort of crossroads." Her lavender glance left the cherub and concentrated on me. "Did I ever tell you about the time I went to a spiritualist in Maida Vale, a fantastic woman?"

"No."

"Well, I did, and she told me I was psychic. Oh, you can laugh if you like," (I wasn't laughing) "but it's true I do have premonitions and sometimes actually see them, you know, sort of pictures in my mind. Maybe poor darling Bruce was murdered, and that's why he haunts me."

"What for? Nudging you into bringing his murderer to justice!"

She scowled at me. "I hate it when you go all nasty and matter of fact. Still, I suppose I can't expect you to understand. Only a very tiny proportion of people are blessed with the gift. That's what the clairvoyant said. She was terribly impressed."

"And that's what you wanted to see me about, to announce you've decided you don't like Heller?"

"Of course not, silly. It's something far more important." She patted the bed, her ruffled temper smoothed out. "Sit down and I'll tell you. But you must promise not to turn all school-marmy and say I can't do it because there's not a hope of your making me change my mind."

Her sleepy lavender eyes under their waxen lids suddenly blazed with excitement. She caught her breath, burst out: "When you fly to London, Toby and I are going with you. By this time tomorrow we'll be in England and I'll never have to set foot inside this horrible house again. It *is* true what they say in the village. It's an unlucky house. Maybe the ghost of that old man who left it to Matthew after he'd shot himself and wasn't found for a fortnight does haunt . . ."

"Do you mind! I don't think I can take any more ghosts."

She blinked, shrugged sheepishly. "Okay, as long as you understand that Toby and I are going to London with you."

"Does Kim know?"

"You must be joking! He mustn't know, not until we're in London. I told you, he and I are through. His black-haired career woman is welcome to him."

"You're leaving him because of Maxime Lennings?"

"No, of course not," she said impatiently, then suddenly raised her head from the pillow, listened to the sound of a car driving away. "They've gone, and do you know why they can go? Because you're here to act as a watchdog. You needn't look so disbelieving. It's true. Kim checks up on me every time I take the car out. This morning he rang the hairdresser while I was under the dryer. She wasn't supposed to let on to me, but she did. And while we were in Troodos he phoned me twice a day and hired a stooge, the doorman, to make sure I didn't take off for the airport." Her eyes widened. "It's the weirdest thing. We both act as if we were scared of each other." She suddenly noticed the folded notes in my hand. "Did Kim give you those?"

"I had to ask him for a loan to get me back to England."

"Six months ago he couldn't have lent you a pound; he hadn't got it to lend. Now you'd think he picked money off trees. That's what the two of them have got tucked away somewhere: a money-tree. Oh, I never thought. Suppose Bruce found it!"

Once in spate there was no way of restraining the stream of Barbie's inventive nonsense. "Barbie," I broke in, "about tomorrow. I'm afraid there's a snag. Donald is driving me to the airport."

"Oh, no he's not. He can't because I'm driving you. It has to be that way. We'll pick Toby up from school early. I'll think up some excuse; I've done it before. If Donald drove you, Toby and I could hardly go along and play a couple of gooseberries, could we? Kim would smell a rat."

"If Kim's as suspicious as you say he is, what's to stop him insisting on driving me to the airport himself?"

"He won't get the chance." She flicked me an infuriatingly smug glance. "That snag is already taken care of; you'll see how when the time comes. Oh, Maria love, I'm sorry to spoil your fun with Donald, truly, but what's it matter when you can get together as often as you want when you're both in London, and the only sure way for me and Toby to get clear of this hellhole is for me to step into the car without taking a stitch with me. You must see that!"

"Suppose I say no?"

She looked aghast. "You couldn't. You just couldn't."

"Why couldn't I?"

"You're part of the family: Toby's and mine and Matthew's."

"I'm not, you know. I've got a perfectly good family of my own."

For a moment she looked frightened to death, then she blurted out: "Because Matthew would want you to. He'd expect you to help me."

Connie popped her head through the door, said to Barbie: "Toby's ready for you to say good night to him. And what time are you two proposing to come down for your supper? Midnight!"

"Tell Toby I'm coming." She swung her legs off the bed. "And you won't have to cook supper for us, Connie darling. We're eating out."

"Nice to be some people," Connie said good-naturedly. "Enjoy yourselves."

"We will." Barbie slipped on her sandals. "I thought we'd go to that hotel beyond Lampadousa. They've taken on a marvellous French chef, and someone was saying last night that the food's out of this world." She glanced up at me. "I'll treat you."

"No." The word shot out of my mouth without the grace of a qualification, an excuse, or thanks. Barbie looked as shocked as if I'd slapped her. "Why?"

"Because I'm half dead on my feet. One glass of wine and I'd be so muzzy I couldn't hold an intelligent conversation, let alone a scintillating one. Plus the fact that I had too big a lunch to face a four-course dinner. Barbie, I'm sorry. It was a lovely idea, but not tonight."

For a moment disappointment at having her generosity thrown back at her turned her sulky. Then her natural good nature took over. "Okay. I admit your sparkle-level's pretty low. What did you two get up to all day? Never mind, forget I asked. After I've said good night to Toby, I'll make us some lovely scrambled eggs and coffee. Connie would fly right off the handle if I told her we'd changed our minds. And I make the most super scrambled eggs. Matthew taught me one time when Mum was ill. He said it made a change from my boiled ones." She stood up, said in a little girl's tremulous voice that might or might not be genuine: "You're not going to let me down tomorrow, are you, Maria?"

"No." Had there been any chance that I would? I didn't know. "What about Connie? Does she know you're off to London with me?"

"Heavens, no. It's not that I don't trust her . . . but she'd fuss, ask a thousand questions, and probably insist on coming with us . . . with all her luggage! I'll telephone her from Heathrow."

While she said good night to Toby, did the eggs, two operations that took her over an hour, I remained in a state of suspended belief. Barbie played games with her imagination, building up elaborate fantasies until there were no more splashes of colour to add, and then, bored with the game, abandoned them. Boredom was probably the keystone of this act of high drama she was intent on playing. She was bored with Cyprus, the house, and her husband. And, I admitted reluctantly, frightened of something. But that didn't mean that boredom and fright wouldn't get lost in the night.

When she proudly handed me a plate of curdled, watery eggs, I asked: "Why the rush? Why not wait until Matthew arrives in three weeks' time?"

"Because I'm not taking any chances. By then he could have changed his plans, be anywhere. But I know he'll be in London tomorrow or Thursday, and that's where Toby and I will be. Matthew will know how to fix all the legal business for me to have sole custody of Toby. I'm not standing for any of that sharing lark. You still don't believe I'm serious, do you? What do you want me to do, swear on a Bible?"

"No, just convince me that you're not play-acting, and that

when you wake up in the morning you won't have forgotten the whole idea."

"The play-acting was my pretending that I loved living in this house, sweltering in the heat, seeing the same people all the time, until I got sick to death of their faces. But it did Toby's health so much good, and Matthew was in love with it, so I pretended. If I'd told him I didn't want to go on living here, it would have been letting him down. And I can't bear that. That's the truth, Maria, I swear it is. Only now I can't pretend any longer, not even for Matthew."

When we'd eaten, she went through her wardrobe, laid a couple of dresses and a baby-crocodile handbag on the bed. "I'm perfectly willing to face the world naked with a cheque book, but I'm damned if I'm going to leave my Pucci and Miss Diorling behind, or the handbag. Actually, it was a Christmas present from Heller. Would you be an angel and squeeze them in your suitcase?"

I promised to try, and when I left her just before ten, Barbie's sole concern was Minnow and her kittens. Connie, she swore, would give a rousing cheer if they starved to death. Athena she still suspected of sneaking the tins of cat-food to take home—Athena, who, finding a hair-grip or a pin on the floor, carefully laid it in some conspicuous place. I had to talk her out of a crazy scheme that whirled up in her head of putting the five cats in a hamper, depositing it with Evangelos at the tavern for us to collect on our way to Nicosia. She'd never heard of quarantine regulations and refused to believe they applied to cats. In desperation, I suggested that Eugenia would care for them for Toby's sake. Tears were still dripping down her face when I said good night.

I left our dirty crockery on the landing until I'd made sure my suitcase would take Barbie's dresses and handbag. I'd stood it by the wardrobe, locked, the key in my purse. When I inserted it into the lock, it stuck and I had to fiddle to make it turn. Peering into the lock to find out what was wrong, I noticed the glitter of fine scratches on the chromium. Someone had picked it.

The files were inside, bound with pink tape, but it was knotted instead of being tied in a bow; they were in a different order, and when I counted them there was one short. I checked through them. It was the thinnest file that was missing, labelled enigmatically: "Hanging Fire." It mostly contained notes in Matthew's private short-hand on situations or personalities that had excited his interest but, being irrelevant to the job in hand, he'd filed away. I could only remember a few of the headings: a peasant farmer in Normandy who claimed—with support from several art experts—that a picture hanging on his wall was a Rembrandt. An eighteen-year-old girl in Southern Ireland who reputedly possessed remarkable powers of healing. A Russian writer who had defected to the West approached Matthew to act as a medium to tell his story to the world and then mysteriously recanted. On the rest my mind was a blank.

One file stolen and no prize for guessing the thief: Kim. I laid the remaining files at the bottom of the case, folded Barbie's dresses, wadded the handbag with tissue, checked that there was enough room for my own clothes, and snapped the case shut. There was no point in locking it.

Accuse Kim of theft? He'd simply deny it. Pin-thin scratches on a lock that had been through customs twenty times, a file that I could, in the haste I'd admitted leaving London, never have taken from the safe! My wits, which had been at their lowest ebb in Barbie's room, were sharp and precise now, evaluating a dozen possible courses which, exasperatingly, refused to cohere into a sound basis for action. Maybe because I was literally seething with anger at Kim's sly little act of pilfering.

Hearing a sound, I opened the door. Across the landing Toby's light was on. I found him sitting upright in bed, nursing his glass jar of snails.

"Sometimes I get frightened in the night that they're dead, and I have to look. I've counted them. Seventeen. That's my favourite." He pointed to a monster with a brown and pink striped shell. "Eugenia fed them while I was in Troodos. I missed them but I don't think they missed me. Snails haven't got hearts, you know, but they've got beautiful faces. I'll lend you my magnifying glass if you like and then you will be able to see them."

I took the jar out of his grasp, put it on the window sill,

pulled up the brilliantly striped blanket Matthew had brought him from Mexico. "Some other time, I'd love it. But not now. Everybody's fast asleep but you. It's the middle of the night."

"You're not asleep. You've still got all your clothes on. And I bet Daddy isn't asleep. It's only eleven o'clock."

"Connie would have a fit if she knew you were awake. So how about lying down now that you've made sure all the snails are fine?"

From the landing, I waited until the hair-line of light under his door had disappeared, and then I took the used crockery down to the kitchen to wash—to find what she called "dirty pots" on the draining board when she came down in the morning soured Connie's temper for the day. When I'd finished I wiped my hands on a roller towel that hung over a door. It was the one that led down to the cellar. I'd only been down there once, but now I found my hand lifting the latch, switching on the light at the head of the steep flight of stairs. The air was chill on my face and bare arms, and half-way down I felt an almost irresistible compulsion to turn back, as though I were guilty of trespassing. Most of the vaulted space was taken up by a wine store, with empty barrels and racks for bottles of which less than a quarter were in use. Partitioned off was a space for the winter store of carob wood and, at the farthest end from the kitchen, a portion that Mannheim, maybe even a previous owner, had converted into a sort of carpenter's shop, fitted with a work-bench and every sort of tool. By the time I'd first visited the house Kim had commandeered it, boarded it in, installed an elementary air-conditioning system, and fitted it out as a studio for his so-called wood-carving. On the door was a new notice: "Workshop. Please Knock!" If you'd pilfered a file, the likeliest place to take it to examine at leisure was your own personal hide-out. I lifted the latch, but the door held against me. Then I remembered Barbie had said there was a lock on the door now. And there it was, a very substantial, expensive lock just above eye-level.

Staring at it, I became aware in the deep silence of an eerie, disembodied feeling of evil at work that made my flesh prickle. I shook some sense into myself. Kim had put a lock on the door to keep his newly acquired ill-gotten money safe inside. And if the file was there, I'd no means of getting at it.

When I was half-way up the stairs leading to the kitchen, I looked back. The lamp above me picked out and high-lighted the white painted door at the far end of the shadowy vaulted cellar. It forced itself on my eye, exerted a strange pull, and hypnotised me into an even eerier certainty: that if I laid my ear against its thin match-boarding, I would hear sounds, a voice. If the telephone hadn't rung above my head, I'd have run down, not up.

Connie could have come downstairs, Barbie could have lifted the receiver beside her bed, but no, it was still ringing when I picked it up and heard the operator ask for my number. Would I hold on, please, she had a call for me.

I sat down on the low carved stool. It was Matthew. In a moment his voice would sound in my ear. What I felt was a lovely assurance, an unfolding of myself as if every crease of fret had been smoothed away. I bore the crackles, buzzes, and snippets of disjointed conversation in three languages without a prick of impatience as the words I would say to him framed themselves in my head.

"I'm putting you through, caller." And on the heels of that professionally courteous voice came a man's shouting: "Matt? Matt? Is that you?"

For a moment the shock of disappointment struck me dumb, and I couldn't utter a word. It was only when he'd repeated his name three times, I found breath to say: "I'm sorry, Mr. McBain, Mr. Grant isn't here."

"Then where the hell is he?"

"In Egypt, most probably in Alexandria."

"Egypt!" It was an exclamation of dismay. By then sufficient of my wits had returned for me to recognise the voice as American or Canadian. "That's mighty queer. Whom am I speaking to? His wife?"

So he was an acquaintance, not a friend. "His secretary. If you want to get in touch with him . . ."

"I do. Urgently. Have you got a telephone number for him in Alexandria?"

"I'm afraid I haven't. He should be in London either tomorrow night or Thursday." I gave him the Curzon Street number, added: "If I see him before you telephone shall I give him a message?"

"Just tell him Lex McBain called. I'm at the Hilton in Beirut. He's to call me back there. It's about the story I gave him last Wednesday night concerning the necklace. There's a follow-up that he should know about. That's all. Tell him to contact me, and impress upon him it's urgent."

"Mr. McBain, what necklace?"

But he'd hung up.

I repeated the word aloud: necklace. For some reason it painted itself in my imagination as some fabulous glittering set-piece of diamonds and emeralds, which in relation to Matthew made nonsense. He regarded all jewellery as baubles. Once he'd bought Barbie a bracelet, another time a pair of ear-rings. On both occasions he'd left the choice and purchase to me.

I switched off the light and sat in the darkness. The necklace dropped out of my mind, and in its place the truth blazed out at me. I saw myself hunched on the low stool, heart and mind and body rocked with joy. A fake, a phoney, a common cheat who, for a whole day had given a flawless performance of loving a man who, when a telephone had rung, had been blotted out of existence.

That sense of catastrophe that had overwhelmed me in the grove, lit by rank upon rank of swaying ghost flowers, had been no more than my spirit's revulsion against an act of treason against the heart. That I'd succeeded in cheating myself was shaming enough; that I'd cheated Donald hung a dead weight of guilt around my neck. My penance was the bleak discovery that I belonged to that arid, unyielding band of women constrained in a lifetime to love only one man; the faithful, lovesick heroines of fiction, self-made martyrs to chastity.

I climbed up to the Crow's Nest, where there were envelopes and paper. I could have telephoned Donald in the morning, but the coward in me shrank from hearing his voice. I wrote the note five times, and when I sealed the envelope it contained no more than a six-line statement that, to give Toby a treat, Barbie had decided she would like to drive me to the airport. The stark signature without a word of fondness or love was a complete give-away. My mind saw the inner lightness falter, the hope wiped from his face. To hurt him cut deep into my heart. Surely that proved that at some far depth of me a grain of love existed! I yearned to believe it, but I could not.

Downstairs I discovered the bulb in my bedside lamp was dead. I had to make do with the main light and turn it off before I got into bed. A wind was rising, and I paused at each window to draw the wide-open shutters closer together. Below in the village half a dozen street lamps high-lighted and set apart from the darkness odd corners of the cube houses, a roof garden, a string of washing, and a group of pepper trees. The wail of a baby, the barking of a dog, the continuous bleat of a goat cut holes in the silence.

From the other window the mountain peaks were ink-black silhouettes against the ebbing moonlight. I was half-turned away, when my eye recorded the headlights of a car on the switch-back road describing descending circles that I lost only to pick up again. Private cars—either tourist or native driven —rarely ventured along that villainous road after dark. A jeep driven by some of the Turkish-Cypriot troops who manned the shell of the Crusader castle? Unlikely, only an emergency would bring them patrolling after dark. One of the United Nations jeeps from their depot a mile out of the village? Some incident that had sent that blue pennant winding up and down the corkscrew road at 2 A.M.? Could be. I followed the illuminated eyes until they reached the point where the road divided, one fork descending to the village, the other to the coast, then I lost them.

By now the stupor of fatigue was building up in my head, and I tumbled into bed. Sleep was a hand's space distant, when I heard the bridge rumble under the wheels of a car. In a reflex action, my wits flamed to life. Kim! If he were alone and sober, this was the moment to tax him with the missing file. He'd deny it, but I'd at least have the satisfaction of serving a warning that he'd not got away with his pilfering.

He wasn't alone. Though the moonlight was fading, three silhouettes were recognisable. Heller, Bengy, and Kim.

The car I'd watched looping down the mountains could have

been another making for the coast, in which case it would have by-passed the village, but the timing was suspiciously tight. I wondered what purpose was important enough to drive three men up that mountain road and down again at 2 A.M. to counterbalance the high degree of risk.

From the landing I saw them, without a word exchanged, go into the sitting-room. I crept downstairs. The door between courtyard and sitting-room was almost but not quite closed. There was an inch of space to which I could lay my ear.

They were at the far end, thirty feet distant from me. The clink of glasses, soda being squirted, the movements of their feet overlaid and interrupted their voices, so that the interchanges were filtered through to me in half-sentences without a beginning or an end.

Heller: ". . . lousy little rat, you disobeyed . . ."

Kim: ". . . no right, no proof. I swear . . ."

Heller: ". . . find his grave, that'll be proof . . ."

And then Bengy's voice, cocky: "Don't look at me, boss. I was off-duty, remember, shacked up with a sweet little bellydancer, not digging graves."

A stream of obscenities burst from Heller, and for half a minute there was a three-part wrangle before Kim's voice cut through it: "For God's sake, keep your voices down unless you want the women in on this. All you've got is a kid's story. Who'd believe . . ."

The voices lost volume, became inaudible until, a couple of minutes later, Heller ground from between his teeth: "Got it? One more botched job and we're through. You're out on your own. Better remember that and make sure she boards the plane. When she has drive straight back to my place. Okay?"

"Okay," Kim said nervously, "except that I've botched nothing, nothing . . ."

I heard the glasses set down, the sound of feet moving across the tiled floor, and only just reached the screen of the first landing before Heller and Bengy crossed the courtyard. When they'd gone, Kim came out of the sitting-room and slid the inner bolt across the great door. That done, he leaned against it. For a second, while my heart thudded, I imagined he was looking straight at me. But his gaze was directed straight into the mid-distance, the gaze of a man who was looking at nothing but the inside of his own head. He drew a great shuddering sigh and went back into the sitting-room to turn off the lights.

I escaped to my own room, lay stiff on my back, the disconnected scraps of that terrible dialogue between Heller and Kim playing itself back in my skull. Whose grave had they not been able to find? Whose?

ELEVEN

I woke to a sun-filled room, astounded past belief that I had fallen asleep, aware of a rock-hard conviction that had built itself in my head while I'd slept. There had been no telephone message from Matthew. The sole evidence that it had been transmitted was Kim's word, which was worthless. It had been an invention, its purpose to be rid of me, a ruse that Connie, Barbie, and I, made gullible by hunger to have news of Matthew, had swallowed whole.

An icy current flowed through me. If Matthew wasn't in Egypt, where was he? What end was served—whose end—by a lie that would be uncovered when I reached London? The answer could only be a playing for time, the introduction of a red herring that would create bafflement and confusion. There was one word spoken by Heller that I held at bay, refusing it admission to my mind. But it lay like a stone in my subconscious, a word as terrible, as final as death: a grave.

For release from a constriction of fear, I seized on one simple step I could take: check with the girl at the telephone exchange. She would have a record of a call from Cairo to Kessima at noon yesterday. I grabbed my dressing-gown. With luck, I could use the telephone in the Crow's Nest before Kim and Barbie were awake to hear the betraying tinkle.

I had climbed three steps when Kim drawled from the landing: "Don't tell me you're going to start typing in your dressing-gown!"

I looked over my shoulder. Go ahead and make the call and he'd only to return to his bedroom, lift the receiver to eavesdrop on my conversation with the girl at the exchange. I turned my head and stared at him. Assuming he'd gone to sleep the moment his head touched the pillow, his night had been as short as mine. It showed. His cheeks were haggard, the skin beneath his eyes puffy, and a piece of the bruised skin had peeled away, letting loose a trickle of blood.

"I was going to check on Matthew's lamp; the one he brought out from England. I happened to notice it wasn't on the table, and I wondered if Athena had put it away in a cupboard. He'll want it when he arrives next month."

He made a visible effort to sound casual. "Oh, you mean the black extending one. It's gone off to be repaired at the electric shop in Kyrenia. Somehow one of its supports got broken. I'm due to collect it at the end of the week." His smile was so bright it was macabre. "Not to worry, I'll guarantee to have it back before he arrives."

I had only to telephone the shop and enquire if it was there. But if he was at pains to be awake, alert to my movements at 7 A.M., he wasn't likely to relax until Heller's orders to watch me climb into the plane had been obeyed. Why was it so vital to get rid of me? My brain refused an answer. For a long moment we stared in silence at once another. I could sense his fear, and my own, growing second by second, made me super-cautious. He possessed the congenital liar's protective inventiveness. To corner him and keep him cornered, I needed irrefutable evidence of one lie. I hadn't got it, not yet.

He gave a sniff. "Can I smell coffee?" He stood, willing me to descend the three steps and go back into my room. I remained where I was. He added with false heartiness: "By the way, give Donald a ring this morning and tell him I'm going to give myself the pleasure of driving you to the airport. Your check-in time's 3.20. We'll take off from here around two."

From the lower landing Barbie called: "What are you two shouting at each other for? I'm dying for some coffee. Aren't you coming down, Maria?"

Kim called back to her: "Ask Connie to bring me up a pot. Nothing else, just coffee."

With him lying on his bed, the extension within reach of his hand, my journey to the Crow's Nest was torpedoed.

When Toby had left for school and Connie was eating her ritual bacon and two eggs in the kitchen, I said to Barbie: "Kim's announced he's driving me to the airport."

Unperturbed, she continued to spread her toast with lemon marmalade. "Don't you remember, I'm driving you?"

"A free fight over who takes the wheel!"

"No." She gave me, for her, a curiously adamant glare. "I told you. I've got it all worked out."

I suggested: "He could follow us."

"You don't trust me, do you?" she accused. "Brainless Barbie who let the eggs curdle last night when she'd boasted how well she could scramble them! But I'm not making a hash of anything today. The three of us will be on that plane, and Kim left behind. So, relax, baby! For once in your clever little life, you're not in control. What are you going to do with yourself this morning?"

I told her about Niko's lost rucksack and water flask, the confiscation of his pocket money, and my intention to buy him new ones, leave them with Connie to give to Eugenia.

She nodded, then warned me: "Lunch at twelve sharp. I've already told Connie."

The morning had the flawless quality that Cypriots take for granted, but which to a Northern European is like a caress. My errand had the virtue of supplying me with a fixed purpose that served to quell the chaos at the centre of my mind. Also there was a public telephone box in the village. From his balcony Kim, drinking his coffee, must have watched me cross the bridge, but he could hardly dog my heels.

Evangelos's general store occupied a corner site. It had been his father's, maybe his grandfather's. Since I'd entered it in February the counters had been ripped out, and instead of leaning helpfully over them, Evangelos was caged behind a home-made check-out.

As I crossed the threshold, he jumped to his feet, ran to switch on the air-conditioning. Its audible purr startled the two elderly, black-garbed women who were tentatively exploring the shelves, seeming unable to lay their hands on what they wanted.

He shook my hand in both his plump ones, his satin-skinned chubby face wreathed in a smile. "Miss Caron! I heard you were in Kessima, and I'm sorry not to see you. People say Mr. Grant has not come with you. Is that so?"

I told him it was, complimented him on his alterations, then looked at the tap within a hand's reach of the till. "But you still wash your grapes even if you are running a modern super-market."

"Of course. Always wash grapes, especially for beautiful young ladies." His hand made an arc. "You like it?" He was begging for praise, and I made it lavish. Even so, he frowned uneasily. "But some of my regular customers they don't care to help themselves," and glanced towards the two black-shrouded women who were edging in the direction of the door.

He abandoned his check-out point to search for the best rucksack and water flask he stocked. As he handed them to me, I took the letter, its sum of grief and shame no lighter in daylight, and asked him if he knew anyone who could deliver it to the Villa Hesperides for me. A click of his fingers brought a nephew from the store-room beyond. He had a bicycle, Evangelos boasted. My letter would be delivered in fifteen, no ten, minutes.

Man and boy waited, smiling at me, wondering why I delayed in handing over the envelope. But in the end there was no choice left to me.

The public telephone box in the village was out of order. I took a right-hand alley that would bring me to the tavern, where there was a telephone behind the counter for customers' use. Four men and Connie's enemy, the butcher, were sitting about two yards from it. One of them, nearest to the counter, had spent his youth in America and spoke fluent English. That, having a telephone at the house, I should use the one in the tavern would arouse their natural curiosity. They would listen, comment among themselves. I decided to wait for a quarter of an hour in the hope of gaining a little more privacy, and went outside to one of the iron tables set under the shade of the carob tree. It wasn't until I'd sat down that I saw the table immediately opposite was occupied. Lois Brown was drinking a bottle of Coca-Cola through a straw.

The absurdity of sitting face to face without uttering a word impelled me to say: "May I join you?"

"If you want."

At least she'd left her hot, woolly cap behind, and there was no sign of her binoculars, although the familiar outsize handbag was wedged between her feet. She laid her gaze directly on me. The expression in her flat brown eyes was not, as I'd expected, hostile; not even particularly ill-tempered, but utterly contemptuous, as though I were a creature whose existence she preferred not to acknowledge. It was a reaction that shocked me into blurting out: "Are you enjoying your holiday in Cyprus?"

"It isn't a holiday. It's a mission. Where's your boss?"

Evangelos came and took my order, and when he'd left us, I said: "Why do you ask? Do you know Matthew?"

She left a pause between question and answer, the effect of which was to render her speech slow and deliberate. "I've heard so much about him, you could say I do."

"From whom?"

Again the heavy pause. "Oh, all around."

Her air of insolent contempt drove me to retaliate. "On Monday I watched you looking at his house through binoculars. Why are you so interested in it?"

"I'm not in the least interested in the house, only the devils who live in it." She added as though elucidating to a retarded child: "You're entitled to snoop if people withhold information to which you have a right. Last Saturday morning Matthew Grant's brother-in-law threw me off the doorstep."

"Kim! Why should he do that?"

"For asking questions he didn't choose to answer, presumably on orders from your boss or Mr. Heller. I'd already received the same strong-arm treatment from him. Put the fear of God into her, scare her off, that was the scheme they cooked up between them. It didn't work. It showed me *they* were scared, and that gave me all the ammunition I needed."

I looked her hard in the face. In manner she was insufferable. Yet there was a quality of resolution in her that evoked a reluctant admiration. "A mission," I quoted back at her. "Do you have to be so mysterious? You say Matthew Grant, Kim Mitchell, and Mr. Heller are withholding information from you. What information do you want from them?"

The straw she was sucking gurgled against the now empty base of the bottle. "I might tell you if I knew which side you're on, but I don't, do I?"

"I'm on the side of the man who employs me."

"Ah, but whose side is he on? My guess would be on the side of his own kith and kin." An ugly, derisive laugh burst in her throat. "Blood's thicker than water, so they say; when an outsider like me comes along asking questions you don't want to answer, you close ranks, go into the old-pals act." She laughed again, a derogatory, mirthless sound. "You lot honestly believe you can get away with murder, don't you? You're too smart to be caught; you've got too much money. Put on a big act and scare the poor little nobody away. It's your bad luck that I happen to be a nobody who doesn't scare easy."

I pleaded, exasperated: "Tell me what you want to know, and I might be able to help."

"You help me! You must be joking! Anyway, I've got all the help I need now: official help." She picked up the outsize bag, rose to her feet. "If it should turn out that your boss wasn't one of the gang of cutthroats, I suggest you try looking for him in the sea."

"Wait, please. You're a friend of Bruce Vernon's, aren't you?"

"Not a friend. I was his fiancée." She held out to me a finger encircled with a platinum ring studded with tiny diamonds. "By now I should have been Mrs. Bruce Vernon, not Miss Lois Brown. He'd got a house, we'd half furnished it. He'd bought a share in a betting shop not half a mile away, and he swore that there would be no more travelling now he'd saved up enough money to set us up for life." She twisted her head out of my sight. "I'm twenty-nine, and Bruce was the only man who ever asked me to marry him. I felt the luckiest girl in the whole world. I wouldn't have changed places with the Queen. Then someone put the boot in, and now all I'm ever likely to get is an empty house. So it's only fair they should pay." She half turned her head, and I had a second's glimpse of a profile wrung with anguish, and then she was gone, blind-eyed with tears, stumbling against the tables and chairs.

I sat there until somewhere near at hand a clock struck half-past eleven. There was no one inside the tavern within earshot of the telephone; even Evangelos was lolling outside with some of his cronies, but it was no use to me now. It had taken a girl with a mission for revenge to shatter the thick skin of calm that had overlaid my quivering fears. Calm, the main component of which was an abiding faith that Matthew was indestructible, a near earthly god who could not be harmed or struck down by a play-boy, an ex-boxer, and a man named Heller. As I stood up, responded automatically to Evangelos's wave, what I had to do formed a black and terrifying picture in my mind.

When it was all at an end, people were to censor me, demand angrily why I hadn't summoned help, averted a tragedy. I was judged criminally irresponsible. There was a police post not five hundred yards from the tavern. But Lois Brown's boast of official help could only mean the police, and I had no wish to tangle with her. Ten minutes' walk would have brought me to Giselle's door, but jealousy is a corrupting emotion and it was not in me to throw myself on her mercy. If Alex was not at the villa, Carima or a member of his staff would know where he could be reached by telephone. I did not trust him.

In the noon heat, as I walked back to the house, I felt completely isolated and alone, with faith in no-one but myself. I was still in a state of shock, appalled by the priceless time I'd wasted. My mental processes were slowed up, totally absorbed in knitting into a coherent pattern all the fast-multiplying threads of evidence. Distress distorts your reasoning-power. Absolute fear can make you mad. Maybe on that day I was half mad.

TWELVE

Kim and Barbie were sitting under the vine drinking. Repeated bursts of laughter broke between them. As far as I was capable of conjecture, I wondered if, during my absence, Barbie had turned an emotional somersault, and that the escape plan had vaporised from her mind.

I went straight into the kitchen, where Connie was preparing salads, handed her the packages on which I'd written Niko's name, and asked her to give them to Eugenia.

She put them on the window sill, took from it an envelope, and gave it to me. It was addressed to Matthew Grant, Esq. Her eyes at their beadiest, she issued an order: "You're to hand it to him the moment you see him, and stand over him while he reads it. I don't want him stuffing it into his pocket and forgetting it for days."

Without a word I slipped it into my shoulder bag.

She sliced a skinned tomato, divided it between three plates—Connie didn't touch salads, being suspicious of the water by which they were irrigated. "Did you hear what I said? It's important."

I nodded. I was rendered half deaf and stupefied by a

mounting torrent of fear that by coming back to the house I had made an error I'd never be able to redeem. Why hadn't I walked a hundred yards to Antinou's garage and hired a car? My rage with myself for the blunder was so intense that, as Kim put his head round the door, his face was reduced to a blur.

"Ah, Maria! Now you're back, come and have a drink."

Barbie in blue denim shorts and a cunningly twisted scarf for a top gave me a sly, secretive smile. "What a time it took you to buy a rucksack and a water flask!"

I actually saw Kim's hand jerk so that a spurt of soda flew wide. Under the dapple of vine leaves we looked straight at one another, then his glance lost focus. With an effort he constrained himself to joke: "I thought you were going on a plane ride, not a hike!"

"They're for Niko." I hoarded the look of fright that had frozen his damaged face and thought if the horror boxed up in my mind were true he deserved to die. But my voice was emotionless. "He lost his, and his father has confiscated his pocket money until he has saved up enough to buy new ones."

He managed a sort of stricken grin. "Interfering between parents and child! Still, it's done now, so here's a drink for a tender-hearted girl."

The atmosphere between the two of them continued so relaxed that when Connie brought out the cold lunch Kim, with rare expansiveness, invited her to have a drink.

She snorted: "You know perfectly well I never touch alcohol until the sun is over the yard-arm." Her father had been a petty officer in the Navy. "And you'd do well to watch your step. Drinking and driving! Some fools never learn."

She stolidly ate through her pile of tinned ham sandwiches while the three of us did no more than peck at the food she'd prepared for us. Insulted, she stalked out to fetch the coffee. I collected the plates and carried them into the kitchen for her.

To my surprise she gave me a searching look of concern. "It's no way to go off on a journey with an empty stomach. All they give you to eat on the plane is a plate of bits and pieces I'd be ashamed to feed to the birds." She unplugged the coffee-pot, set it on a tray with the cups. "I'm going to put my feet up for an hour, but I'll be down in time to make you a nice cup of tea before you go off. And maybe you'll fancy a biscuit or two then." As though my face were a mirror that reflected the terror that wrenched at my heart and nerves, she added kindly: "And don't you go fretting yourself. Matthew will soon sort Master Kim out! Get him back on the straight and narrow. He's had plenty of practice!"

When I carried the tray outside, Barbie and Kim were still drinking, neither of them ready for coffee.

"Ugh!" Barbie squealed, "too much soda," and took her glass of Campari to the drinks table inside the sitting-room. A second later she popped her head round the door. "What about yours, darling? Want a refill while I'm up?"

"Thanks, baby."

When she drifted in to fetch Kim's glass, she placed herself with her back to him, contorted her face into a grotesquely contrived wink. "By the way, Kim's decided he wants to drive you to the airport, so I'll stay home. Okay?"

Presumably I answered yes, though I'd no space in my mind to spare for their infantile games. No-one was going to drive me to Nicosia airport. My resolve that, an hour ago, had been a miragelike nightmare now screamed to be set in motion. But how? If I walked out, hired a car from Antinou, Kim would be on my heels and, hard on his, Heller.

I examined them both as though they were my enemies, as indeed they were. If that caricature of a wink meant anything, it was an indication that Barbie's escape plan was still on. If so, she'd have to put on a dress for the journey. Equally, if Kim drove me, he'd change out of his denims, spruce himself up for the drive into the city. Say twenty minutes while one or other of them changed. A small margin of time, but it was all I was likely to get. And it only took care of one of them.

I waited, my eyes never far from my watch-face, while my brain counted and tabulated: a crystal ash-tray and a lamp smashed, Kim's bruised and torn cheek, his damaged hands. Heller's worsened limp. A telephone call from a stranger. A man high in the mountains crying out for help to a scared, running boy, and a girl with a mission. A car weaving in circles down the switchbacking mountain road at 2.00 A.M. Disjointed accusations and counter-accusations bouncing between three desperate, frightened men . . . and now at last I spoke it in my mind: a grave they'd not been able to find.

What jerked me back to the present was an awareness of Kim's slurred speech. From six feet away Barbie, her face shadowed by the chair canopy she'd pulled forward, was watching him with catlike intentness, as though he were some sort of prey. When his head slipped sideways, she stretched, got up.

"There you are! He'll not be driving anyone anywhere this side of six." She tweaked a hand that dangled limply over the chair arm. "Out cold!" She threw me a look of triumph. "Three soneryls dissolved in a glass of Campari. Even the colours matched!"

At that moment in time Kim's state of health aroused no mite of concern in me, yet I heard myself register a protest. "Alcohol and barbiturates could kill him."

"Oh, phooey. It would take a hell of a lot more than three. He'll live, but not noticeably until we're about due to land at London airport. Then if he swings into action, Matthew will have Toby made a ward of court, and there won't be a damned thing Kim can do about it."

She stood like a child waiting for praise for a good deed. I'd none to give her, though by doping Kim she'd removed one of the prime obstacles to my escape. Now, with Connie napping, I had only to rid myself of Barbie, and I'd be free.

She said, cross with me: "Oh, don't look so self-righteous. How else did you suppose I was going to do it! Handcuff him or something!" She glanced down at her watch. "There's over an hour before we have to leave. I'm going to have a shower and a teeny siesta. If I'm not down by a quarter to two, give me a call."

I promised and listened to her sandalled feet climbing the stone staircase. The ease with which I'd regained the freedom I'd forfeited by returning to the house momentarily unnerved me, as though it were some sort of trap. But Kim slept on, and from the first floor I heard the gush of water. Within ten minutes Barbie would fall as deep asleep as a child on her bed.

I walked up the incline of the garden, the white scorching sun hammering my head, my inside freezing and faint. Minnow and her kittens in the shade under the lemon tree squinted in wild alarm in case I was their arch-enemy, then, reassured, closed their eyes. Beyond the screen of olive and cypress trees, I sat on the crumbling stone wall and looked up at the mountains, tracing the levels where the olives gave way to carobs and carobs to pine, and higher to the peaks where there were no trees, only a cruel, perpendicular terrain that repeated itself hundreds of times. I counted the hours between Friday and Wednesday and, when I arrived at the total, began to shiver. For comfort I did a second count from Monday afternoon, when Niko had fled down the mountain.

I walked back down the garden and studied the positioning of the two cars. Barbie's Triumph was parked at an angle on a slope. Release the brake and I could back it, with luck not have to gun the engine until just before I reached the bridge.

I crept upstairs. On the first floor vapour was drifting from the bathroom, but there was no sound from Barbie's room. On the floor above, pausing outside her door, I could hear Connie's ladylike snores. In the Crow's Nest, I collected a torch Matthew kept on hand for use as emergency lighting during a power failure, a brandy flask, and a double-knit sweater. From my own room I snatched a cardigan from my suitcase. Downstairs before I filled the flask, I took a long hard look at Kim. His head had fallen so far forward that his chin touched his chest. I forced myself to feel his flesh and take his pulse. It was steady enough, and his colour was good.

With the flask and torch wedged into my shoulder bag, the two sweaters suspended from the strap, I clicked open the door of the Triumph, closed it on the half-catch until I was out of earshot of the house. As I eased it down the incline, the tyres squeaked on the ground-down rock. I coasted half-way to the bridge before I had to turn on the ignition. In the hot silence the engine firing sounded like a thunderclap in my ears. With eyes riveted to the rear mirror to catch the opening of a shutter, Connie or Barbie shouting from a balcony, I nearly missed the sharp-angled turn on the far side of the bridge.

In the shadow of a doorway an old woman's fingers flew nimbly in and out of her lace bobbins, Aristo, returning to his wheel after lunch, waved to me, and through the open doors of the Primary School children's voices floated, Toby's among them. Apart from these visible and audible signs of life the village, under the breathless heat, was reduced to a sun-struck somnolence.

Soon after I'd taken the left fork, I stopped, strained my ears to catch the sound of a following car. All I heard were the grunt and grind of the afternoon bus.

Until I reached the United Nations Post, there was a narrow strip of metalled road bordered by sandy tracks that lost themselves in loose banks of crumbling rock which, disintegrating, cascaded into the road. On the perimeter of my vision there were olive groves, every silver leaf tarnished with dust, and beneath them a shimmering gold carpet of scorched grasses, with here and there, in little groups or big ones, the ghostlike candle flowers. Once I'd passed the pale blue United Nations flags, I was committed to a corkscrewing switchback of hairpin bends. Matthew had driven Toby and me up it one cool, sunny day in February on our way to the monastery where Niko's uncle swept the cloisters, watered the flowers and vegetables, and higher to the Crusader castle poised half in and half out of the sky. The journey had called for no effort from me. Now, distracted by giant fears and a raging impatience, there was no let-up between one blind corner and the next, beyond any one of which I might run into the hazard of a flock of sheep, a tourist driving dangerously fast, or a donkey plodding homeward with a towering load of carob wood on its back, and its owner three-parts asleep. I met them all and emerged unscathed. Mile by mile the sheer drops grew more precipitous until the sweat poured down my face and ochre dust was caked on every inch of bare skin. Even with dark glasses my eyes were tormented by the white, scorching glare as I desperately searched the horizon for one landmark: the word Enosis painted on a wall of rock in huge blue letters. When it came into sight and I had crossed over to the far side, where the folds and overfolds of the mountain peaks were nearer, for a few seconds my pent-up breath eased. But the pressure of time dispelled even that momentary relief. I was driving too slowly, using up twice as much time as Matthew had taken. As I swung round another hairpin bend, I noted with alarm the tips of violet shadows touching one mountain peak. As I swung the car again, I glimpsed far off a great thunderhead of cloud building up behind another, turning it into a smoking volcano. Was a violent storm going to rob me of an hour of precious daylight? With despair I saw behind me the wasted morning, and behind the morning four days when, from hindsight, I seemed to have put my wits to sleep—as though I'd deliberately laid myself under a spell, the first word of the incantation spoken when I met Donald at the airport. Guilt at love mocked and debased was like living with a wound that was never likely to heal.

I prayed soundlessly for the particular formation of mountain peaks that marked my goal to define itself on the skyline: one blunt-topped mountain joined by a saddleback to a higher peak shaped like a crooked nose. A hundred feet above the track was a cave that had been an Eoka hide-out and an arsenal of weapons for Grivas's men. Their lair uncovered, three Greek Cypriots, one Niko's uncle, had fought for their lives and lost them. When the domed summit and the crooked-nose peak came into vision, my sharpened, quivering senses remembered every detail of that other day.

On the way home Toby, who had been briefed on the family saga of heroism by Eugenia or Niko, and knew the exact location of the cave, plagued Matthew to stop. Matthew said there was nowhere to park unless he blocked the road to uphill and downhill traffic, and drove on a quarter of a mile where there was a rough lay-by.

Toby, suspecting he'd been cheated, complained vociferously: "I wanted to climb up to the cave, and now you're going to say it would take too much time to walk back, and we've got to get home."

"I guess that's about what I am saying. After all the climbing we've done today, if I were you I'd settle for the last bottle of Coke. A cave's a cave, and we've covered practically every known variation."

"But that cave is special, it's a haunted cave. If you go near enough at night, you can hear voices. They call out to you."

"But not in daylight." Since Toby refused to be deflected by a bribe, Matthew fetched the Coke, pried off the cap, handed it to him. As a further sweetener he loaned Toby his binoculars, focussed them, and led him to a high point that would give him a clear view of the cave.

We sat among the tiny arbutus trees, my feet curled under me to avoid damaging the brilliant patchwork of cyclamen threaded with thyme.

"I'd have thought," I remarked, as he kept one eye on Toby, "it would be a shrine rather than a haunted place. Brave men —or boys—who died for a cause they believed in. Why should the villagers be scared of it?"

"The graves in the village cemetery are the shrines. This is where bullets flew out of the sunlight to slaughter two youths of eighteen and one of twenty. The blood, the bitterness, the horror of violent death are locked up in that cave making it a place of evil memory as long as there is anyone alive who has heard the story from his father or his grandfather, which he'll pass down to his own children."

As we waited for Toby, we talked about the bone-deep enmity bred for generations by a civil war, the present pseudo truce-calm that was shattered by minor incidents when the tension between the two races exploded into violence, and the ever-burning never-dying hatred of a minority for a majority. About Enosis and Gribas.

Toby stumbled back breathless, and flung himself between us. "I could see it, but not into it. How do caves get made, Uncle Matthew?"

"By erosion. All through these mountains there are strata of soft rock. When the rain pours down, it washes out the soft rock and leaves the hard. And there's your cave."

"Athena's always praying for it to rain. Every Sunday she buys a candle and lights it and asks God to make it pour."

"Every Sunday?" Matthew queried. "Even when it's poured for the last six days?"

"Nearly every Sunday. She took me inside her church once and showed me the little silver legs and arms and bits of people's bodies that hang over the ikon. You see, they prayed to the ikon to cure them and when he did, they gave him a present to say thank-you."

Walking back between us to the car, he glanced first at Matthew, then at me. "It's been a super day even if I didn't go inside the cave where Niko's uncle was shot dead." He gave me a smile that when, as now, he was especially happy, even with the gap in his teeth, was as beautiful as his mother's. "You liked it, didn't you, Maria?"

"Yes, I think it's been a super day, too." Above his flaxen head Matthew's and my glances locked, and on a sudden there dawned in his a wholly new expression, tender, almost wondering that set on a light to the spark of hope in my heart that had no right to be there.

Toby, ever ready to push his luck, went on: "The next castle I'd like to see is Kantara. Miss Nash says it is the best of all because the sea is so near. If you fell off the top you'd drop right into it."

And Matthew, with that haunting light transfiguring his gaze, while my senses began to spin, promised that we'd make the pilgrimage to Kantara in October. But next morning, he'd regarded me with the old platonic fondness, reducing me to equality with his close friends, who were legion. Had his head overruled his heart, or had the look of tender near-love been a mirage of the mountain light?

When the crooked-nose peak revealed itself on the sky-line, to cool the engine and top up with water from the jerry can in the boot, I stopped the car as Matthew had done on the upward trip. And while the engine was cooling, I scaled the highest tumble of rock that gave me a bird's-eye view of the descending spirals of the road. Far below, I could see a scarcely moving smudge that was probably the donkey that had passed me. Nearer, a jeep was emerging from a forestry post, but it turned down towards the coast. No car was coming up.

With the ignition switched on, my eye was caught by a dialface I should have checked before I left the village. The indicator in the petrol gauge hovered over empty. I'd never possessed a car with an accurate petrol gauge, but the Triumph was barely a year old, and it made sense to assume the marking was correct. Which meant that even if I had enough petrol to reach the track below the cave, I'd have none to get back to Kessima. But I was so totally obsessed with the immediate objective that the query mark over the return journey made a negligible impact on me.

The petrol lasted for twenty minutes. I ran the Triumph down a descending inlet in the scrub that overhung the mountain, braked a second too late, and when I got out of the car saw I'd missed precipitating myself over the edge by six inches. My knees were useless and my arms numb with the strain of wheeling round what seemed in retrospect a thousand hair-pin bends. From the road I glanced back. The cream Triumph was instantly visible for anyone interested, but, with daylight fast running out on me, I dare not spend precious minutes in camouflaging it with armfuls of scrub.

I slung my bag over my shoulder, slotted the two woollen sweaters through the strap, and took a bearing. I'd not done too badly. At least the cave was in sight.

The sun still blazed, but it was lower in the sky. I calculated that I had, at the most, an hour before sunset. For half the distance I kept to the road, and then took a short-cut obliquely upwards, tramping across the silver and grey scrub, boobytrapped with tumbles of rock, gullies that were too wide to jump and had to be circumnavigated by time-devouring detours. I had been clambering, breath labouring my lungs, for over half an hour before I saw, immediately above me, the hollow mouth of the cave. By now the light was no longer golden but lavender, and there was a rim of brilliance outlining the western peaks.

In absolute stillness, with no sound but the pumping of my heart, I looked up. Without a second's warning, my burning, invincible faith that Matthew was inside collapsed. For a second my head swam with the huge effect of letdown; my flight from the house, the headlong drive, my unshakable conviction that Matthew would be there were reduced to the naïve reasoning of a child. With sweat pouring down my face I shivered with the onset of complete despair. A snake uncoiled itself and slithered across the path. I was too numbed to experience a qualm of revulsion.

But if hope had perished, its memory remained, drawing my feet upward. There was no single path to the cave. I had to negotiate half a dozen on different levels, climbing the last hundred feet on hands and knees, clutching at rocks, some of which loosened and rolled away as soon as I grasped them. Once I paused and called his name, and the echo of it came back to taunt my ears. I saw, poised like a threat, a drift of cloud over the far peaks, trailing scarves of carmine across the opal sky.

The entrance to the cave was half screened by rocks cemented together to form a baffle wall. Inside the floor was smooth, and the air cool against my throbbing temples. I called his name into the hollows. There was no breath of sound except, buried farther back than the torch would reach, the tinkle of dripping water. With the feeble beam, I examined every foot of the cave's emptiness. Someone had swept it clean. There wasn't a footprint in the sandy grit but my own.

I sat on a crag and learnt what total fright was: a shivering of the nerves, a cooling of the heart, a rigidity of the flesh, and a deathlike blankness of the mind. When darkness came I disentangled the thick sweater, tugged it over my head. It was chestnut brown mohair, raggy at the elbows where Connie's darns had pulled away from the old, frayed wool. The faint scent of tobacco filled my nostrils. I hugged it to me, and spoke his name under my breath.

Until the stars spread across the luminous indigo sky and the moon rose, the torch was my only light. I couldn't remember how old the battery was, only that it wasn't new, its life probably nearly used up. Now the help for which I'd been too proud, too jealous, too vain to ask was inaccessible; I would have begged for it under any condition, at any risk. I could not guess how many hours it would take my legs to stumble down the mountain switchback to the U.N. Post, or upwards to the Crusader castle, which was garrisoned by Turkish-Cypriot troops. The will to reach either was there, but without physical strength it counted for nothing. I could go back to the car, use it as a shelter for the night. But at some point near where I sat a man had cried out for help on Monday afternoon, and Heller and Kim, with Bengy along, had spent half last night searching for a grave they'd not been able to find.

Those two hard facts sent me lurching to my feet. As long as the torch battery stayed alive, I would search. I would call and listen, then call again and again and listen again and again. The area in which I could operate restricted by the radius of the feeble beam, I descended to a track that wound itself round the mountain, throwing a man's name at its flanks, and having its echo flung back at me.

Twice I stumbled, once suffered the horror of nearly having the torch jerked from my grasp. The rope sole of my left espadrille was ripped in two and my knees were wet with blood. I had sat down to try and calculate by swinging the torch backwards how much ground I'd covered, when it skimmed over a small, smooth object. I stood up, directed the light in such a wild series of arcs that for a number of anguished minutes I couldn't find it. When I did, I literally dropped the six feet that separated me from it. A wallet, black sealskin, its corners clipped with gold, the initials M.S.G. stamped into the hide.

As I held it in my hand, hard under the beam of the torch, every ache and pain vanished from my body, the constriction of despair lifted from my heart. I could have climbed every one of the wicked teeth of the mountains, walked a hundred miles. And when I called his name it was with a calm resonance. He was near. My single prayer was that the torch battery would hold out until I found him.

When its faltering beam reached him, he was lying in a miniature crevasse, his head overhung by a shelf of rock, the lower half of his body buried under a mound of stones. His right hand was unreachable, his left lay across his chest. When I burrowed under the overhang, there was a moment of shocking pain. Blood from a wound on his head had caked over his face. I went through the correct motions: wedging one sweater under his shoulders and the other over him, supporting his head while I struggled to dribble brandy into his mouth. But it ran out again and trickled into the stubble on his chin. His flesh was lethal cold. I pressed my lips to his, but they stayed cold, untouched by the warmth of a breath. Once, when I felt for it, I believed I detected a pulse, the second time I could not find it. I had come in search of a live man. I was isolated, alone, and threatened by the natural elements that were my enemies. The appalling horror in my mind was that time—time that I had wasted—had cheated me.

THIRTEEN

I spoke under my breath the most terrible of all words: my love is dead. He will never speak or laugh again. The voice that enchanted my ears was forever silenced, the great heart of compassion stilled. Memories crowded in: big ones, little ones, gestures that belonged uniquely to him, the smile that was echoed in his eyes, and his unconscious air of splendour, in a ribbon strip of film that spun through one half of my head. The other half, separate and split off, was visualising the process of resuscitation as I frantically measured distances: whether to climb up to the Turkish guard post or race down, a much longer distance, to a telephone box. I decided to run down.

One half of my split mind ordered me to put my shoulder bag beneath his head, provide comfort for an injured man, while the ice-cold inhuman half insisted there was no comfort on earth that you could give the dead.

I hauled myself out of the crevasse. A half-moon was rising in a landscape of eerie monochrome, and once I reached the road I calculated I would be able to see without the torch. As I stood upright, I was shriven of fear. I had no memory of terror, and, miraculously, my split mind had healed itself. Matthew was not dead and he was not going to die. As though absolute faith had rendered me weightless, not one of the rocks or boulders to which I trusted my feet foundered under me. When I reached the rough sand-packed road, I looked back to memorise the exact positioning of the frieze of dark peaks now silvered at the edges by moonlight. I decided they provided too imprecise a landmark and scuffed with my fingers to clear a patch of smooth yellow earth between two patches of scrub. On it I laid down a rough cross of stones.

For maximum speed I found I still needed the torch. I had covered maybe half a mile when I heard the sound of a car travelling up the mountain road. On an instant the terror I'd lost came virulently, consumingly to life. I persuaded myself it was a detachment of Turkish-Cypriot soldiers returning to the Crusader castle, in which case they'd be travelling in a jeep or a Land-Rover. For an endless minute I waited until it started to round the coil of the road immediately beneath where I stood. Not a jeep, not a Land-Rover, but Kim's Volvo. Seconds too late I switched off the torch. If they had been looking up, and where else would they be looking as they swung round that steeply ascending bend, I would have been as starkly visible as a lighthouse. In that freezing moment only one intention stayed fixed in my skull: to put as long a space as I could between them and Matthew's half-buried, living body. To play decoy and run towards them, not back to where he lay. Until time ran out, as it must do when they breasted the last bend, I kept to the road, running it so fine that I expected the beam of the headlights to overlap me. Before they did so the car slurred to a halt. They'd found a sign-post I'd completely forgotten: the abandoned Triumph.

I dived for the scrub, and as long as the silence lasted, ran and scrambled until there was no breath left in my lungs. When I heard the car engine burst into life, I slithered forward on my hands and knees until I found what touch suggested was a substantial fall of rock that, short of digging myself a burrow, was the only pitiful hide within reach.

The car came forward at a crawl, and then a hundred yards from where I crouched it stopped. Kim got out first, then Heller, and, last of all, Bengy: three dense-black figures against the blaze of the headlamps, which divided as Bengy went behind the car, returned with three flash-lamps, and switched off the headlights. They advanced in close formation, Heller and Kim just ahead of Bengy, the road, wedged between the flanks of the mountain and a precipice, swept by the beams of lights they wielded. The farthest edge of one thrust of radiance revealed to me the puniness of my hide. It was no more than a rough corner piece of stones. It hid me from anyone approaching, but I was instantly visible from the rear or above. Bengy's progress was faster than that of the other two. He loped ahead of them, swinging his flashlight to cover the widest possible area. He whistled between his teeth, having fun like a boy on a treasure hunt! I was the treasure.

On the rough, uneven road Heller, limping badly, advanced at a lumbering uneven trot. Level with me, he raged: "Bengy, keep that beam down. Do you want to bring out the troops? They're edgy enough as it is. Keep it down, I tell you. With her car ditched, she can't have got far."

Kim's protest was a feeble, unconvinced bleat: "We don't know how long ago she ditched the car. She could be miles away by now."

"I saw her not five minutes ago. So would you, if you hadn't been blind-drunk. Don't forget, you're the reason we're searching for a stupid bitch who knows more than's good for her, so get going and find her. I told you to keep a check on the phone. That's all you had to . . ."

They passed me, and the voices fighting one another grew inaudible. For a second the radius of the down-swinging beam reached high enough to illumine Heller's face. Its fat was covered by a skin-tight mask of savagery. When I judged them to be beyond earshot of small noises, I twisted in my makeshift hide, and when I was crouched lower than the rocks about me, I willed the three of them to turn and retrace their steps, counting off the seconds on my fingers. I'd used two hands once and one a second time, before the beams of the torches were reversed. Once they had passed me, the moonlight was bright enough to guide me not downhill but uphill through the sheltering rocks and stubble to the Turkish-Cypriot guard post. All I had to do was to keep as motionless as a hunted animal, ration my breath, and wait.

When they turned they separated, making three intermittent ribbons of light. Heller limped along my side of the road, Kim on the other, every now and again tipping his beam over the precipice, sliding it down the mountain. Bengy abandoned the road, took to the slopes, bounding and leaping, the light in his hand ascending and descending erratically. With hands crossed clasping my shoulders I bent forward, transformed myself into a crouching ball of numbed bone and flesh, half stifling myself, robbed of vision, with only the sounds of their feet to measure their nearness.

When they came level, and the space separating us began to lengthen, my hope brimmed high until a blast of light from Bengy's torch hit me. He let out a cry of manic glee and came running, leaping from rock to rock. I should have run too, but the beam dazzled my eyes, and I wasn't dexterous enough to struggle out of my hide, which had become a trap. His hand grabbed my hair, and my feet left the ground as he held me up like a prize he'd won. "Got her, got her," he screeched, and shone the torch directly into my face. "Where do you want her, boss?"

Kim came in a shambling run, then stopped, bent over as though he'd suddenly gone sick in the stomach, as Bengy snapped my hands behind my back and gripped my two wrists together.

Heller's cumbersome form did not move from the road. The torch he held down illuminated the lower half of his body, the rest was a thick, menacing shadow. "Back in the Triumph. If she won't walk, carry her."

Bengy released my wrists. "You heard the boss man's orders. Walk nice and fast, or we'll have to carry you, and it won't be a piggy-back ride." He gave me a punch between the shoulder blades.

Kim beseeched: "No rough stuff."

Bengy cackled. "Gentle as a lamb provided the little lady behaves herself. Getta move on, baby. I'm right behind you, so don't you get any smart ideas about cutting loose; they'll get you nowhere." Playfully he wound a strand of my hair round one of his fingers. "There, that should keep us nice and near one another."

Heller closed in. Kim lumbered behind, an outcast from his dream landscape of getting rich by playing liege man to a sadistic crook with a smile on his face. A pretty landscape in which there was no spot of blood, not a raised fist, and certainly not an unfinished grave on a mountainside in which a man had been half buried alive.

Heller led the way down the slope to the Triumph. Once he stumbled, half pitched forward, triggering off in my head a wild conjecture of escape, but even before he righted himself, Bengy's hand clamped like a vice on my shoulder. Heller opened the rear door, motioned Bengy to thrust me in the back seat, get in the front. As Kim made to follow him, Heller slammed the door. "No room for squealers. Outsiders stay outside."

"I've a right," Kim spluttered.

"Prove it," Heller shouted back. "Prove it," and shut the three of us in a lighted cage with Kim pounding helplessly on the window with his fists.

Bengy turned in the front seat to relish a close-up of the injuries to my face, knees, and hands, the rips in my clothes. "My, my! Who'd have thought such a tidy, pretty little bird would have got herself so messy!"

Slowly Heller turned his head, and, engulfed in the bloated ruddy face, the slit grey eyes fastened on me with a limpet gaze. I was too obsessed with a time schedule of minutes, even seconds, to suffer the familiar heaving revulsion. How long could a man's chilled flesh endure more cold? How long without aid would a pulse so faint you couldn't find it a second time continue to beat?

The clown's smile crept back into place on his bulging red lips. "You and me have played games before, haven't we, Miss Maria? That time you won, or maybe you didn't . . . it depends on the angle. But this is no game, it's for real. The way we played it with that high and mighty boss of yours. He got a bullet through his brain for prying into what didn't concern him, and for trying to threaten me. No one stays alive who threatens me. You'd do well to remember that, Miss Maria.

Maybe you'd like to know who shot him. That's him beating on the window. Shot him dead and buried him with me watching him to make sure he didn't turn yellow. And that's what you've come up here looking for, isn't it: your master's grave. Why, to lay a bunch of flowers on it! Or to run to the police crying your pretty eyes out!"

I stared straight in front, closing ears and mind to his boastful gibberish. Matthew was alive; wounded but not dead.

His hand wrenched my chin sideways. "You come clean and maybe you'll get off with a caution, or maybe not. When you were getting that yellow-livered squealer out there drunk what did he tell you?"

I got my chin free, glanced through the window at the sheer drop that was so close I couldn't see the edge. Heller jeered: "That side you've nowhere to go except down, so far down you'd never reach the bottom alive. High and mighty Miss Maria, smart as a whip, proud as a peacock, how old is she? Twenty-three, twenty-four? And all that's going to be left of her if she doesn't talk is a mush of smashed bones the police will scoop up with a shovel! So your only chance is to talk, and fast."

Suddenly the air we breathed was rent by an explosion of shattering glass as a missile smashed through the off-side window, lost momentum, and bounced on my foot.

Heller gave a roar like a bull. With one hand he pinned me back in the corner and, with the other maimed one, brushed away the blood that was streaming down his forehead into his eye.

Bengy reached for the door: "I'll get him, boss."

"And finish him."

Kim didn't run. He stayed, legs planted apart, not five yards from the car, swaying on his feet, punch-drunk with terror. The shot was so muted the gun must have been fitted with a silencer. There was no cry, just the sound of a body that had been an upright block of shadow hitting the ground.

Bengy came back to the car, opened the rear door, gesturing over his shoulder with the gun. "Where do you want him, Boss?"

"In the boot."

Heller's splayed right hand forcing me back into the corner was an immovable weight against my chest. He spat with venom: "Now that makes a whole lot of difference. You two have dug your own graves, or shall we say built yourselves a funeral pyre, a nice little family cremation."

I'd read somewhere if you were content to limit yourself to one objective, and pursued it relentlessly with undivided heart, counting neither cost nor sacrifice, you won it in the end. But to win mine, I had to be quicker and sharper-witted than the cold, inhuman thug beside me.

With Kim in the boot, the hand brake released, the ignition turned on, Heller planned that both our bodies should burn to bones in the blazing car. Before that happened I had two cards to play, and if they were trumps, I'd survive. The first was that the petrol tank was dry.

As Bengy flung open the lid of the boot and, maybe encumbered by Kim's weight, lurched against it, the wheels slid forward. It was plain that with wrists weakened by the switchback drive, I hadn't pulled hard enough on the hand brake when I'd abandoned the car. Heller screamed, reached over the seat to grab it. Before his hand touched it, I played my second card: a sliver of glass from the window Kim had shattered and which my fingers had found and hoarded. I scored it down Heller's cheek with my right hand and released the door catch with my left.

Bengy was groaning and shouting, hauling at his master's heavy, cumbersome body to get it free of the car. With the wheels gathering momentum my margin between life and death was only a split-second wide. I knew as I tumbled out it wasn't wide enough. All I could do was to fling myself free of the hurtling car. As the blackness hit me, my last thought was that by dying I'd condemned Matthew to death.

I was marooned in a silver and black landscape with no memory of how I came to be hitched to a tree on a mountainside in the depths of the night. The upper half of my body was suspended in space. There was a thunder in my head and a dull ache in my ribs, and no certainty of what—if any—purchase lay behind me. When I cautiously shifted one foot, the tree creaked and I felt the roots tug to free themselves from the earth. Fraction by fraction I disentangled my legs and feet, explored blindly with my toes, and gradually, terrifyingly, came to my knees. My numbed fingers found and measured a ledge. Widish, but its length was no more than the distance between my outstretched hands. I crouched and, bathed in the ghostly sheen of the moon-glow, had the eerie displaced feeling of being enmeshed in a nightmare. If I were patient this terrorising scene would fade inconsequentially into another, either more or less terrorising. I closed my eyes, and then as if a blind had shot up I remembered how I'd come to be where I was, and heard again the hideous rending sounds of a tumbling, somersaulting car. The time sequences were impossible to calculate: minutes, hours, half a night? The spur that hauled me to my feet was the memory of a grey face glimpsed in the light of a dying torch, an ice-cold hand, a faint, barely perceptible pulse. I twisted away from the sheer fall into space behind me and clawed with my fingernails to seek a crevice in a face of rock that was smooth as marble. I was feeling the clutch of the first pangs of absolute despair when a blast of light struck my eyes and blinded me. The shock sent me back on to my knees. Thrown down from the sky, a voice called my name, sending it echoing round the empty lunarscape. When the echo died for the tenth time, I recognised it. It belonged to Alex Theocharis.

A young policeman lowered on a rope hauled me to the top. Another, older, stood behind Alex as he eased me on to level ground, wrenched himself out of his jacket, and spread it over my shoulders. In the headlights of a car, the runnels on his satyr-face were contorted into grim anguish. "Maria, don't try to talk, not yet. We've radioed to the guard post for an ambulance. It will be here in a very few minutes."

I half sat, half lay down, while he bent over me, pouring brandy into the cup of a flask. On the rim of the radius of the light, I glimpsed a long hump that appeared to have a dark cloth spread over it. I pushed the brandy aside so violently that it spilled, and, speechless, pointed.

"My child," Alex said, his voice as gentle as though I were

indeed his child. "Kim is beyond human help. You are our concern."

The elder of the two policemen spoke with authority. "Perhaps, sir, the lady can inform us who shot the gentleman you have identified as Mr. Kimberley Mitchell. Now the young lady is safe, our first duty is to find the . . ."

The name I shouted with all the force in my lungs reached the air as a whisper, but Alex caught it and repeated it after me in a hushed, skinned voice. "Matthew! It was he who . . ."

Now I could speak. "No, Matthew's up there." I pointed. "Wounded, half buried in a gully. We've got to find him, now, quickly."

Alex's glance, those of the two policemen turned in unison to focus on the ink-dark crags rearing against the silvered sky. How abysmally stupid they were! How criminally, perhaps fatally slow. I scrambled upright, got far enough to lay a hand on a flashlight before my knees buckled.

Alex caught me. "Maria, if it is true that Matthew is there, we will find him. But you must remain calm. You are too weak and hurt to exert yourself."

I tore myself free from his grasp. They'd never find Matthew until the breath had left his body unless I led them instantly to the half-grave in which he was buried. "We have to find a cross. I made one on the ground . . ."

There was a sheepish, patient expression on the faces of the two policemen, pity and distress on Alex's. I shouted: "Take the car, I'll tell you when to stop. It's three or four bends up."

It was four, and when I got out of the car, I beat off Alex's supporting arm and raked the flashlight through the undergrowth until it found my cross of stones on a patch of golden earth.

From that point the four of us climbed, but to me we seemed to take an eternity of time clambering over the spilled stones and rocks down which I'd skimmed. He lay exactly as I'd left him, his head supported by my shoulder bag, the upper half of his chilled body padded between two woollen cardigans. As I went to drop down to his level, Alex grabbed both my arms, held them with such force I was made a prisoner. "The police will get him free quicker if we do not impede them. They are experienced, we are not. Maria, restrain yourself for Matthew's sake."

Under the flashlights that Alex and I held, the two policemen worked in dead silence until they could ease him out. His face beneath the stubble was the colour and texture of marble except where the blood had hardened into black crusts. And when the policemen laid him on the stretcher they had brought from their car, one arm fell free and swung heavy, inert like a dead limb. I had it cradled in my hands when I heard a heavy car swinging down the mountain sounding its siren. Alex said in my ear: "The ambulance from the guard post. If there is not a doctor with it there will be a medical orderly."

An officer in khaki fatigues spoke to Alex. "You are Mr. Theocharis?" Without waiting for a reply, he bent over the stretcher, then motioned the two policemen to carry it to the ambulance. To give them room to manoeuvre, he stood back. He was a tall, broadly built man, neither old nor young. It was the stillness of his face, marked with pity and solemn reverence, that tore from me a wild cry of denial. "He's alive. I know he's alive."

His glance by-passed me, and he spoke to Alex in Turkish. Alex nodded sombrely. In the second they were engrossed I regained the muscle power in my legs, and when the two policemen lifted the stretcher into the ambulance, I was behind them, my foot on the steps.

Alex seized and held me back, spoke sternly. "Maria, they must have room, be unimpeded. There are treatments they must administer instantly, even before they reach the hospital. It is better for Matthew that you follow in my car. Come, we will travel right behind the ambulance."

But he had not reckoned on the elder policeman.

"Sir, I appreciate your concern for the young lady, whom you inform me is Miss Maria Caron. I do not ask her to make a detailed statement, but a murder has been committed. We must know who fired the gun that killed Mr. Mitchell, who was at the scene, and in the car that . . ."

Alex raised his hand to silence him. "Maria, just the names. Who was in the car when it went over the mountainside?"

I gave them Heller's and Bengy's names, a capsulated account in short, impatiently spoken sentences. I did not know whether Bengy or Heller, or both of them, had been in the car when it catapulted over the mountainside. I did not know how Matthew Grant came to be wounded and half buried in a grave.

"Enough." Alex dismissed them. "Later, you or your superior officers will be at liberty to question Miss Caron."

Until we had caught up with the ambulance and were parted from its tail-lights by no more than one tight bend, Alex did not speak. "You were afraid I would not keep my word! There, we are as near him as it is safe to be."

He did not ask me a single question. Later, I was grateful to him for his forbearance; at the time I was incapable of any such emotion. I could not understand why he should find it necessary to talk to me, to fill a silence I did not want filled. As though there was any space in my mind or heart for curiosity, to learn by what means he and the police had reached the point on the road where they had seen the Triumph somersault over the mountainside. Barbie's rage when she discovered that I had tricked and betrayed her were paltry irrelevances. With the car gone, she assumed I had connived with Kim to prevent her escaping to the airport. She'd poured black coffee into him, and when he was partially sensible, had attacked him for duplicity. It had been nearly five before either of them was rational enough to telephone the airport and confirm I'd caught the London plane. B.E.A. had informed Kim that I'd failed to pick up my ticket.

Kim had stormed out of the house. Immediately Barbie had telephoned Giselle, and later Alex, but it had been six before he had arrived home to be confronted by an hysterical Barbie raving about a stolen car. When he had unravelled her accusations, he set enquiries afoot that eventually brought information from the U.N. Post that a white Triumph driven by a girl had been seen heading towards the pass during the afternoon and had not been observed coming down, though that was no guarantee that it had not done so.

Alex, fearing I'd had a break-down or an accident, had summoned a police car equipped with stretcher and ropes to cope with any emergency to follow him. They had spotted lights moving on the mountainside, and were less than a quarter of a mile away when the Triumph had hurtled into space.

When he came to the end, the only question I asked: "How many days is it since Friday?"

"Five," he said softly.

We were held up at the hospital gate by a second ambulance that slipped in behind the one in which Matthew lay. By the time we entered, they'd whisked him from sight. Against my will I was handed over to a young doctor and an even younger nurse with a gentle smile and lustrous, doelike eyes, who promised: "We will make you clean and comfortable."

It was a time-wasting operation to which I was not prepared to submit. To overrule me, Alex placed me forcibly in front of a mirror. It showed me a face that was covered in blood, a mat of hair caked with earth. "You like the look of yourself?" he queried. "Your lovely hair filthy, your pretty face scratched and cut?" When I shook my head he counselled: "Go with the doctor and the nurse. Meanwhile I will telephone Barbie and Carima." He touched my cheek, said gently: "Barbie must be told before rumours begin to spread." The face with its satyr folds, the eyes that pierced deeper than most, was flooded with pity. I looked away. I'd no need of pity, so why spend it on me? For a moment I despised him, yet in the dark terror of that night, he was to be my only support.

My injuries amounted to no more than bruised ribs, multiple bruises and abrasions. When the doctor had examined me, strapped up my ribs, he abandoned me quickly for a baby in the next cubicle who had been brought in with scalded feet. The little nurse sponged away the blood and dirt, applied salve and sticking plaster to cuts. Finished, she told me to wait. I was not prepared to do so; I had already been away from the room in which Alex had promised to remain for nearly an hour. She pointed to the ripped dress that hung over a chair. "You wish people to see you in your bra and panties? I think you are not that sort of girl. I will find a cover for you."

In ten minutes she returned with a white nylon hospital overall. "You may wear it to take you home, and then, in the morning, you perhaps will be so kind as to return it."

I hope I thanked her, but I can't be sure.

In the waiting-room Alex was no longer alone. Close to him were Barbie and Giselle, their backs to me when I opened the door. Their heads swivelled, and from a death-white face, weirdly distorted out of shape, Barbie's hyacinth blue eyes fastened on me without recognition.

Giselle took an uncertain step towards me, asked in a shaky whisper: "Maria, are you hurt?"

Before I could answer the door I'd just closed opened. A thick-set, elderly man in a white coat, with a deeply tanned face, quick-darting eyes, said: "I am Andreas Staphos, the senior physician at this hospital. Which of you ladies is Mrs. Grant?"

"There is no Mrs. Grant. I am his sister, Barbara Mitchell."

He addressed Barbie formally. "Unhappily, it is best that I tell you that Mr. Grant's condition is highly critical. He has suffered a moderately severe scalp wound, a gun-shot wound in the left thigh, plus a number of other injuries. None of these would normally have proved fatal, but they have been left untended for a number of days, and in addition he has been subjected to prolonged exposure, and is severely dehydrated."

Alex cleared his throat. "What are his chances?"

"He is in a small intensive care unit we have only recently installed here. I would like you to be consoled by my assurance that everything possible is being done for Mr. Grant. It is my opinion and that of my colleagues that it is highly unlikely there will be any definite change in his condition for some hours. I think it would be a wise course for these ladies to return home where they will be more comfortable than we can make them. Perhaps, Mr. Theocharis, you would be good enough to return."

"I agree the ladies should go home," Alex said. "I will be back within the hour."

I demanded in a voice that burst in a harsh and ugly sound over Alex and the doctor's subdued, courteous tones: "He's alive, isn't he? And he's going to live?"

Maybe my white nurse's coat confused him, maybe he was not clear as to my relationship with his patient, but the doctor gave me no more than a sombre, reproving glance. Without a word he left us alone. We none of us had breath to speak.

Giselle's Fiat was nearer the hospital entrance than Alex's

car. As he opened the door for her, she pleaded in a breaking voice: "Whenever there is any news, whatever it is, however bad, you'll promise to telephone me?"

He promised, speaking to her with the same caressing gentleness he'd used to me. She kissed Barbie, who made no response, then turned to me, words hanging on her tongue but never leaving her lips. Because she was a strong person accounted by people who knew her as a super-woman, she was striving with all her might not to go to pieces while her world reeled out of orbit. Looking at her taut face, her anguished eyes, which were dark and dull, I thought: She's afraid in the marrow of her bones, already accepting that Matthew is dying. It was a weakness that fractured the perfection with which, to me, she'd been endowed. I could not conceive of love acknowledging defeat. And what was death but the ultimate defeat, one that endured forever!

Barbie sat in front of the Mercedes with Alex. I could see him talking to her in an undertone, but she did not utter a word in reply. Except for that bald claim of kinship with Matthew, she seemed to have been struck dumb.

Connie had been watching for the car and was waiting in the courtyard. Silently she held out her arms to Barbie, closed them about her, and looked at Alex. While she rocked Barbie, who had begun to shake violently, racked by dry sobs, he gave her the gist of the doctor's bulletin.

All she said was: "She needs her bed," and led Barbie upstairs, guiding her feet from one stair to the next.

Alex touched my shoulder. "And so do you. Let me help you upstairs."

"I can manage. There's nothing much wrong with me. I just look a mess." And then I found myself saying stupidly over and over again: "I'm sorry . . ."

He gave me a puzzled, astonishingly sweet smile. "My dear child, what have you to be sorry for? Is there something you wish to tell me?"

I shook my head. I could hardly explain that I was apologising to him for a distrust of which he'd never been aware.

He took me to the foot of the stairs, made me the promise

he'd made Giselle, and exacted one from me that I would try and sleep.

When he'd gone, I climbed the stone slabs. From Barbie's room came the muffled sound of rending sobs, and Connie's soothing voice.

I undressed, hung the white nylon coat on a chair to be washed and returned to the hospital in the morning, and got into bed. When there was no sound from the room below, I heard Connie go downstairs, close and lock the courtyard door, and after an interval climb up again.

She was carrying a tumbler of hot milk in one hand, two aspirins in the palm of the other. She sat down on the edge of the bed. With her spirit blunted, her shoulders sagging, an air of being overwhelmed with grief and confusion, she was transformed into a shadow of her dauntless self.

Her upper lip trembled, but she quelled it. "It's a bad do. Terrible. I don't know how much she's taken in except about Matthew. But she knows Kim's dead. She said it to me, threw it off, as if it meant nothing: 'Kim's dead!' Who killed him?"

"Bengy shot him on Heller's orders."

"Murdering devils! Hanging's too good for them. Did the police get hold of them?"

"I don't know."

Horror plus a blazing righteous indignation put some spirit back in her. "What's been going on? You acting all innocent, then pinching Barbie's car, going off on your own, never a word, up into the mountains to find Matthew, when none of us knew he was there. But you knew, you must have or you wouldn't have gone. Why didn't you tell those who had a right to know?"

To have regathered and collated all the cobwebs of suspicions that had driven me on that desperate ride was beyond me. I told her so. She scolded me but without much heart. "Acting on your own like that! Going off . . ." She broke off grumbling, and offered me the aspirins. They were the only pill she took, or administered to the household. Her panacea for every indisposition. If aspirin didn't cure you by morning, you needed a doctor.

She stood on guard until I'd swallowed them, drunk the milk, then she shook up my pillows.

Half-way to the door, she turned on me, made a stark appeal. "There's Toby. Nobody's given a thought to him, poor lamb. He'll have to be told his father's dead. And Matthew . . ."

"Matthew's going to live," I shouted.

She said, grief pinching her face into premature age: "That's one miracle we're all praying for tonight."

FOURTEEN

It felt as though my face were being stroked by a feather. When I opened my eyes Toby, through the gap in his teeth, was licking the tip of the feather into shape. "You woke yourself, didn't you?" he said guilelessly. "Connie says Mummy's got a headache and I'm not to wake her. And Daddy hasn't come home yet. I know because his Volvo isn't in the car park." With barely repressed glee he minutely examined my scratches and bruises. "Did you have an accident?"

"Yes. A car accident."

"With Mummy's car?" I said yes. "On your way to the airport? Is that why you're still here when you should have been in London with Uncle Matthew?"

"Yes." I looked for my watch, but somewhere I'd lost it. "Do you know what time it is?"

He consulted his near saucer-size nickel-plated diver's watch, complete with second hand and date. "In two seconds it will be twenty-six minutes to seven. What will Uncle Matthew say because you bashed yourself up in an accident? Will you fly to London today?"

I was saved from replying by Connie's entry. Her hair was

tousled out of its corrugated waves and there were smudges of shadow under her eyes, but her smile at Toby was normal: fond but ever ready to admonish him for his own good. "So there you are, and me looking all over for you!"

"Only over the house," he corrected. "You could see I wasn't in the garden. When I've had my breakfast can I go and wake Mummy?"

"Depends on whether you eat your breakfast."

In one of what Connie termed his answer-back moods, he retorted: "Depends on what it is."

"What would you like?"

Temporarily thrown by the unexpected soft answer, he recovered himself, took advantage of a dispensation from providence: "Sausages, four."

"Please," Connie prompted.

"Please," he added while he returned to making an inventory of my visible scratches and cuts. "I could lend you my snails. Would you like to have them to keep you company?" When I'd thanked him for the offer but refused it, he trotted off to fetch me a book: *Myths and Legends of Ancient Greece.* "It's one of my favourites, that's why it's got my best pressed banana leaf as a bookmark."

When he'd left us, I struggled to pull myself upright, but every joint in my body was locked, and the room slowly revolved until the ceiling changed places with the floor.

"Better lie still," Connie cautioned. "Mr. Theocharis telephoned at half-past six. There's been no change during the night. He's as bad as ever."

At the door, Barbie, half dressed, swayed on her feet. She still wore her dead-eyed zombie look. In a harsh staccato voice she announced: "I'm going to the hospital to see him. No matter what any tin-pot doctor says, I'm seeing him. Since my car's been stolen, I'll get Giselle to drive me."

"You're not going anywhere until you've had some breakfast," Connie warned, obsessed, as always, with food.

Barbie gave no sign of hearing her. She advanced upon me like a revenging goddess. "You knew he was up there, shot to pieces, half buried under a mountain, and what did you do! Keep it a secret, steal my car . . ." She heaved out her shudder-

171

ing breath. "And launch into a solitary heroine act! What could you have done on your own? Nothing but sit and watch him die if Alex hadn't called the police and followed you. Is that what you wanted, to sit beside him while he died?"

She wasn't waiting for an answer: she didn't want one. "Why should anyone want to kill Matthew? Who put him where you found him?" She bent over me, her face contorted to the ugliest shape of all: hate. "You knew what had happened to him. You must have. And all the time you put on a pie-eyed innocent act, doing damn all. Jaunting off on picnics, never breathing a word that you didn't intend to catch the plane to Heathrow. You know what you are, Maria Caron, a sly, double-crossing little cheat, and worse, much worse, Matthew's dying, that doctor as good as admitted it last night, and it's written all over Alex's face. I'm not blind. Nor stupid. So who killed him by keeping quiet until it was too late?"

Then she closed her eyes as if the sight of me nauseated her, and stumbled out of the room.

"Take no notice," Connie said gruffly. "She doesn't know what she's saying. She's more than half out of her mind, proper crazed." She paused, added: "Though why you had to be so sly and secretive I'll never understand till my dying day."

Soon after Toby left for school I heard the Fiat arrive and depart. When Connie came upstairs to reclaim my breakfast tray, seeing her good food spurned, nipped in the corners of her mouth.

"Connie, were *you* able to eat any breakfast?"

"I had some on the run." Softening fractionally, she ran a hand over my forehead. "Doesn't feel as though you've got a temperature, but maybe I better play safe and take it."

I dissuaded her, swore I was perfectly all right, and she was only too ready to take my word. It wasn't that her natural kindness, her concern for anyone in discomfort, had ceased to operate, rather that it was shoved out of sight, in a kind of mental deep-freeze. Half of her was locked in the hospital with Matthew. The remaining half was claimed by Barbie and Toby. It was an equation I understood. Only I was even more steely single-hearted than she.

It took me a full hour to shower and dress. When I'd finished, the worst of the crippling pain and stiffness had passed, and, climbing like a snail, I managed to reach the Crow's Nest and telephone home. By now, by telephone or telex, Matthew's name would be on the desk of every news editor and telecaster in London. By noon it would be plastered over the lunch-time editions, on the radio in "News at One," which my father listened to.

This time I was out of luck. My mother answered. "In an accident? What kind of accident? What about you? Are you hurt?"

I managed to break through the torrent of alarm. "I was only marginally involved. I'm perfectly all right."

"Marginally involved? What is that supposed to mean? You know how anxious your father will be, and what that will do to his heart and blood pressure!"

"That's why I'm telephoning. So that he shan't worry. To prove to you that I'm all right."

"But Mr. Grant isn't!" She paused, and I could sense her brain clicking. "Is he going to die?"

"No. He's going to recover."

That let her off the hook of a precept she would never have broken: speaking ill of the dead. "I'll never have an easy moment as long as you work for that man. He's got no conscience. What's more, he's too full of himself. If you'd any sense you'd have realised years ago that all that concerns him is his own glory, flaunting himself on television, his name in big type in the newspapers. The truth is that he mesmerises you."

I forgave her because she was worried out of her reason as much for my father as for me. I spent three more minutes on calming and reassuring her, and promised I'd telephone again tomorrow. Then I telephoned Gladwin. Shocked, he couldn't, he protested, make head nor tail of my story, and was incensed and alarmed that I was "leaving him in the dark not knowing how it had all happened." All I could do was to promise faithfully to keep in touch.

Connie put her head round the door. "It's the police. They're asking for you. If you don't feel up to it, I could try asking them to come back later, though they don't look in a mood to have a door slammed in their faces. I've put them in the dining-room."

It was the least used room in the house, one Barbie had never got around to doing up, still filled with the heavily carved furniture that the Mannheims had probably brought from Germany. Its single window faced a steeply rising bank that blocked out most of the light.

Two men who rose to their feet as I entered were sitting at the dining-table. One was the hefty young policeman who'd hauled me from the mountain ledge to level ground. His companion was a middle-aged senior officer, spare of figure, spruce in appearance, with the direct, uncompromising manner that comes naturally to those accustomed to issuing orders that are automatically obeyed. In a sharper and more incisive voice than you normally find among Cypriots he introduced himself as Inspector Stanos and, drawing out a chair for me, apologised for intruding when I must still be suffering from the after-effects of yesterday's ordeal. There were, however, matters of extreme urgency on which only I could supply them with the information that they required. He trusted I understood the position.

I replied I did; the rotund young policeman retired to a corner, switched on a table lamp, and took out his notebook.

First the Inspector demanded a recapitulation in detail of the grounds which had led me to suspect that Mr. Grant was lying severely wounded on a mountainside beyond the pass.

As though not to embarrass me, he kept his gaze in the mid-distance until I reached the telephone call from Lex McBain, then his glance swung to focus sharply on me. "Can you recall his exact words? Also his address in Beirut?"

His address required no effort of memory, and the words that had passed between us were so few they were soon repeated.

"And that was all? No details about this necklace he referred to or his meeting with Mr. Grant in Beirut? Merely that there'd been a follow-up to the story?"

"That is so."

He said in the tone of one delivering a stricture rather than a compliment: "You are a young lady of considerable courage and fortitude. You are also an extremely reckless one. You matched yourself against desperate criminals armed with guns and prepared to use them. What did you imagine that you alone, without equipment for rescuing and transporting an injured man, could do to assist Mr. Grant? Why did you not confide your suspicions—or convictions—to someone who would have been in a position to lend you support, and above all, Miss Caron, why did you not confide in the police?"

"It's difficult to explain. I was shocked, not very clear-headed. As nearly as I can explain because I was living in the same house as Kim Mitchell. If my suspicions were correct, he was a member of a gang of murderers. I wasn't prepared to share my suspicions with any relative, friend, or contact of Kim Mitchell's."

"That doesn't answer my last question. Why did you not report what you overheard and deduced to the police, not behave like a lady knight-errant in an English fairy story?"

There was no logical come-back to that but the truth. "To some extent because Miss Lois Brown had already contacted you, and . . ." To throw in the mutual hostility we roused in one another, her hysterical charges against Matthew, seemed so ludicrously time-wasting that I left a silence.

"Why should the fact Miss Brown had seen fit to contact us preclude you from doing so? I would like an answer, Miss Caron."

"She's convinced that her fiancé, Bruce Vernon, was murdered. She also appeared, when I spoke to her yesterday morning, to believe that Mr. Grant knew this, was part of a conspiracy of silence to keep the true facts from her."

"And was he?"

"No. He was in London when Bruce Vernon was accidentally drowned or murdered."

A silence clamped down on the room, unbroken by a sound in the house, a raised voice or a donkey's hoof-beat from the village. When he spoke it was with heightened gravity. "You are Mr. Grant's personal secretary. I assume, therefore, you enjoy his fullest confidence. It would not be unreasonable to suppose that you are aware of certain events that culminated in last night's tragedy. You must have formed some theory as to why Mr. Grant was kidnapped from his own home by a relative and a close friend, and left to die where it was unlikely he would be found, either dead or alive. To know that theory might be of assistance to us."

"I haven't one to give you. I can't conceive of a reason why Kim Mitchell should bury alive a man who'd supported him, his wife, and child for years."

He had the poker-face of a professional policeman. It was impossible to guess whether or not he believed me. That point settled—or not—to his satisfaction, he moved briskly forward to the next. "Now, Miss Caron, would you tell me of the last occasion on which you were in contact with Mr. Grant?"

Together with the dates of my departure and return from Cornwall, the words Mrs. Pratt had written in red ink on a sheet of my typing paper were recorded by the constable. When Inspector Stanos had double-checked them, he made a signal for the constable to close his notebook.

"I understand that Mrs. Mitchell is at the hospital. Meanwhile there is certain urgent work that my men need to carry out in the cellar. It may be necessary to demolish certain parts of it. I would naturally have preferred to have warned Mrs. Mitchell in advance. Perhaps, on my behalf, you would apologise for any disturbance my men cause. I assure you, it will be kept to a minimum."

As he rose, although my curiosity, together with every other emotion of which I was capable, to keep my reservoir of hope filled, was no more than a flickering candle power, I asked a single question. "Heller and Bengy, where are they?"

"Heller was trapped in the car. He died on impact of multiple injuries. The man you refer to as Bengy, whose passport bears the name Bernard Sissons, was arrested shortly after 1 A.M. this morning. He has voluntarily made a statement. Our immediate task is to obtain corroboration of that statement." His smile was openly cynical. "With Heller and Vernon dead, grave doubt as to whether Mr. Grant will regain consciousness, Mr. Sissons' métier, understandably, is to pose as an innocent pawn compelled under duress to execute the orders of his employer, who is in no position to contradict any part of his statement."

"I saw him shoot Kim Mitchell."

"Yes, indeed." This time his nod was one of congratulation.

"If you would be good enough to explain to Mrs. Mitchell that my men will be working in the cellar this afternoon, I will be in touch with both of you after I have made contact with Mr. McBain."

Avoiding Connie, her strings of questions to which I had no answers, I left the hot, airless room, went and sat on the wall at the top of the garden with my back to the mountains. I picked a small, hard lemon without a streak of gold and rolled it in my palms. From the place I'd chosen I had an unimpeded view of the bridge and was able to spot the Fiat the moment it started across.

To obtain an instant sight of their faces, I stood up as they got out of the car. It was the expression on Giselle's that made my heart pause between one beat and the next. When Connie came running into the courtyard to lead Barbie indoors, as though she were an exhausted child incapable of placing one foot before another, Giselle stood with an air of overwhelming uncertainty, as though she were lost in an unknown landscape. For a long moment her gaze hung on the house, then she freed it to allow it to travel up the garden, where it found me.

Again she hesitated before she opened the gate, climbed the path. When no more than a yard separated us, she told me what I already knew. "Matthew's still in a coma. There's no change from last night."

Her eyes fell away from mine, focussed on a clump of dying Michaelmas daisies Connie had brought from England, their roots wrapped in wet cotton wool. Grief and fright had not touched the delicate bone structure, but it had drawn the flesh that covered it taut, sharpening her profile, and doused the glow of unshakable self-confidence. Like me she was suspended over a chasm; unlike me, she had no faith that she would reach the other side. Again, I thought, the hair-line fracture in her perfection both diminished her and made her to another woman more human, likeable. But only for a moment.

With a surge of envy that made her voice bitter with anguish, she cried out: "If Matthew lives, he'll owe you his life."

I tasted hate on my tongue: as though gratitude was a bonus that would win me the prize she craved.

It was the sound of stampeding feet, a continuous high-pitched screaming that swung our heads in the direction of the house, set us running, and brought Connie and Barbie out into the courtyard.

"Uncle Matthew's dead!" In a paroxysm of outrage, Toby flung himself on his mother, shaken by spasms of racking grief. "He was shot dead, near the cave where Niko's uncle was killed. That's what they are all saying at school."

Unforgivably, Barbie, Connie, and I had not given a fleeting thought to the adult gossip that would be picked up and relayed by the children. Barbie knelt down to Toby's level, held his flailing figure tight to her. "He's not dead. Toby, I promise you, Uncle Matthew is not dead. He's terribly, terribly ill, and he's in hospital, but the doctors and nurses are doing all they can so that he shan't die." She and Connie had to repeat the words a dozen times before the jerking shudders eased from his body. He stood with bowed head, the tears rolling down his cheeks. "Then Daddy's not dead either? Is he in hospital too?"

His mother either could not or would not answer, and it was Connie who knelt down to his level. "Daddy's not in hospital, my lamb." They stared at one another, and when the first tear I'd ever seen Connie shed slid over her eyelid, he said in a voice terrible to hear from the mouth of a child: "Somebody did shoot him dead?"

Connie reached and cradled him in her arms. "No one shot him, lovie. He was killed when his car overturned last night."

She had, for reasons of her own, told a lie that any child at school would lay bare, but it soothed him a little. Thereafter, the traumatic effect of the shock was to make him cling to his mother, to demand that during the day either she or Connie was within his sight, and at night he slept in his mother's bed.

Later in the morning Alex and Carima arrived to plead for the four of us to move to the Villa Hesperides. When Barbie, Connie, and I refused, Alex went away and returned with his most trusted house-servant, Christos, whom he posted by the big blue outer door into the courtyard to receive the constant flow of villagers who crossed the bridge over the ravine to present their gently spoken, grieving condolences, to request the latest hospital bulletin on Mr. Grant, and to whisper of candles they had lit for him in the white-domed Greek Orthodox church in the square.

In the peak of the afternoon heat, while Barbie and Toby, with Minnow curved into the crook of her back, slept under the gilded cherub, a truck with three policemen and a sergeant armed with picks, shovels, and sacks took possession of the cellar.

Connie and I sat in the sitting-room. She grumbled: "I always knew he'd got his loot buried down there, but that's no excuse for bringing the house down about our ears. That police officer who was here this morning must have told you what they're looking for. Or is that another of your little secrets?"

"He might have told Barbie if she'd been here, but he didn't tell me."

"She wouldn't care if they tore the whole place apart. She wouldn't even know they were doing it." For a moment she looked distracted, before she pulled herself resolutely together. "I'll make us some tea, but they needn't think I'm traipsing up and down the cellar steps with a pot for them."

They worked until dark. I watched the four men cross the lighted car park. The sacks were as empty as when they arrived, but one had tucked under his arm the file Kim had stolen from my suitcase.

Every hour on the hour Barbie telephoned the hospital. The bulletin never varied. The condition of the patient was unchanged.

At ten o'clock Alex returned to the house to deliver personally the last one of the day. Matthew was locked in a deep coma; he was barely alive.

I imagine it was Barbie's face, chalk-white, immobile, as though she was imprisoned in some nightmare trance, that decided him to stay the night.

FIFTEEN

It was 2 A.M. when the telephone shrilled once before the receiver was snatched off. Alex, who had chosen to sleep in his clothes on the sofa in the sitting-room, the telephone on the floor beside him, was fumbling for his glasses to read the number on the instrument.

The telephone number confirmed, a woman's agitated and high-pitched voice was clearly audible. Since it wasn't a call from the hospital, I went into the courtyard, where Christos was lying on a folded blanket, his body an extra barrier against the door, until I heard Alex replace the receiver.

Rumpled, his thinning iron-grey hair wispy instead of smoothed over his head, the runnels on his satyr face pressed deeper by fatigue, he gave me a blank-eyed look, said in a chain-smoker's hoarse voice: "I never knew Matthew had a wife. She'd just heard he's in hospital, and sounded panic-stricken, almost crazy. Did you know he had a wife?"

There was a purely physical jolt, a sort of giant body-blow. "No."

"Well, he has. In Manchester. Marigold Grant."

I felt hysteria rising, clamped my teeth together to prevent it escaping, but it beat me. It was minutes later, with Alex removing the brandy glass from my lips, before I was capable of speech. "Matthew and Marigold were divorced years ago . . . I'd guess five or six. She married again, and now her name is Marigold Fairley."

"Then why did she announce herself to me as his wife, which she most certainly did?"

I shook my head. "Maybe to substantiate her claim as a close relative, which an ex-wife isn't. And . . ."

"And?" he prompted when I paused.

"Women who fall in love with Matthew don't seem to be able to let go . . . surrender him."

His glance was at once quizzical and tenderly affectionate, but he said nothing. He had no need to. With his needle-sharp perception, I'd probably given myself away to him a dozen times. I felt a bite of anger. I resented his lack of faith in Matthew's recovery infinitely more than Barbie's, Connie's, and Giselle's. I challenged him. "Why don't you believe Matthew is going to make it?"

"Believe . . ." He looked troubled, for once uneasy at having no placating answer. "You want the truth? Yes, I know you do. Because the odds are stacked against him. So you believe, and I hope. Is there all that much difference?"

"Yes. Matthew's not an ordinary man. He's immensely strong, physically and mentally. And he loves being alive."

He smiled and looked into my face for a long moment before he spoke. "And you're no ordinary woman. Who knows, between you, an extraordinary man and an extraordinary woman, you may accomplish a miracle." He laughed beguilingly. "Come, child, even miracle-workers need sleep."

As he guided me towards the stairs, I tried to thank him, but he stopped me. "Hush! Why do you assume that because I have made myself rich I have lost my heart!"

At eight in the morning, promising Toby that she would be back in two hours exactly, Barbie went with Alex to the hospital. Toby stood on the parapet of the Crow's Nest to watch the car until it was out of sight, then Connie sat with him at the walnut table and played his favourite card word-game at which he always beat her.

This was the day when the telephone never ceased ringing. I sat by the master instrument in the sitting-room and answered enquiries from friends and colleagues that seemed to span half the world.

At half-past nine Inspector Stanos was driven into the parking space, followed by Kim's Volvo. He enquired if it were possible for him to see Mrs. Mitchell. Apart from other matters he wished to advise her that the inquest on her husband would be held at 8 A.M. the following day. If Mrs. Mitchell was not well enough to attend, her presence would not be obligatory, but in that case he would require a sworn statement from her. My presence at the inquest was obligatory.

I explained that it would be well over an hour before Mrs. Mitchell would return from the hospital. Would he care to wait?

He checked his watch, did a calculation. "Mr. McBain is due to land at Nicosia airport in just over an hour. A police car is meeting him and driving him to headquarters, where my senior officers and I hope he may be able to enlarge on the information he has already given us over the telephone. His corroboration of Sissons' statement is, naturally, a vital factor in the case. I am afraid I must insist on seeing Mrs. Mitchell this afternoon without fail. I suggest 3.30. Will you be so good as to advise her I will be here at that time?"

"Yes." I added: "I'm afraid she is still in a severe state of shock. She may not find it easy to understand your questions."

"We do not harry bereaved widows, Miss Caron. You may rest assured that Mrs. Mitchell will suffer the minimum of distress at my hands." He reached into his breast pocket, withdrew a small cellophane envelope padded with wadding, opened it, and with reverent fingers laid the object it contained on the table. He held my gaze with imperative directiveness. "Miss Caron, I have to ask you if you have ever seen this article or a similar one, either in this house or in the possession of anyone who resided in this house or visited it."

The telephone rang as he completed his question. It was the editor of a London newspaper. As I made the routine responses I stared at the small coil of vivid, near-iridescent green wire, the ends of which formed overlapping snakes' heads. When the call ended I went and stood over it. "It's a bracelet, isn't it? I've seen ones like it in museums. In Athens, I believe, but I can't swear to it."

"You would not have to travel as far as Athens, no farther than the Cyprus Museum in Nicosia. It was made by a craftsman who lived maybe as long as three thousand years ago, part of our national heritage of priceless antiquities, one piece among many others that was stolen from us by Julius Mannheim. Is his name familiar to you?"

"He once owned this house. Before he committed suicide he made a will bequeathing it to Matthew Grant."

"He was a skilled amateur archaeologist who, in the postwar period, secured for himself a place on one of the international teams excavating the tombs of the late Bronze Age. One day he was caught leaving the site with some gold buttons secreted in the toe of his shoe. He was summarily dismissed. Unfortunately it did not occur to anyone that this was not his first theft, and his house was never searched. Today such criminal laxity could not occur, but I am speaking of over twenty years ago. In fact, he had previously stolen many gold and copper articles of jewellery, several small cult figures, and a necklace of gold and agate that from Sissons' uninformed description would seem to have been a particularly superb example of the Mycenaean period. He hid them in a hollowed-out cavity in the cellar in that section which first he, and later Mr. Mitchell, used as a workshop. This copper bracelet, wedged into a crevice, is the sole article my men found.

"According to Sissons' testimony, Mitchell discovered the cache roughly a year ago. He informed Heller, who realised that, provided they could smuggle the articles out of the country without risking the enormous penalties for exporting antiquities, and dispose of them secretly, they stood to gain a considerable sum of money. Sissons is vague about the means they employed. It has now come to light—through our enquiries following Miss Brown's accusations—that Heller had a police record in England, was wanted for armed robbery. Hence he was in no position to return to that country and act as his own underground salesman. For that job he co-opted an old friend of his Bruce Vernon. His was a task requiring considerable skill and guile. No reputable museum in Europe or America would have bought such antiquities without exhaustive enquiries as to their source and exact knowledge of how the seller obtained them. What in the art world is called a provenance.

"But there exist wealthy, eccentric collectors in Europe, North and South America who are prepared to pay large sums for paintings or rare antiquities, ask no awkward questions, and make no display of their purchases except to trusted friends sworn to secrecy. It would appear that Bruce Vernon was successful in contacting at least two of them."

He glanced at his watch, checking the margin of time. "Now it is my duty to ask you, Miss Caron, had you any prior knowledge of the facts I have related to you?"

"No."

"Would you have any reason to suspect that Mrs. Mitchell was in her husband's confidence, that she was aware he was a party to illegally exporting and selling stolen antiquities?"

"I'm positive she wasn't. I'll swear it if you want me to."

"It is Mrs. Mitchell who must swear on her own behalf." He wrapped the bracelet in wadding, replaced it in the cellophane envelope, returned it to his pocket. "You will inform Mrs. Mitchell that I will be calling on her at 3.30?"

"Yes. I know you're in a hurry to meet Mr. McBain's plane, but could you tell me how he comes to be involved?"

"Very briefly." He spoke quickly, tersely, his eye constantly checking the time. "Mr. McBain is a Canadian journalist. He spent the month of August in London with relatives, among whom is an uncle who is on the staff of a world-famous firm of auctioneers. He repeated to his nephew a story on which he himself placed no credence, that genuine Cypro-Minoan jewellery and other antiquities, including a remarkable, quite unique necklace, had been sold by an Englishman whose body had later been washed up on the northern shore of Cyprus. Fortunately for us newspaper men are by nature of their trade credulous, prepared to spend time investigating wild rumours. Mr. McBain worked hard to verify the truth of the story in London but without success. At the beginning of September he was posted to Beirut. Last Wednesday night he met Mr. Grant in an hotel bar. Knowing his close connection with Cyprus, he repeated the story to him. According to Mr. McBain, Mr. Grant listened with interest, asked him a number of pertinent questions but could throw no light on the mystery. Nevertheless, Mr. Grant was aware of Julius Mannheim's record of theft. Bruce Vernon, the drowned man, was a close friend of Heller's, as was his brother-in-law. The following day he flew to Nicosia to pursue his own investigations. Meanwhile, last Thursday, Mr. McBain received a letter from his uncle informing him that the story appeared to be true, as the buyer of the necklace had been traced. That is why he telephoned.

"What precise form Mr. Grant's enquiries took we have no means of knowing. We can only pray that he will recover consciousness and be able to tell us. Sissons swears he knew nothing of any confrontation between Heller and Mr. Grant on Thursday or Friday. Friday was his day off. He spent it in Nicosia, the night at the house of a prostitute, not returning to Kessima until midday on Saturday.

"He is equally unforthcoming on Vernon's death. It is possible that Vernon, who drank heavily, let fall a hint of his activities which filtered back to Heller. Equally it is possible that he turned blackmailer, demanded a bigger cut for his services as the price of silence. And now, if you will excuse me, I must be on my way to meet Mr. McBain's plane."

When I accompanied him as far as the courtyard, there was a visitor sitting on Connie's stool by the well. Christos gave me a look of humble apology that he had failed to dislodge her.

Geoff had persuaded her to wear one of Doris's scorched sun hats, but the pink sandals, now scuffed of all colour, were still on her feet. When she saw me, she stood up, gabbled: "You'll think I'm making a nuisance of myself, what the newspapers call intruding on private grief, but before I called I made sure Mrs. Mitchell wasn't in. When I've misjudged someone I don't have an easy moment until I've apologised. That's the way I am and I can't help it."

"You don't owe me an apology."

"But I do," she insisted dogmatically, and glanced meaningly at Christos. "Can we go into the garden?" She walked ahead of me until she reached the carob tree, then turned with a defiant twist of her ungainly body. "I've heard most of what happened. Geoff found out for me. The police told him things they wouldn't tell me. That's how I know now that Mr. Grant had nothing to do with Bruce's murder. So it's only right I should apologise for misjudging him."

"It's all right." I found it difficult to concentrate on what she was saying. "Please don't worry about it."

"But I do," she flung at me. "I had a pretty shrewd idea that Bruce was in on some sort of deal that was not, well, strictly legal. There'd been other times. He more or less admitted as much but said it was safer for me not to know. So I never asked. All that mattered to me was that he was going to make enough money to buy a house so that we could get married." Her voice faltered, then picked up strength and defiance. "I didn't care what he did so long as he loved me enough to marry me, but I can't expect you to understand that."

"I think I do. Lots of women feel the same way."

She looked offended, as though I'd denegated her. She rushed on: "Just a lot of old bits and pieces they found stowed away, a sort of treasure trove. No one would have been hurt or a penny the worse off if they hadn't tried to double-cross him, cheat him out of his share. That's what happened. Lots of people made the mistake of thinking they could cod Bruce. He looked so easy-going. But inside he wasn't. He'd fight to the last ditch before he'd be taken advantage of. So they murdered him." Her eyes were like two stones in her stiff pudding face. "But with Heller and Mr. Mitchell dead . . . there's a fat chance of proving it." In the intense heat she shivered, then pulled herself together. "Well, I've got that off my conscience."

She moved away, she must have, but I've no memory of saying goodbye, only of seeing Alex's Alfa Romeo drive into the parking space. One glance at Barbie's face, and Lois Brown was obliterated from my mind. Tears were pouring down it in a torrent, and without Alex's arm she would never have reached the courtyard. A woman bereaved and desolated.

I could not move. I was made as cold as arctic ice by the touch of death, by a world that had been transformed into a wasteland. For a long minute I was literally blind and deaf.

Then Alex called me, and enough vision returned for me to see tears streaming down Connie's cheeks, enough hearing to hear Toby's hiccoughing sobs.

As I crossed the threshold of the courtyard, Barbie lifted her head above Toby's, who sat on her knee. My eyes registered the lovely smile on her lips, and I thought grief had crazed her. I looked at Connie. Her face wore a dazed grin. She was moving her head up and down like a nodding Chinese doll. "He's come to," she repeated over and over again. Christos was silently clapping his palms together, and on Alex's face relief overlaid the aftermath of forty-eight hours of unremitting devotion: bone-deep fatigue.

Barbie chanted: "He's going to get well. He knew me and he knew Giselle. He could talk a little, couldn't he, Alex? The doctor says he's still terribly weak and ill and that we must be patient." She laughed like a happy child. "That's all we have to do, to be patient."

When Alex had left and Connie had knocked up a snack lunch none of us could eat, Barbie went up to her bedroom. As I passed her open door she called my name, held out a limp but welcoming hand. "Matthew wants to see you." She gave me a baffled, querying look. "Why didn't you come to the hospital with me?"

Because she could not have endured me in the car. Because I'd wished to spare Matthew the emotional strain of having two women who loved him at his bedside. When his spirit was fighting to survive, I'd believed, rightly or wrongly, the only gift I could give him was absolute peace.

"Until he was conscious, as long as you and Alex and Giselle were with him, that was enough."

The old look of affectionate teasing twitched her mouth. "You're a queer one . . . little Miss Keep-herself-to-herself, that's you. Heaven knows what goes on in your head. I've given up trying to guess." She plaited her fingers between mine. "But I love you for saving Matthew's life, and I always will."

The memory of yesterday's abhorrence and lashing accusations was expunged clean from her mind.

Without warning the calm broke and she bowed her head between her hands, so that the tears slid down her wrists.

"Now I can mind about Kim. What Alex told me about him. I couldn't until I was certain Matthew wasn't going to die. If Kim had killed . . ." She shuddered into silence. I sat on the bed, my arm round her until she could speak. "I can't pretend . . . He two-timed me a hundred times . . ." Her hand fell and the tear-drenched lavender eyes stared dazedly into mine. "But he was the only man I ever slept with. In this day and age . . ." Sobs wrenched at her, so that the words seemed to be shaken out of her. "Do you know what terrifies me? Going to his funeral. I won't go. I can't . . ."

I comforted her. "Alex and Carima and I will be with you. Now listen while I explain something. At the end Kim found more courage than most men dredge up in a lifetime. He must have known he was asking to be shot when he threw that rock through the car window to give me a chance to get away before Heller released the brake and sent it over the edge with me inside it. And remember if I'd been killed Matthew would never have been found."

She nodded solemnly, hearing the words but not absorbing them into her mind. A moment later she took refuge from tragedy too overwhelming for her to handle in the trivial. "But what will I wear?" she wailed, distraught.

I promised her we'd sort that one out, and broke the news that Inspector Stanos would be calling at 3.30 to ask her a few very simple questions.

She looked at me with stark fright. "I'm ill. I'm not going to see him. I can't." The tears gushed over her eyelids. "Can't you understand, I just want Matthew to take me away from here so that I can forget it ever happened."

"I'm afraid you can't get out of it, but I'll stay with you, make sure he doesn't bully you, though he wouldn't be likely to anyway."

It was Connie who brought him up to the Crow's Nest, where I'd gone after supper to take the telephone calls so that Barbie, who was reading Toby to sleep, wouldn't be disturbed.

As Connie closed the door on him, he said jerkily: "How are you? I haven't worried you until it was certain that Matthew had turned the corner. But Alex has kept me in the picture."

He was a figure from the past, a ghost, but as the light struck his face, I had to blink hard to keep the tears that stung my eye-balls from overflowing. I'd not wept for Matthew, for Kim or for Barbie, but now I could have wept my heart dry for Donald Hardwick, for the freak in me that withheld from him the love he deserved, the love I yearned to give him.

We sat inside the window that opened on to the parapet, the mountain shapes barely perceptible in the velvet darkness. For a moment he examined my face closely, then looked away, said in a voice made as dry as sand by remembered hurt: "I'd have come with you. I mind that most, that you didn't trust me, that you had no instinct telling you that I would do any mortal thing for you, even hand you Matthew Grant on a plate!" He turned his glance to me, made a conscious effort to recover himself. "Now there's nothing I can give you, is there?"

"You could learn to hate me."

He smiled, but it was a smile of relinquishment. "Why? You tried. If you'd been less honest, you'd have brought it off."

"I believed I loved you."

"You lied to yourself, but the lie back-fired as we were walking back to the car. It literally sickened you, made you ill."

"Hate me," I cried passionately. "Despise me for playing the cheapest trick in the world."

He gave me a half smile, sad as tears. "It tricked me into happiness. Why should you despise a girl who gave you one perfect day?" He paused, finished on an abrupt note. "Do me one favour: don't say you're sorry."

I promised. I asked him if he would like a drink. He refused and told me formally he was flying to London the next day and would not be returning to Kessima for a month.

The thick, muffling silence that fell between us was an unbearable weight, but I knew what it was to love without return; that there were no words in the dictionary with power to ease or comfort. I whispered: "Forget me," but he either did not hear or did not choose to do so.

He got up. "I hope he deserves you. Are you going to marry him?"

"He's not likely to ask me."

"Why?"

"He was married once. Maybe it turned him off marriage for good." Or maybe, I thought, he was waiting for Colonel Nash to die, for Giselle to be free of her beloved tyrant.

Suddenly rage burst in him, overflowed. "Can you bear the waste? Men and women get obsessions, become possessed. But if they want to be free, in time, maybe a long time, an obsession can be exorcised."

"Donald!" I pleaded. "You're preaching to yourself!"

His face, stricken with grief and rage, all kindness and joy pinched out of it, might have been another man's. Maybe to a degree it was. Punishing disappointment can warp and distort, and though some of the mis-shapening rights itself, a residue is left.

He lashed out at me. "He's not worthy of you. Yet he lives in your heart and mind. No matter how far away he is, he's with you. That's true, isn't it?"

"Yes."

He thrust the chair in which he'd been sitting aside so violently that it skidded across the polished floor. I stood motionless and listening until his stampeding feet no longer sounded on the stone slabs.

I opened the door so silently that he didn't hear the hushed movement. He was asleep. I stood at the foot of the white hospital bed and looked at him. His left arm and hand were bandaged, and so was his head, the strands of hair that were visible on his crown unnaturally dark against the snow-white cotton. A drip feed was attached to his right hand and the bed covers propped high over his right leg. I checked the breaths he took with my own. They matched. He was living, as I'd believed he would. Joy subsided into peace.

The flesh on the marvellously drawn planes of his face was paper-thin—white paper, the eyebrows indrawn as though, even in sleep, his brain was harried, but his mouth was quiet, its lovely generous curves untroubled.

I looked for a long while at the man who was wrapped close in my heart forever until I grew afraid that his eyes would open and he would read mine before I had time to mask them. On silent feet I moved to the window. Outside a jacaranda tree dropped some of its hyacinth-blue petals on to the sill, where they lifted and drifted in the gentle shift of the breeze.

Alongside the window was a white painted chest. On it stood vases of flowers—roses, carnations, orchids—with gift cards attached. In the central place of honour was an arrangement of white and spun gold: stems of tall white flowers and glittering thistle-heads, so airy it seemed to float. There was a card on which were written two words: "Love, Giselle."

A high oblong of a room, a counterpart of a hospital room in England except there was an electric fan that hadn't been turned on or didn't work. My roving glance returned to the bed. His dense blue eyes were half open, watching me. A face with its eyes closed is inscrutable, half dead; even now, with his lids parted, it told me little except that it was the face of my love. I smiled, but he did not smile back.

The voice I'd expected to be weak was only husky: "Are you real?"

For an answer I went to the side of the bed where his bare hand lay on the white quilt, laid mine lightly on it. The last time I had touched his flesh it had been deathly cold. Now it was warm, alive.

The husky voice said: "Every hour of the night I was sure that you were lying somewhere with your lovely bones broken and that no one, not even Alex, had the guts to tell me." A shadow of his old, gently mocking smile touched his lips. "All very macabre!"

"Worthy of Toby, frightening himself to death for the hell of it. Barbie does too. Maybe it runs in the family."

I sat down in the high-seated chair, and when I eased my hand away, he stared at the cuts on my palm, the raking scratches on my arm. "Ugly, but don't worry, in a week I'll be as good as new."

His eyes came to mine, stayed there so long that I had to will mine to remain still. "Tell me," the husky voice asked, "what do you say to a girl who saved your life?"

I laughed a little. "Look at you, already thinking in headlines! Who's been feeding you on melodrama?"

"Alex, the police. Not melodrama, the truth. I asked you a question."

I kicked aside the gratitude that would constitute a lifetime's penance. "You say thank-you, and she replies: Think nothing of it. Any time."

Some emotion I couldn't read tightened his mouth, and he moved his head on the pillow, looked straight down the bed. "Why didn't you come to see me?"

"Mainly because of Barbie. The shock literally stupefied her. You were all she had to hang on to. It seemed to me best, at least until you were conscious, not to butt in. She's coming round now. She stood the interview with the police inspector yesterday much better than I expected."

He remembered where I'd spent the early part of the morning, at the inquest on Kim, and asked about it. The proceedings had been no more than a formality, with Bengy, under his real name of Bernard Sissons, being named as Kim's murderer.

When I'd told him, he said: "I asked Alex to look after you. Did he?"

"Like a stand-in father. If we'd been his nearest and dearest he couldn't have been kinder. He's propped all of us up."

"Good," he whispered. His lids sealed over his eyes. He seemed to sleep. When my ration of time ran out, I eased myself out of the chair. His eyes flew open. There was a tincture of the old ring of authority in his low-powered voice. "You're not to go."

"I have to. The doctor gave me fifteen minutes and I've used up fourteen. Barbie will be here this afternoon."

His eyes searched mine with a terrible naked anxiety. "Will you forgive me?"

"What on earth for?"

"Telephoning you." He drew in his breath so sharply there was a faint rasp in his lungs.

I smiled to coax him to smile, and failed. "Who else should you telephone? And talking of apologies, I owe you one. You see, Arabella fell down and broke . . ."

He wasn't listening, only looking at me, with a dark-blue fire of enormous intensity. "I want to explain . . ." His voice dried up on him, and his face became so bleak, so wounded, that terror pinched. I touched his hand to reassure myself that it was still warm and alive. The doctor hadn't trusted me. He'd sent a nurse to remind me that I must leave.

I whispered, my mouth level with his ear: "I'll come back tomorrow."

He whispered back: "What time?"

"Half-past ten."

On the way to the door I paused to glance at the central vase on the chest, and his voice, suddenly doubled in strength, spoke across the room with a clarity that startled me. "Are you thinking that while you kept your promise I broke mine?"

My promise had been to put no flowers on his desk, not to stir the sugar into his coffee. Stupidly, I could not remember what promise he'd made me in return. I parried the question. "I was only wondering what the tall white flowers are called."

"Squills," he said, his voice weakening again.

I found it an ugly name. "I call them ghost flowers," I said quickly, and went out, not trusting my face sufficiently to let him see it.

I took my portion gratefully. In that moment of peace and thankfulness I did not ask for more. The savage craving for what I could not have was tamed; it would return to claw me, but today there was a nimbus of joy around my heart.

SIXTEEN

Next morning the drip-feed had been removed, he was lying higher on the pillows, his smile was echoed in his eyes, and his voice less husky. I laid a folded sheet of paper on his bedside table. "I brought you a list of all the people who've been worrying about you."

He ignored it. "I fixed it with the doctor. A full half hour's visit. So sit down and let me look at you."

"You mean you bullied that nice young registrar!"

His smile had a glint of mischief. "Only to a permissible degree. As you well know, I'm not an unreasonable man."

I laughed. "I don't even have to enquire if you're better!"

"Sufficiently to insist, all right, plead if you like, that this time you listen while I explain why I telephoned you last Friday morning. It's important to me, damned important."

"If that's what you want."

"It is." He paused, as though selecting and marshalling words in his head, and when he spoke it was in short factual sentences. "When we arrived at the house on Thursday evening I faced Kim with McBain's story. He denied there was a word of truth in it, challenged me to prove it. My answer was that as soon as I could lay hold of Heller I'd do precisely that. But Heller was off on his yacht, not expected home until Friday. I left a message with his housekeeper for him to contact me immediately he set a foot inside the door.

"If Lex's story stood up, and there was sufficient evidence to suggest that it would, I'd have no alternative but to lay the facts before the police. Kim would be arrested, charged with theft, and either heavily fined or, more likely, sent to prison. My first priority was to get Barbie and Toby off the island before I contacted the police. By Friday morning I'd decided to have Barbie drive them from Troodos direct to Nicosia airport, meet them there, and ask you to fly out and take them to London." He gave me a flying sardonic glance. "You know Barbie! How she reacts to a sudden emergency, tends to go to pieces. She'd probably have refused to board the plane without all that gear she's got stashed away. Also, marooned in a London hotel, I doubt whether, in the circumstances, she could have coped alone.

"Twice early on Friday morning I tried to telephone you and each time Kim lifted the receiver downstairs. I hung up. I couldn't risk him short-circuiting my plan by ordering Barbie to jump into the car and drive home, thereby using her and Toby as blackmail counters. Around eleven, that radio girl-friend of his from the American Network drove in. He went out into the car park to talk to her, and I seized the chance to phone you. You weren't there. I put the date forward until Sunday, but it was an appalling line, and I couldn't be certain that woman of yours got the message. By afternoon I was praying she hadn't. But she had."

"Not all of it, not, for instance, which file you wanted."

"The 'Hanging Fire File.' Before he killed himself Mannheim burnt all his personal papers except one that Athena found, months later, tucked at the back of a drawer in the dining-room. It was a list written in German, in a cramped, barely legible writing. I clipped it to some notes I'd made on the history of the house, intending to translate it, but never got around to doing so. On Thursday night it occurred to me it might conceivably be a record of the objects he'd stolen." His eyes came slowly to mine. "What it amounts to is that telephone call was literally an order that could have brought you to your death, either by being shot to pieces or burned in a blazing car."

"I'd run the petrol tank bone dry. I doubt if the car could have caught fire."

Searing perplexity, a sort of creeping despair that was entirely foreign to him closed on his face. "To me it matters that you should understand why I telephoned you. Why does it upset you so?"

To be a burden of gratitude that constrained him to temper his words, to be a permanent reminder that I must forever receive the privileged treatment due to someone who had saved his life! "I'm not upset, but I like to have the record straight. I wasn't killed, just scratched and bruised. I didn't save your life. You saved your own by staying alive and shouting for help to Niko, Eugenia's brother."

For the first time a flicker of humour came back to his face. "What dear Annie would have called peacock-proud! You prefer your version?"

"If you don't mind. It's the true one."

"Don't go all meek. It depresses me. And depression in a patient is a cardinal sin. Doctors and nurses combine forces to jolly you along. You end up wearing a fixed docile smile, but behind it you're grouchy and evil-tempered."

"Bored," I corrected.

"And guilt-ridden as hell that I over-estimated my power to force the truth out of a lame hoodlum and a scared kid. That I never for one moment visualised the issue as one they would resolve by brute force. Minutes after I telephoned your flat the two of them stormed the Crow's Nest. Heller armed with a revolver, Kim with an iron bar with which after I'd landed a couple of punches he cracked me over the head. I came to after dark when they were packing me into the boot of the car. Kept alive because the job was easier if I were mobile and saved them a long haul with a body. Where they were going they weren't even put to the effort of digging a grave; there were a hundred gullies into which they could dump me, cover me with mountain debris and boulders. Heller's plan was that I'd walk to the edge of the grave, be clubbed or shot into it. What he overlooked was his own physical disability in covering rough ground when they daren't, for fear of rousing a nervy garrison, use more than a minimum of light. Kim was ahead, with a small flashlight, Heller behind, prodding a gun in the small of my back. That's when he fell, headlong, and I ran, or deluded myself that I was running. Heller screamed at Kim to keep the light on me, and fired. He hit me in the thigh. I passed out until I found myself in a sort of slit trench, with Kim piling rocks and stones over me, and Heller, somewhere in the dark, yelling at Kim to make sure I was dead. But by that time Kim was a gibbering idiot. Then, he was a born loser, about the worst lieutenant you could pick for a murder job. They panicked, both of them, were reduced to concocting the story I'd phoned from Cairo which half an hour's expert investigation would have exposed as a lie. I played dead, which was easy enough. Kim could have believed I was dead; more likely he wasn't in a state to determine whether life was extinct.

"When I saw the car drive off I had just sufficient leverage to free my head and shoulders. The rest of the rubble beat me." He gave me a look so deep and moving that my heart melted. "It isn't having half of me buried alive that haunts me. It's you, a small, utterly reckless avenging angel . . ."

I interrupted him. "Stanos's version was that I fancied myself as a female knight-errant straight out of a fairy tale. He didn't intend it as a compliment, quite the reverse."

"Then he doesn't know you. I do. How did you know or guess? This is what baffles everyone."

I told him, or as much of it as I could put into words. As I finished a nurse put her head round the door to announce there were two more visitors waiting to see Mr. Grant and that his lunch would be served in exactly one hour's time.

He scowled. "Why must they serve hospital meals at such ungodly hours! Lunch at noon, sharp!"

I surveyed the flowers and fruit, the bottles of champagne and whisky. "Is there anything you want? That's what everyone is asking."

"Just be sure to arrive tomorrow . . . sharp!"

I touched his hand so lightly that it was barely a touch.

"Tell me what day it is, I've lost count."

"Sunday. Half the candles in the church have been lit for you. Athena lights a new one for you every morning."

"Bless her. That puts me into a state of grace that should last an hour or two."

Matthew remained in hospital ten days, during which a timetable established itself. The hour from ten to eleven was mine, during which he dictated replies to the mountain of telegrams and letters he'd received. By the end of the week he was handwriting a few personal notes, including one to Marigold.

Barbie, once with Toby and once with Connie, went to see him each afternoon. Friends on the island, or passing through, visited him. Alex and Carima looked in most days. Sometimes Giselle paid her daily visit as I was leaving, other times she went in the afternoon. Always she left behind her some exquisite votive offering of fruit or flowers; failing that some piece of nonsense that would amuse his eye.

As he grew stronger his humour surfaced, the radiance came back to his smile, and he was issuing orders, not obeying them. For me it was an interim period of unreal calm, a suspension of time during which I negotiated with a London pre-prep day school for Toby's entry at half term, found a furnished flat in South Kensington for Barbie, Connie, and Toby, and booked our flight tickets to London for a week after Matthew was due to leave hospital.

In order that he should travel in maximum comfort Alex and Carima collected him in an old Daimler—one of Alex's fleet of cars. On the threshold of the courtyard Barbie, Toby, Athena, and I were spectators of what amounted to a royal progress as villagers cried their joy or tried to touch his hand through the open window. Only Giselle was absent because Dadda had developed a cold on his chest and refused to be left.

Aristo had abandoned his potter's wheel, Evangelos his tavern, Antinou his garage. The Merchant Tailor was waving a Union Jack; Eugenia's mother and Niko were among a score sweeping him home on a tide of loving good will.

Barbie and Toby raced to the car while Connie, Athena, and I waited in line. The bandages had been unwound from his head and replaced with a surgical dressing, but he still walked with a stick. In the merciless midday sun, I saw for the first time the new lines laid on his face, and, under the glowing air of magnificence, fatigue suppressed. As his lips touched my cheek, as they had touched Connie's, the heart of me, unaffected by the surface joy, was withered by that public embrace.

After lunch, when Alex and Carima had left, and Toby, despite well-marshalled and forceful arguments, had been dispatched to school, to leave Barbie and Matthew alone, I went to help Connie with the dishes. Handing me a plate to wipe, she asked: "What's to happen to this place when we're gone? Is he going to sell it?"

"I've no idea." He'd never given me a hint of his plans for the house that he and Giselle had made together.

I enquired if she would stay with Barbie and Toby in London. She looked affronted. "She could hardly manage on her own, could she? And Toby's got another year before, poor mite, he is shunted off to boarding-school. Who'd get him up in the morning? Jolly her out of the doldrums?" She was referring to the interludes of physical and mental inertia that attacked Barbie, not so much melancholy as a severance from everyone about her. "And then there's those blasted cats of hers. Oh, I know Eugenia's going to be paid to feed them, but she'll fret about them, you mark my words. And the only way to stop her pining will be for her to buy another, as like as not a whole litter, from the first pet-shop she passes. Before we've been there a month, I bet the flat will be crawling with the nasty, sly creatures."

She paused, her hands deep in soap-suds. "Of course when Toby goes to school, and Barbie's on her feet, I'm not saying I wouldn't like a little place of my own, with a bit of garden where it rains once or twice a week, and you're not scared to death of treading on snakes every time you set foot in it. Not to mention being able to pop out and buy a nice bit of filet steak." Her face cleared and the chronic tiredness of the last fortnight lifted from it. "Besides, it would be somewhere for Toby to spend a piece of his holidays. Snails by the pailful, not to mention caterpillars."

When she went upstairs to her room to put her feet up, in order not to disturb Matthew and Barbie, who were talking in the sitting-room, I climbed the garden path and sat on the wall between two cypresses and stared at the house. I heard the echo of the Turkish-Cypriot driver's voice. "It is unlucky house. Whoever lives there someone dies." Not the house, I thought, but the men who had invaded it. A German exiled from his homeland traduced by ancient spoils; a money-hungry playboy who, sniffing a rich reward, had stolen them for a second time. And Heller, a common thief whose record for three armed bank robberies in London and the Home Counties was now in the hands of the island police, plus a hoard of thousands of pounds of used notes found in a safe in the villa.

Below me two of Minnow's kittens were spitting and fighting over a lizard, a fresh sheet of cerise bougainvillaea had spread another curtain of flame over Connie's garden shed; the grapes on the terrace had been picked and nearly all the lemons were gold. I examined house and garden minutely, as though I were saying goodbye, as indeed I might be. In it a spectre of death had stalked me for days, invisible because I'd refused to recognise its existence. Yet, paradoxically, it was not the crippling terror that I remembered, but the sensation of peace combined with delight of the days and nights when Matthew and I had been under the same roof.

I'd left my dark glasses in the house, and, to shield my eyes from the merciless sun—and maybe because I could bear to look no longer—I turned to go indoors. On the threshold of the courtyard, Matthew called to me from the parapet of the Crow's Nest. "Maria, can you come up?"

He was sitting in a chair by the window that looked over the ravine into the village. On his blotter I had laid some letters and a couple of cablegrams that had arrived that morning. As I stood by them waiting, a most wondrous thing happened. I was purged of the corroding resentment at the waste of love, washed clean, made as light as air, my chains weightless. In that moment to love was bounty enough. I glanced towards him, but he did not seem aware that I had entered the room. The house had a tomblike silence under the great cushion of heat that had stilled voice and step, put crying children to sleep.

For no reason I reversed the order of the two cablegrams.

"Be still." His face turned to me: a graven face of dignity

and reserve, all the gaiety it had worn before and after lunch lost. "Be still," he repeated, "with me."

I felt his fatigue as if it were my own. "You should have let Connie do what she wanted to do, put a bed for you in the dining-room, saved you from having to climb the stairs."

He made a gesture of disagreement. "Let's get one fact straight. I left my nurses behind in hospital. A splendid band of women; I'm eternally grateful to them, but for a while I'll be allergic to saucy caps and white uniforms, and voices that jolly me along for my own good."

He got up, pulled a chair for me into the shade alongside his. Be still, I repeated to myself, and unquestioningly treasured the silence that made a sanctuary from words that could inflict mortal hurt.

Yet the first words that left his lips, pitchforked me head first out of it. "What's happened to Hardwick? Donald Hardwick?"

"He's gone back to London." I wondered who'd told him about the day we'd spent on the island. Barbie might have done so, but it was likelier to have been Giselle.

"Perhaps I should rephrase the question. What's happened between you and Donald Hardwick?" Looking down at my hands, I would feel the weight of his penetrating gaze. "For instance," he went on, "are you considering marrying him?"

"No."

"Why not?"

I laughed. There was no mirth in it, no gladness, only an aching bitterness, a degree of astonishment that he should be curious enough to ask that question. He went on: "He's eligible, pleasant-tempered, good looking, with a promising career ahead of him, and he's so desperately in love with you that every time you appear on the horizon he practically sits up and begs!"

I saw us in the sandy grove, the ghost flowers swaying; I felt for a moment that wrenching terror of the heart that was like a forerunner of death. I saw him standing at the precise spot Matthew was sitting, the evening of the day on which the spectre I'd refused to recognise had been put to flight; a man who was averse to fighting for a lost cause, but fighting nevertheless.

"You don't do him justice. You never have."

"Ah," he said softly. "It distresses you to talk about him!"
"Yes."
"Because you're in love with him?"
"Because I'm not."
"And having banished him, you weep for him?"
"Is that so unnatural?"

The telephone rang before he could answer. I heard Marigold's breathy, high-pitched voice. "I want to speak to Mr. Grant. The hospital say he left this morning and I don't know where he is."

I laid the receiver down. "It's Mrs. Fairley." I walked on to the parapet, to the farthest point where I couldn't eavesdrop.

In five minutes he came to look for me, his smile wryly self-condemning. "I reproach you for weeping for Hardwick, and yet I do the masculine equivalent of weeping for Marigold! Come back inside unless you want to be fried alive." He gave me a sharply slanted glance of enquiry. "Barbie must have talked about her to you?"

"Only once that I can remember. A tramp or a tart, I forget which she called her, and that she's a weight on your conscience."

"Actually she's neither a tramp nor a tart. She has a compulsion towards respectability. We were twenty-two and twenty-five when we got married. She was a model girl with everything going for her except stamina to stay the course. When we'd been married for eighteen months, I was shipped off to the Far East. It was my first solo job writing under a by-line. I was out there for just on two years before I got an instant recall home. When I telephoned the Hampstead flat from Hong Kong I couldn't get a reply, so, naïve as a boy, I decided to give her a surprise. When I did just that there were a man's clothes where mine should have hung, and he was asleep in her bed. They'd been living together for a year. It was a surprise that exacted a monstrous revenge on her. Caught out, she swore she was only waiting for me to return to ask me for a divorce so that they could get married. I gave it to her. Ten months after the marriage he was killed in a pile-up on the M.1. and Marigold, pregnant, lost the baby. She went back to modelling, but she'd lost her place on the ladder, new girls had raced ahead of her. She met Vic Fairley, who had some vague connection with a film company. She boasted he was going to make her a star. She had a few walk-on parts before he deserted her, and, three years later, she divorced him. So far she hasn't married again, and for the last couple of years she has been working as a beautician in a Manchester store."

"And clinging to you for comfort and support."

"You could say so."

"Barbie's right: she is a weight on your conscience. Why do you feel guilty for *her* unfaithfulness?"

"I feel guilt for marrying a girl whose sole motive force was her looks, which were a spectacular but steadily diminishing asset, and then abandoning her to ply my trade, assuming she loved me enough to sit home baking pies, knitting sweaters, when droves of men came drooling every time she flicked her eyelashes. Guilt, you could say, for my arrogance."

"Do they still come in droves?"

"Probably not in droves. I haven't seen her for five years. To do so might inflate hopes I couldn't fulfil. My conscience isn't that guilty! I ensure that even with galloping inflation she'll have a comfortable income in her old age. She's scared of that . . . getting old and being poor." His glance sought mine, as he said with deep gravity: "That is an honest accounting of my marriage."

I wondered if it was not a misplaced kindness—or a man's natural conceit—to keep himself in the forefront of her life, even if only by telephone, letters, and the management of her money. Wasn't it a refinement of cruelty to provide the tiniest spur to hope? If so, it was unintentional.

I asked, hungry to know: "After lunch Connie asked me what you intend to do with the house, if you were going to sell it."

"Sell it . . ." He sounded vague. "That depends on a factor outside my control." Very slowly, almost in slow motion he turned his face towards me. There was neither ice nor compassion in it, only a vulnerable look I'd never seen there before, as if he were afraid, which, since fear wasn't a part of his make-up, could not be. "Maria, will you be patient with me?"

Lost, grasping for the meaning behind the words, I nodded. "Endlessly, but how?"

"In that half grave I had intermittent periods of quite astounding lucidity. Death might have come, a wrapping up, the final closure, an end to all chances of redeeming my sins of omission." Gradually a smile flooded his face, lay like a wreath on his mouth. "When it doesn't, your reward is that life becomes so infinitely precious you swear that never again will you waste a second of it. Am I being tedious?"

"No."

There was a long pause when his eyes held mine as though they loved and cherished me. The single-mindedness that was at the core of him seeming miraculously diverted to me. "Well then, my love, will you marry me?"

For a second I lost the power to think, which in itself was a kind of ecstasy; desire almost destroyed my reason, but not quite.

I heard my voice blurt out the only crystal clear thought in my head. "Giselle loves you. You must know she does. You can't deny it."

"I don't." His glance clouded and then cleared. "What I do deny is your assumption that love automatically buys a return of love. That it is an emotional *quid pro quo*, as though the heart were an adding machine."

"You don't care . . ."

"Maria!" So much feeling welled up in one word that I was silenced.

I got up, walked to the table, turned my back on him, stared through the window at the mountains, and when I was calm said: "You didn't see her the night they brought you into the hospital. She was bereft, inconsolable, nothing but grief in her." The silence that hung between us obliterated the words of love he'd spoken; they became insubstantial as a dream.

His answering voice was quiet, measured. "Maybe I should love Giselle, but I don't. To me she is, and always will be, a remarkably gifted and attractive young woman. I admire, appreciate, have great affection for her, and, yes, a kind of pity for the narrowness of the life forced upon her. But I don't love her. I don't want to share my home and bed with her." The tone of his voice changed to one of absolute nakedness. "I want to share them with you. I love you, Maria."

"But it's been so long," I whispered. "So long."

I heard his uneven step, I felt the closeness of his breath, his hand clasp my arm, but I could not stir.

"Listen, my love, please listen. When you scarcely recall the last time you fell in love, you distrust that bolt to the heart, the transformed face of a world that suddenly shimmers with radiance. You wouldn't remember that afternoon when, on our way back from the castle, we stopped for Toby to look into the cave through my binoculars. You were sitting cross-legged among the flowers, your long silk hair streaming about your beautiful face. That was the moment of a blinding revelation in which I did not wholly believe."

"In February!" I turned, freed myself from his grasp, a whisper of belief touching my heart.

"In February!" He held my eyes. "If you want to count the months there were seven of them, months I wouldn't choose to relive." A wryness touched his mouth, but his voice was driven by a ferocious anxiety. "The stakes were so high they made a coward out of me. A jealous coward. One word, a touch and you'd have taken to your heels, and I'd have lost the sight and scent of you forever. I was terrified."

"You! Terrified!"

"Of Hardwick and an impressive young man with a lean and hungry look who paced the pavement waiting for you every single Wednesday night you were in London."

"You can't mean Kevin Walsh!"

"If he was your Wednesday-night date, yes."

"I've known him since I took him to kindergarten. He's a year younger than I am and his parents lived across the road from us. Mr. Walsh died a month after Kevin entered medical school and, not much over a year later, his mother remarried and moved to East Anglia. He doesn't approve of his stepfather, so he refuses to accept any money from his mother and scrapes along on his grant. Actually, Kevin approves of very few people."

"I can imagine! But he approves of you?"

"Because I'm a once-a-week meal ticket. He's perpetually hungry. We have a deal, every Wednesday night I'm home I cook him as much food as he can eat; when he qualifies he's to buy me dinner at Claridge's. On Sundays my mother has him to lunch and so between us he keeps reasonably well nourished. He's dedicated to own his future, with a single-track mind filled by a picture of himself as a top-flight surgeon, a sort of Christiaan Barnard. And when he comes to needing a wife he'll pick one to suit the job, *his* job!" Suddenly I raged: "I simply don't believe that Donald or Kevin terrified you for seven whole months. I know you!"

"Yes," he said in a gentle, wondering voice. "You do indeed, as no one else does. But I didn't know myself, not until I'd been half buried alive on a mountainside. That, my darling Maria, alters your angle of vision pretty drastically. What bothered me was not so much dying, as you dying because I'd telephoned you, given you no warning of what lay in wait for you, and myself living without you, which would have been another species of death."

I said slowly: "But you're not a coward any longer. Why?"

"You climbed a mountain to find me. You did it alone, throwing fear, danger, even sanity to the winds. Doesn't that suggest there is a particle of love somewhere deep inside you . . . for me?"

The dreams in my head were no longer dreams. I was borne up on light, a stillness within me so beautiful I dare not speak and break it.

He lifted my chin, and I looked into his face with its long planes and flying eyebrows, the eyes that were melting with love. "What do you want me to do, my darling, go down on my knees and beg?"

I was the beggar, a happy beggar made fabulously rich. As he kissed my mouth with trembling fierceness, we seemed to breathe joy into one another.

Night had come, Barbie, Connie, and Toby were sleeping, and the dark, silent world was wholly ours when I asked: "What did you mean when you said that selling the house depended on a factor outside your control?"

"Why, you. What would be the point of keeping it if you couldn't bear to come back here?"

"But I want to." It was where a love had been born that reduced the ugliness and horror to ash that the wind would blow away the fierce, scorching light of the sun.

"Then it's yours," he said simply. "I endow you with it, like the rest of me, all the great chunks of bad, and the few particles of good that come from loving you. Twice a year we'll come back and live in it together." He turned my face so close to his that our lips brushed in understanding, love, and joy. "Are you happy?" he whispered.

It was such a commonplace, overused, and inadequate word to describe a whole inner world turned from darkness into light, but, bemused by love, I couldn't find another.